GREEN'S HILL

Werewolves

Volume Two

AMY LANE

DSP PUBLICATIONS

Published by

Dreamspinner Press

5032 Capital Circle SW, Suite 2, PMB# 279, Tallahassee, FL 32305-7886 USA
www.dreamspinnerpress.com

This is a work of fiction. Names, characters, places, and incidents either are the product of author imagination or are used fictitiously, and any resemblance to actual persons, living or dead, business establishments, events, or locales is entirely coincidental.

Green's Hill Werewolves, Vol. 2
© 2017 Amy Lane.

Cover Art
© 2017 Anne Cain.
annecain.art@gmail.com
Cover content is for illustrative purposes only and any person depicted on the cover is a model.

ISBN: 978-1-63533-684-9
Digital ISBN: 978-1-63533-685-6
Library of Congress Control Number: 2016916564
Published September 2017
v. 2.0
First Edition of Becoming published by Torquere Press, 2011.
First Edition of Being published by Torquere Press, 2011.

Printed in the United States of America

This paper meets the requirements of
ANSI/NISO Z39.48-1992 (Permanence of Paper).

Rampant, Vol. 2

"With the intensity (and the stakes) jacked to eleven, *Rampant, Vol. 2* is a white-knuckled thrill ride of a resolution, leaving the reader with a tantalizing peek into what's in store in the next book in the series."
—The Novel Approach

Rampant, Vol. 1

"I think *Rampant, Vol. 1* is my favourite book in the series."
—Prism Book Alliance

Bound, Vol. 2

"As usual, Amy Lane blew my socks off with this story and left me in a huge book hangover because there simply isn't other books out there written like hers."
—Inked Rainbow Reads

By Amy Lane

The Green's Hill Novellas
Green's Hill Werewolves, Vol. 1
Green's Hill Werewolves, Vol. 2

LITTLE GODDESS
Vulnerable
Wounded, Vol. 1
Wounded, Vol. 2
Bound, Vol. 1
Bound, Vol. 2
Rampant, Vol. 1
Rampant, Vol. 2
Quickening, Vol. 1
Quickening, Vol. 2

Published by DSP PUBLICATIONS
www.dsppublications.com

Becoming

PROLOGUE

TEAGUE WASN'T the only one who had bad dreams—at least not this night.

Two days after the Werewolf Debacle, as Jack was starting to think of it, he lay beside his lovers. He should have been hearing their breathing in the dark, but instead he was sweating, trying to recapture the dream that had ripped apart his night. Jack had been a big reader as a kid, and he'd spent much of his childhood in stories of knights and ladies, quests and battles—silly, idealistic bloodshed for a sheltered, bloodless boy. This dream had been just like them. He remembered bold lines and fairy-tale colors—just like a comic book or a kid's story. And just like a comic book or a kid's story, the movements had been broad and stylized—it hadn't looked real at all, but the beautiful parts had been more beautiful and the scary parts had been terrifying....

Unlike in real life, where she was a rather plain college student, Lady Cory was very beautiful in the dream. Her hair was a glorious scarlet waterfall, and her eyes flashed green-brown fire. There were no freckles to make her average, and her cheekbones seemed to have moved up and gotten a little narrower. The results were lovely and terrible and terrifying—there was nothing of the friendly, frightening human being Jack had been humanly jealous of. In her place was an inhumanly beautiful, cold and bloodless monarch, the kind men would die for and women would kill to serve.

Teague stood before her—wearing armor polished to a sheen, of course. He held his helmet under his arm and knelt with his head bent forward in servitude.

"I give to thee, my lady, all that is in my power...." Not Teague's words in real life, of course, but Jack could see the sentiment was real. The lady could too, and she bent her head and replied. Her words were humble, but her face was haughty and indifferent, and Jack felt a blaze of anger in the dream because he knew—just knew—that bitch had no idea what it was she was being offered.

"Your sacrifice is unnecessary, sir knight. You serve us well. Be happy, go home to your lovers. Be well."

Of course Teague wouldn't just let that stand, now would he? He'd have to go and do the noble goddamned thing and make *her accept what he was offering.*

Jack watched in horror as Teague turned the sword inward, and—grabbing it by the blade—thrust it into his chest. Of course, in real life this would be impossible since he was wearing two tons of armor, but just for Jack's dream, because he was horrified and freaked out, that fucking sword slid in like the steel plating was butter. And the damned lady of the house, she did nothing. She did jack-fucking-diddly-shit as Teague reached inside that wreckage of metal and chest cavity and pulled out his still-beating heart.

In the dream Jack started to scream—one of those terrible screams you make when you're asleep, where your mouth is open and your chest is working like a bellows but no sound comes out. Teague looked at him with that beautiful fuck-me grin and winked. When he spoke, blood frothed and bubbled from between his lips. "Don't worry, Jacky. There'll be enough for you when she's done."

But Lady Cory was gnawing on the thing, flashes of scarlet blood coating her cheeks and dribbling down her chin, and Jack was pretty damn sure there was going to be nothing left.

Jack's eyes opened in the dark, and his heart—still securely in his chest, unlike Teague's dream heart—hammered blood in his ears.

He turned to Teague, that bantam, wiry body back-spooning into Jack's arms, just in time for Teague to gasp like a swimmer who'd been under for too long. He struggled to sit up, making what sounded like suppressed screams in his throat, but Jack tightened his embrace and forced Teague to lie down.

After a few moments, Teague's body relaxed. He turned away from Katy, who was soundly asleep, and let Jack kiss his forehead and nuzzle his cheek. As Teague's breathing calmed down and his terrible shivers stopped, Jack spoke, his voice startling in the dark.

"What do you dream about, beloved?"

Teague hauled in another breath, and Jack felt one final, convulsive shiver rock his scrawny, tree-root body.

"Letting you down," he said after a moment. Jack kissed his forehead. It was still clammy from the dream, and Teague made a rough sound in his throat before his shoulders came down in that self-protective cocoon Jack recognized so well.

"Impossible," Jack said fervently. He was thinking that his dream could wait. Teague had enough on his mind.

Personal Debt

WHEN TEAGUE Sullivan was fourteen years old, he made a miraculous discovery.

Girls wanted to touch him.

Boys probably wanted to touch him too, but he didn't figure that out until Jacky, and it was beside the point. The point was, Teague had never been touched unless he was getting beaten. When Michelle Campos—with glossy dark hair in rolled curls, vivacious brown eyes, and the sexual confidence of a girl who knew she was wanted—pinned him behind the boys' lockers after sixth period gym, whispered breathily into his mouth, and put her hands on his shoulders, Teague was mesmerized. Not by Michelle, although she was pretty damned awesome, but by the feel of her palms on his flesh.

He opened his mouth to her kisses, and she tasted like soda and chocolate. He didn't get a lot of sweet in his life, so he learned to love sweet, although he never ever asked for it. She pulled up his shirt and rubbed his bare skin with her whole hand, and he must have whimpered in complete surprise when she hit his nipples and his whole body tingled, because she laughed into his mouth and kissed him harder.

Before he could protest—not that he would have—she had unbuttoned his jeans and was on her knees in the dark of the locker room with his hard, aching cock in her mouth and her hands massaging his thighs. He couldn't have said at that moment which one felt better. When his vision went dark and his body exploded and his eyes rolled back into his head, he might have said it was the mouth on his cock, but it was a near thing.

He didn't know what to do then.

He stood there, stroking her hair as she laughed some more into the closeness of his thighs, and then they heard voices.

"Oops!" she said, standing up and wiping her mouth with the back of her hand. She had a wicked smile, and he found himself answering it, feeling shy and dumb and inept. It didn't matter. She gave him a quick kiss on the mouth, letting him taste himself, and then held her finger to her lips and disappeared through the back entrance to the boys' locker room, leaving Teague to haul up his jeans and continue breathing, although that second one was somewhat of a stretch.

He'd felt vaguely ashamed of that moment.

Not of her mouth or her hands or anything she'd done—that had been wonderful. So wonderful, in fact, that sex became like soda or chocolate—that sweet thing he would never reach for but would take only when it dropped into his lap. Which it did frequently, much to his constant surprise and puzzlement. He didn't *do* anything! Why did women keep wanting to feel him up and blow him?

No, he felt ashamed because of what he *didn't* do. He hadn't *done* anything to deserve that miracle of firing nerves and human touch. He'd just smiled at her a little in math, that was all. But she'd kept smiling at him, and he'd kept returning it, every day a little longer, and then… then on this day, she'd blessed him with human touch and orgasm, and he hadn't paid his debt.

He never got a chance to pay that debt. Michelle's boldness had been an act of desperation and goodbye—her parents were moving her to an even smaller school in an even smaller town, because the assumption was that sex doesn't happen in small schools in small towns. Anyone who's ever been to one could tell you different, but parents are often afraid of sex, and there has never been any reasoning with them.

So Teague learned his second lesson.

He learned that if you don't see the person ever again, any mistakes you made, any fuckups or uncomfortable moments could be pretty much forgotten.

Teague lived to be fourteen because he learned quickly and acted on that knowledge. He learned to be a fucking awesome lover in the same way. He never wanted to feel that sense of shame and debt for not giving back. He also learned to only go home with girls who wouldn't want to know his name in the morning.

Teague had been almost thirty when he woke up in Green's bed after being healed of what should have been a mortal wound. He never said a word to Green—he never had to—about how Green's touch was like food to a starving man and balm to a ravaged soul. Green knew. But when Teague found himself sharing a bed with Jacky and then Katy, being touched constantly, especially in sleep, became a sweet and terrible part of his life.

Sweet because it was the thing he craved most of all and never wanted to admit to needing.

Terrible because he could not see how, in his entire history, he had ever come to deserve such kindness. How could he repay it? It was like that long ago blow-job—perfect, exquisite, and stolen from the pain the world should be.

So that touch as he went to sleep haunted his dreams. Whether his lovers were being chased by a dragon with his father's face or whether he was locked in his head, screaming in his skull as his traitorous body destroyed what he loved best, it was all about being touched and how if it didn't hurt, Teague Sullivan didn't deserve it.

Now that he'd had love for a couple of weeks and learned that it hurt sometimes worse than no love at all, he would have thought the dreams would ease up a little, but they hadn't. Life became a crapshoot. One day he was sitting with his family and ready to reach for them like he had a right to be happy. The next day he was howling his chest raw because he had no right to be happy, none at all. It was almost easier when he'd expected to be beaten all the time—at least then he'd known what was coming. It had sucked, but he hadn't been touched then. He hadn't known the opposite of "suck." He hadn't known that sometimes heaven might allow "rock" as opposed to "suck."

The dreams hurt, gleeful demons frolicking in the viscera of his broken heart.

That was what love should feel like, right? That was all he deserved.

He certainly didn't deserve Jacky holding him, rocking him, kissing his forehead tenderly, making him feel protected and safe. He definitely didn't deserve Katy's softness—Katy pressed up against his back in sweetness, better than chocolate and soda and softer than cotton candy or puppy fur. He didn't deserve them—he knew he didn't. But they wouldn't let him up, wouldn't let him out of bed into the cold and the dark and the wet.

They wouldn't let him go, and so he accepted them. He had to, because even when he didn't deserve them, he knew better than to hurt them when punishing himself. Any asshole knew that was a debt you could never repay, and Teague always paid his debts.

The next morning, Katy woke him with a sleepy kiss.

"Last two days were nice, baby, but today I've got to work." She smelled spicy and exotic as she kissed him—something about the soap she'd bought to use in the shower. He liked it. It was like cinnamon and bay leaves—warm and sharp, just like her.

"You have a good day, Katy," he mumbled, and she surprised him by keeping her face close and regarding him with warm brown eyes.

"Last time I told you to sleep in, Teague, you didn't. You got all hurt and then went on a run and then you and Jacky almost got killed, and then we had to sit on you to make you sleep in. I know you've got to meet werewolves and be all functional today, but… could you, just for me, let me think of you tucked in here with Jacky for an hour? Don't get into no fights, don't get all hurt on your inside. Just sleep. Make love. Try a do-over, okay?"

Teague blinked. "Maybe I'm just not designed for sleeping in. You ever think about that, Katy?"

She shook her head and swore softly in Spanish. "I think you got some time to go before your heart's all better, that's what I think. And you might kill us first while it's mending. 'Bye…."

"Katy…." He'd hurt her, though he didn't know how, and she scowled at him and gave him a flipped wrist with an open palm. *Talk to the palm, Teague. I'm done talking to you.*

"Fine, damn it!" he snapped before she could slam the door. "I'm staying here in bed. Are you happy?"

She looked over her shoulder as she got to the door, and he couldn't help but think that even the sulky thrust of her lower lip was charming. "You gonna get laid?" she asked, considering.

Teague risked a look at Jacky, who squinted one eye at him and went back to feigning sleep to keep out of the argument.

"No," he said punitively, and as Jack sat up in bed and protested, "*No?*" Katy let out a musical laugh and slid gracefully out the door.

Teague grunted, a reluctant smile twitching his usually compressed mouth. "Serves you right," he grumbled. Then he hauled the comforter over his shoulder and retreated to the corner of the bed where he usually slept when he was by himself.

Jack scooted next to him and grabbed him around the waist in spite of his startled squawk, and Teague found himself hauled up back-to-front with his lover.

"What in the…."

"Humor me." Then Jack… *fondled* Teague, for lack of a better word.

"I thought we were supposed to be sleeping," Teague complained, but he wasn't protesting very hard. God—Jack's touch, Katy's touch—it really had become his drug, hadn't it?

Jack's hand slid across Teague's chest, rubbing deliberately against Teague's sensitive nipples and down his stomach, and Teague arched into it, appreciating the pure touch of skin on skin.

"You go ahead and sleep all you want," Jack murmured into the sensitive hollow of his ear. "Just let me touch you while you sleep."

Teague bit back on a half-strangled sound. It might have been "please" before he killed it.

"Please?" Jacky asked plaintively, and then Teague felt like a coward for not saying the word first.

"I really do need to run today," he protested half-heartedly. "That's not just bull… sh… eeeet…."

"Bullsheet?" Jack chuckled. He had just wrapped his arm over Teague's shoulders and framed Teague's throat with his long-fingered hand. It was an intimate position, a vulnerable position—especially when the hand was large and it was attached to a tall, strong man. Teague's vulnerability slammed into his chest, and it occurred to him that he was giving Jack his safety, his life, just with that one gesture.

He wanted to run, and his shoulders quivered with the urge to push himself out of bed and head for the cross-country track. It took all his will to simply lie passive under Jack's seductive touch.

Jack seemed to sense this. Carefully he stroked down from Teague's throat and whispered, "Shhhhh… take it easy, big man" into his ear.

Teague swallowed. "I wasn't kid—"

"I know." Sometimes these exchanges got heated, sharp—Teague's driving need to run coming up against Jack's possessive need to keep him in their bed. But not this time. Maybe it was the enforced intimacy of the day before, or maybe Jack just knew what Teague needed, but this time Jack's voice only grew gentler.

"Here, beloved," he whispered. Teague blushed under the endearment just as he blushed under Jack's hands. "Here, I'll make you a deal."

"Yeah?" Teague hated the note of pleading in his voice, but his insides were still raw. The day before he'd had an emotional pain dump of epic proportions, a 9.9 on the Richter scale of internal cataclysms. He couldn't have another argument right now—he wouldn't do it. He needed something easy…. God help him, he needed to give in. But he was stubborn. He would negotiate. He wouldn't go too far into the debt of touching… he couldn't. That was his code. It had kept him sane for thirty soulless years. *Yes*, whispered his traitorous body, *but those years were before Jacky*. He told the voice to shut up—Jack was offering him a way out.

"Yeah." Jack nibbled on his ear again. Teague's hips started to arch and wiggle. He tried to make himself stop that—it was impossible to stay out of personal debt when your body was taking touch on credit.

"What's the deal?" Teague tried to turn, thinking he would pin Jacky down, ravish him, take his long, drooling cock into his mouth and make his lover crazy. Jacky would touch him then unreservedly, and Teague could earn the touches that way. But Jack kept his arms around Teague's chest and tightened the embrace, not letting him move unless he jerked his body out of Jack's control. That would lead to a fight, to a conflict, and Teague… oh Goddess… he was still bleeding from thinking Jacky was dead, from having his lovers tend to him like a fraught, weepy child.

"The deal," Jack told him, gently biting the nape of Teague's neck and then laving it with his tongue, "is that once—just once—you stay here and let me make love to you. No running away, no fighting to be on top, to be in charge. Stay here, let me touch you. Touch back if you want to, but don't take over."

Teague's supreme discomfort with the idea came out with the whine in his throat. "I'm… I've got to…. Jacky, I'm not good with that…."

Well, it was obvious he wasn't good with it—his body was straining against itself—and Jack's hands started rubbing his shoulders in more insistent circles. "Just let me, Teague." Jacky pushed on Teague's shoulder without comment or weakening, and Teague found himself rolling over onto his stomach. "Let me. I promise, you let me take care of you, and I'll let you go running. No strings attached, no drama—you'll just put on your shoes and go."

Then Jack sat up and straddled Teague's thighs while his hands worked big-palmed magic on the twisted, knotted steel bars at Teague's shoulders.

"Damn, Teague. You just woke up—how can you be this tight?" Jack wriggled, and Teague could feel the long muscles of Jack's inner thighs against the corded muscle of his flank. Jack's semihard cock nestled between Teague's legs near the crease of his buttocks, and Teague kept wanting to clench his asscheeks to keep it there or bring it closer, which surprised the hell out of him in general.

He grunted a noncommittal sort of reply to Jack's question and forced himself not to move, not to respond, to just lie there and accept the wonder of Jack's touch as it was bestowed on him.

"So," Jack asked, leaning forward so his lips would touch Teague's spine between his shoulders, "do we have a deal?"

"I'm not good at this," Teague temporized, because he wasn't sure he could. To lie down and just accept touch? To not give anything in return? To exercise complete trust that another human being, even Jacky, would not hurt him when he had relinquished control?

"Not good at accepting love?" Jack asked, still bent over Teague's back. "I never would have guessed." He rained some more kisses along Teague's back and then shifted so he was no longer straddling Teague's thighs, the better to knead the muscles in Teague's lower back and buttocks.

Teague made a sound of loss for Jack's cock, no longer wedged near his bottom, and tried to think of something to say to the sarcastic truth Jack had just given him.

"You'll just let me go?" He ended up whining and wondered when he'd turned into a six-year-old girl.

"After we're done," Jack affirmed. Teague, mesmerized by the absolute wonder of Jack's hands moving from his lower back to his scrawny, muscular ass, couldn't do more than grunt and agree.

"You like that." Jack wasn't asking—it seemed obvious, because Teague couldn't stop himself from arching into Jack's strong, massaging pushes against his skin. "May I…." A thumb traced the furrow of his cheeks and brushed on the scars Teague knew were there on the backs of his thighs and toward his opening.

Teague whimpered. He couldn't help it. He didn't want Jacky to know, to think about the pain, to worry about the shit that had happened to him when he'd been helpless. He didn't want Jacky to think about him that way, period.

"They're just scars," he managed to say, glad his face was turned away. "I've got lots."

"I know," Jack said softly against the side of his bottom. "You've got lots. And they all hurt both of us. How about you let me touch these, and then they won't be able to hurt us anymore, okay?"

I am not worth all this pain.

He was almost biting his tongue in an effort not to say it. Instead he pulled his arms underneath him in an effort to escape.

Jack threw his long body on top of Teague's, pinning him to the mattress. Teague kept his shoulders tight, because they both knew he could throw Jack at any time. He'd proven that two nights ago. He was the meanest, most aggressive werewolf in the pack. They both knew it.

And Jack was a beta—not anywhere near as strong as Teague, and certainly not as tough.

He defeated Teague's intentions with two words.

"You promised."

They stayed there, frozen, for a couple of heartbeats, Teague's breathing harsh in his own ears. Teague's glance slid sideways to the red-numbered clock on the end table, and he saw they had a good long time before he was going to have lunch with Cory and talk about the werewolves locked in the basement.

Eventually that's what decided him. He didn't want to burden Cory and Green with any more of his bullshit—Cory, especially. She took too much on her narrow shoulders as it was. She wouldn't talk about the werewolves in the basement until she knew if Teague was going to be okay. So he had to make himself okay, had to make it okay with Jacky, right there in the privacy of their bedroom, before he left it.

Teague's shoulders softened, pressed into the mattress, and Jack's tackle became more of an embrace. "They're just scars," Teague repeated stubbornly, but they could both hear the catch in his voice, both feel the way his whole lower body clenched against the memory of a long-ago bastard with a broken bottle.

"We both know that's a lie," Jack countered. Teague snarled into the pillow—a human sound, but still visceral and angry.

"Can't we just leave my shit alone, Jacky? We've been doing this for a few weeks. Can't we just stick to that pattern? It was good, right? I didn't let you down in the sex department?" Jack sat up, but he kept the flat of his hand between Teague's shoulder blades to keep him pinned down. "We were all good," Teague finished helplessly, and Jack's other hand came up to ruffle reassuringly through his hair.

"The sex was great, Teague. Never doubt it," Jack said, scooting back until he was straddling the bottom of Teague's thighs again. "It was just one-sided. You gave, I took. That's not fair, man—don't you want to get a little back?"

I get it back when you let me touch you. "I don't want to be a pain in the ass."

Jack laughed breathily as he contorted impossibly forward and kissed the base of Teague's spine. "You are—frequently. I like it."

In spite of himself, the slowly burgeoning erection unfolding under his belly, and his discomfort with this situation, Teague found himself chuckling. "Didn't we do enough of this yesterday?"

"Yesterday was about comfort. Today is about you letting me give you something."

Jack's tongue carefully traced a crooked path across Teague's right asscheek and descended into the tender skin of the cleft. His movements were so deliberate that he must have been chasing a scar across Teague's skin. Teague gasped, all words gone, and held his breath. Jack used his palms to separate the halves of Teague's bottom and continued that torturous path, replacing pain and fear with love and joy.

Jack paused, right where… where….

Teague tensed again, hoping that would be the end of it, praying that it wouldn't. "What are you doing, Jacky?"

Jack's breath puffed against his secret skin when he spoke. "Giving you better memories."

Teague almost came off the mattress when Jack's tongue touched home. "Oh God…. Jacky…."

It was warm, and it was wet, and it was invading, plunging into him, teasing, laving, and Teague was held in place only by the pleasure, the drug of touch, as Jack licked and penetrated and gave. Teague's vision went black behind his clenched eyes, and he gasped and moaned softly. Jack shifted off his thighs and between them so Teague was lying spread-eagled and vulnerable beneath him as his fingers came into play.

It was… it was… oh *God*… it was sweet. But he wanted more. His hips started undulating, pressing against the mattress, and he let a whimper slip out, a begging sound. Jacky pulled away and gruffly whispered, "Roll over," and God help him, Teague did.

Jack didn't take up where he'd left off. He straddled Teague's stomach instead and started kneading the muscles of Teague's shoulders and chest.

Teague's cock was so hard it hurt.

He scowled up at Jack fiercely, unable to articulate his pain or his want or his need. Self-denial was too deeply ingrained in him to break the habit now.

Jack grinned in his face. He was panting slightly, and his own cock was hard on Teague's belly, but he was smiling. Teague was even more affronted—and more than seven-eighths tempted to whip his body around and fuck that smile right off Jacky's pretty face.

"You want something, Teague?"

Teague closed his eyes and counted to ten. "I'm fine, Jacky. No worries. Never… nnnngghhhhh"—because Jack's fingertips had found his nipples and pinched—"better."

Jack scooted his hips backward until they were groin to hard, aching groin. He hovered over Teague's face for a moment, lips to lips. "Because it would be okay, you know, if you wanted something. I'd be happy to give you whatever you wanted…."

Teague wanted Jack to kiss him. He'd always thought kissing overrated until he'd first kissed Jack. It had been passionate and intimate, the way kissing a stranger wasn't. He'd kissed Katy too, and the sweetness had been a surprise, but that passion and intimacy—he'd learned it all from Jack.

He didn't have any words. Teague lifted his lips up to Jack and prayed the boy would forget his game and just kiss him, without strings or caveats…

And oh God, his mouth was glorious. It was hard and fierce and wanting. Jack wanted Teague as much as Teague wanted Jack, and their tongues meshed and mated and their lips whispered. Teague groaned and lifted his hands, not in mastery but in need. He needed to wrap his arms around Jack's shoulders and hold him—it was imperative.

Their bodies ground together as they kissed, just the friction of their cocks between their stomachs and the terrible, terrible want between them.

Jack tried to move. Teague knew it was to finish what he'd started, to take Teague's erection into his sweet mouth and try to suck his brains out of his dick. Teague didn't let him.

"Stay," he begged between kisses. "Oh God… please stay…." Because he needed an anchor, someone to hold onto, so he didn't disintegrate, fly into outer space, lose himself completely in the unbearable high of being touched. He needed Jacky, whether he came and—oh… oh… Christ, he was going to come—or not. Teague needed to hold Jack. It was more important than orgasm, more important than his pride, more important than breath.

He needed to hold Jacky. He just did.

His climax shattered through his synapses and exploded out of his skin. He held on to Jack, clenching him so tight Jack could barely move, could barely breathe, even as Jack's own climax shot a scalding path across Teague's belly. They clung together, breathing hard while Teague's arms convulsed around Jacky's shoulders.

"Anything," Jack panted. "I'll do anything you need me to."

They were touching, skin to skin, sex to sex. Jack had touched him, without reservation, without reciprocation.

It was a debt Teague could never repay.

Being the Royal Bank

I LOOKED at the shiny silver knife in the werewolf's shaking hands and was completely baffled.

"You wrapped that in bubble wrap and shoved it up your *ass*?" The sincere dedication to hatred in that act was really out of my league.

Behind me I heard Teague grunt. "So I smell, my lady." He sounded as baffled as I was. Bracken wasn't confused in the least—he was cracking up.

Fucking awesome. Bracken was in fine form today, which, considering how rocky things had been between us after the werewolf thing, was a good sign. I don't like it when the people I care about put themselves in danger. I really don't like it when they do that and I'm left out. It makes me all pouty and irritable, and Bracken gets the brunt of it. Especially when he's the dumbshit who gets shot!

Teague also seemed to be in good fighting trim, and this heartened me to no end. We'd heard him—hell, the whole hill had heard him—have a class-six emotional hurricane two nights before. I didn't blame him—I'd been in the process of a similar storm myself—but Teague… well, shit. Teague was so damned repressed, so sincerely sure that he didn't deserve anything, much less honest emotions—man, the fact he'd walked out into the living room, fresh from a shower after his run, looking like he could take on a biker bar and then some, was a testament to the guy's resilience, that was for damned sure.

A good thing we were all hunky-dory, because this negotiating thing wasn't going so well.

"Shut up, cunt, and let me the fuck out of here." The guy we were "negotiating" with, the werewolf with the bubble-wrapped knife, was a mixed bag of genetics with straight black hair, cinnamon-colored skin, and light gray eyes. He was also about seven buckets of terrified, pissed-off crazy.

I looked around the bare steel room and at the four other werewolves in it. They were at the opposite end of the room from MacShitsyerpants and looking at the guy like he smelled really, really bad.

According to Teague, he did, and not just because his hands were covered in feces. There was something otherworldly going on with this one that was setting off the werewolf sensors like alarm bells.

And since his hands *were* covered in feces, he didn't smell that great to me either.

I squinted at the guy. "I've got to say, I'm at a loss. What in the fuck was your plan?"

Because really, this was a lose/lose situation for the guy. After we'd taken him and his buddies out two nights ago, we'd brought them here. We were pissed—I mean *seriously* pissed. The fuckers had set up a "peace treaty" meeting and then tried to ambush us. We should have taken them out before the ambush even had a chance to take effect, but Teague had brought Jacky, and shit had gone down, and… well, we were as pissed at ourselves for walking into the trap as we were at these assholes for springing it.

Since we'd killed fifteen out of twenty of them, we figured we'd let these five sit in lockup until we didn't feel like annihilating them on general principle.

And it wasn't like lockup was that bad. It had a bathroom—one of those little portajohns, but still, odds were they'd seen each other's junk before, right?—and food and water. We'd even given them a big warm soapy bucket for a sponge bath, and some clean clothes. We'd put cots in and given them blankets. Hell, someone had even brought in a box of untouched paperbacks. I mean, we wanted *negotiators*, not *hostages*, right? And we'd thought it might be going well, until Bracken, Teague, and I had walked into the vampire vault, so called because that's where we put our brand-new or out-of-control vampires, and this guy had reached into his soiled shorts and pulled out what had proven to be a knife.

I looked at him again, waving that knife in front of me, the word "cunt" echoing in my ears like a dying cat. "Do you have *any* idea how many people are outside who would be willing to kill you if you lay one finger on us?" I asked, hoping for sanity. "Besides the fact that the three of us did some serious damage to your entire pack two nights ago for shits and giggles?"

"I don't give a fuck!" the guy screamed. Spit flew out of his mouth, and with that and the smell, I was really glad I was across the room from him. "Just let me the fuck out of here and I won't fucking kill you!"

"Or maybe," I said with a grimace, "you put that thing down and we won't kill *you*?"

I was charging power as we talked. Of course I was. I had a shield at the ready, because I was standing between Bozo MacShitsyerpants and my beloved and my friend. I'm not stupid—just mortal. The plan was that nobody else got to shed a drop of blood because these guys were brain-damaged assholes with no sense of family, honor, or organization.

He'd shoved a silver knife up his *ass*?

I looked at the guy in complete disbelief, shaking my head and wishing I was the type of power-mad psycho bitch who could just fry all these fuckers where they sat and get rid of this little problem.

"I just want the fuck out of here!" the guy sobbed, and I sighed. He was so pathetic.

"Okay, Junior," I said, trying to take the irritation out of my voice. "I'll make you a deal. You put away the pig sticker, and we'll take you outside for a bit while we work this out. Does that work for—"

The dumbshit rushed me—knife out, arms flailing, shouting, spittle and drool, the whole nine yards. He didn't even use his werewolf speed, and I was in the process of throwing a shield up between that knife and me and the guys when Teague did something supremely stupid.

He *threw himself in front of me.*

And took the silver knife right in the middle of his ribs.

Teague screamed and fell at my feet, and I screamed and used my shield to slam MacShitsyerpants back against the steel wall with enough force to make his head crush in a little bit. I wasn't sure if he was dead yet, so I kept him mashed there like a gurgling bug and sank to my knees in front of Teague, glaring at Bracken to stand back so the guy wouldn't bleed out.

"Green!"

He was coming.

"Jesus, you dumb Irish motherfucker, what in the *hell* did you think you were doing?" I fished in the pocket of my jeans for the bottle of herbal salt wash that counteracted silver in werecreatures and iron in the sidhe. Our lives were risky enough that I never went anywhere without it.

"Protecting… my… queen…."

Christ, spare me from heroes. With a yank I cleared the knife from under his ribs, grimacing as the blood welled up from it. The knife wasn't that long—five inches, maybe—and on a werewolf, this sort of wound was normally cake. A few minutes panting, some beer, some salty meat, and he'd be good to go.

But it was long enough to drive the silver deep into Teague's body, and that was bad. That made the wound worse than it would be on a human. Teague was starting to froth blood at the mouth and turn gray, like a guy with a really fatal infection, and wherever Green was, it was time for me to pony up and do some first goddamned aid.

"I was throwing a shield up," I muttered, squirting about half the bottle of salt wash on the wound.

He hissed. "I'd forgotten you could do that, Lady."

"Well, goddammit, remember! I can protect you. It's my *job* to protect you!" I parted the wound to see how deep it went. It was already turning a dark gray, like Teague's skin. Shit. I knew what I'd have to do.

"I… beg… to… differ…."

"Fuck." I would *not* argue about this right now. I swore again, and then without wincing or cringing or any of the girly shit I *really really really* wanted to do because I was *so* not a healer, I shoved the little plastic bottle as far into his flesh as I could before the icky, squishy give stopped. Then I took it in both hands and squeezed as much of the salt wash as I could into the wound.

Teague gasped again and made a "manly pain" sound. *"Green!"* I called in my head, with all the shock and terror I was *not* voicing, and he was suddenly next to me, holding his hands to his ears.

"Holy blue fuck!" he snapped. "Even in my head, that's worse than a grieving bean sidhe—now move!"

I did, looking helplessly at my red-dripping hands, while Green moved in to bend down and kiss Teague on the lips. Sex was the hallmark of his healing—the kiss was as necessary to Green as a bandage would be to a human doctor.

"Cory?" Nicky said. He'd apparently arrived on Green's heels. "That guy on the wall—are you going to kill him, or is he going to be art?"

I looked at the guy. His skull was reshaping itself, so apparently I hadn't killed him straight off. "He's too ugly to be art," I snarled, and I was a werewolf's whisker away from squashing the guy flat. MacShitsyerpants yelped, and there was a sudden rank smell of urine as five frightened werewolves voided their bladders.

"Lady, please don't."

The voice was soft but sound. Teague had apparently broken away from Green's best healing kiss to stop me from killing Dumbfuck MacShitsyerpants, and I was damned if I knew why.

"Any particular reason?" I asked, skeptical.

Teague sat up and nodded respectfully to Green, who in turn gave Teague a hand up. His skin was already flushing, and his wound had knit while Green was touching him, but his dark blue T-shirt was split wide down the middle, and blood—red and the infected gray—saturated both the T-shirt and the gray-green flannel shirt over it.

"It's my job," he said tersely. "Tomorrow, fair fight. These guys"—a nod at the other werewolves—"can see whose dick is bigger."

"These guys" were crouching in a puddle of their own piss making puppy-whimpering noises. I think if someone had asked them at that moment, they would have told me my alpha was five feet nine inches of pure dick with a topper of dark blond hair.

"Awesome." I glared at my hands and forced down nausea. I'd had blood on my hands before, but it was usually from someone I'd killed or fought with. And it hadn't been turning gray. "We'll have a gladiator death match, complete with audience and are-you-fucking-shitting-me, asshole?"

Teague blinked and gave a thin smile of retribution, not even surprised at how fast I'd downshifted. "I want to kill the guy who just knifed me, Lady—and if I recall, he was the one shitting."

"Auuuugghhhh…." I wanted to scrub my gory hands through my hair and over my face, but I couldn't. I was just going to stalk outside to the anteroom at the bottom of the stairs when I heard Green clear his throat. This werewolf thing was my barbecue. I was Teague's entrée to the new world of the preternatural, and wolves got really confused with too many leaders. With a sigh, I looked around again at the odd assortment of frightened young men who had signed on for what they'd thought would be an everyday gang rumble and ended up the surviving members of a massacre.

"You! Assholes!" I barked. "Are you ready to go get a shower and change out of those dumbshit clothes?" They'd come dressed as their own little brown-and-green gang—they looked like big fat dorkfish.

They nodded hopefully.

"Excellent. Nicky?"

"Yes, my liege." He bowed ironically, and it was all I could do not to flip him a gore-crusted bird.

"I want you and seven of your closest werecritter friends to escort these guys upstairs. They can wait in the anteroom for now, and as soon as the vampires wake up, let them know they're breakfast." The vampires would be able to keep track of the werewolves for a little while after the blood donation. It wasn't a sure-fire security system, but these guys had never been fed from. They looked scared enough for it to act as a pretty darned good threat.

Nicky nodded and trotted up the stairs to gather suckers to help him, and I looked at the four saddest werewolves on the planet.

"You! Assholes! Strip to your skin, leave your nasty old laundry in here, and meet us out in the anteroom." I gave MacShitsyerpants a squeeze, just to hear him gurgle. Then I raised him up to the ceiling and dropped him, smiling with some sick satisfaction as he yelped at the crunch of an ankle bone. It would take that a good couple of hours to heal completely.

"You! Dumbfuck! You get to stay here all night. And we're not cleaning *jack.*"

Teague was looking at me beseechingly, or I really would have killed the fucker who'd knifed him. Bring a knife to a negotiation? MacShitsyerpants deserved to die just for being that ass-stupid. As it was, I led the way outside of the anteroom to let the werewolves get naked. Just as I cleared the vault, I was thrown into the side of the door hard enough to see stars.

"What in the fu—"

"What, you're not happy that he's got to serve you, you want to fucking get him killed too?"

I glared at Jacky, wondering when my head had exploded. "Jacky?"

Suddenly Bracken was between me and Jacky, growling, which is never a good sign, and Teague was hauling at his partner's arm.

"Jacky, it was my own dumb-fuck fault, you hear me? She was throwing a shield up, and I just—"

"You say that, but you're the one with the blood—"

I reached behind my head to feel the bump back there—it *felt* like it was actually bleeding—but Green got there in time to stop me.

"Don't want to mix Teague's blood and yours, beloved," he warned softly, and I jerked my hands away. Don't want to mix. No making vampire werethings, no having the werecritters bite the sidhe, no werecritter sorceresses or vampire sorcerers, nope, nuh-uh, no thanks. We'd seen where that ended, and it wasn't pretty.

He passed his hand over the bump on my head and it went away. So did the pain, which was good—because if Bracken thought for one minute that Jack had really hurt me, he'd kill him, and then we'd be fucked.

"Bracken! Down, boy!" I snapped, jumping into the fray. Bracken glared at me.

"He hit you!"

"He pushed me. It was an accident!" I hoped Brack would take it at that. It had felt more personal than that, but I wasn't going to cry foul.

"You!" Jacky turned away from Teague, who was gruffly ordering his beta out of the room. "You got him hurt. Are you happy? Is there anything else you want from him? More blood? You fucking ghoul—"

My eyes widened with shock—not so much at the harsh words, since I give out plenty of that on my own, but from the anger aimed at me. Jacky closed in on me and grabbed my arm, shaking me, forgetting he was a werewolf and I was not. My head was smacking back against the wall, even though Green had my shoulders and was trying to keep me still. Jacky's grip on my arms *hurt*, but I fought the urge to throw up a shield. If Bracken knew how rattled I was getting, he really *would* kill Jacky, but ouch… damn it… I couldn't focus—and then Teague jumped in and stopped the whole thing.

He went wolf, and Jacky—bonded to him in his heart and probably his body as well by now—went with him.

In a heartbeat, even less, Jack was on his back, his furry body tangled in a puddle of jeans and a thermal shirt, whining in submission. Teague's blond hackles were up all along his spine, and his jaws were locked—without biting—around Jacky's throat.

Green, Bracken, and I stared at the wolf tableau for a moment, shocked and saddened.

Christ. What a fucking choice. It was one I'd never want to make— but it was also one Bracken or Nicky wouldn't force me to make either. We all loved Green too much to hurt him that badly.

Teague growled and backed off, staring at Jacky's puzzled, hurt wolf with fierce, ungiving eyes. This was his wolf's decision—support the pack over his lovers.

Jacky whined and bumped noses, and Teague licked him resignedly, and that much giving, that much forgiving, made him abruptly human again.

Teague was much less assured as a man than he was as a wolf. He looked down at his mate, who was now human and lying on the floor looking stunned and devastated.

"Jacky…," he mumbled. Jack looked away.

Teague didn't have a whole lot of resources in him to deal with a lover turning his back. In fact, he only had one. In a moment he was a wolf again, hauling ass up the stairs for the main room. I said, *"Fuck!"*

Green touched my face and the back of my head again, then said, "I've got Teague. You get this goatfuck!" And then he was gone. He breezed by

Nicky, who had returned and was looking at us with horrified eyes, and I squinted at him, wondering if it was the adrenaline or the tears making my vision so blurry.

Then I couldn't look at Nicky anymore, so I turned toward the goatfucker in question. "Nicky, help him up," I said numbly. Jack looked at me with unfriendly eyes.

"You know—" I stopped for a minute to wipe my eyes with the heel of a shaking hand. "—I could have grown old and died without forcing him to make that choice."

Jack dropped his glare, misery suffusing every line of his long, nearly unblemished body. "I thought he'd choose me."

"He did," I snapped, wiping my eyes again. Fuck. The blood on my hands was making them sting. "If he hadn't done that, Bracken would have killed you." I was deadly serious. I could feel Bracken's entire body vibrating behind me. Jack had yelled at me. He had gotten in my face, he had grabbed my arm through my sweatshirt with bruising, supernaturally strong fingers. Green hadn't known about the bruises to heal them. They throbbed now under my sweatshirt, and I made a mental note to hide them until they could be taken care of. Nobody did that to me, not with Bracken at my side.

Jack looked up, startled, and saw Bracken. My beloved's lips were drawn back from his teeth in a horrible snarl, and he was growling like a true wolf. Jack turned pale and looked at me, really looked at me. I am small—a lot smaller than he is—and my hands, and by now probably my face, were covered in Teague's blood. My face was cold, so it was probably pale, and all in all I looked little and plain and human.

And Jack had hurt me—and hurt me on purpose. But I didn't think he was a dishonorable man, not at heart. Teague couldn't love somebody like that.

"I'm sorry," he said weakly, gazing into space at something I couldn't see. "I didn't mean to—"

"It's okay," I said automatically, but I wiped my eyes again.

Bracken snarled, "The hell it is."

"All right, it's not," I sniffled. "But we've got other stuff to do. Jacky, get your clothes. Nicky needs to go find us some more wolves. Go with him. If you don't want to do that, go to the common room, or back to your bedroom, or… hell, anywhere but right here, right now, okay?"

"I'm so sorr—"

"*Okay!*" I was nodding, trying to get him to find his good sense and go. Clumsily, as though not actually seeing what he was doing, he gathered his clothes in front of his groin and did just that. I found myself hoping his good sense was wadded up somewhere in his jeans and boxers, because I certainly hadn't seen it from where I was standing.

As he wobbled his way up the stairs, I turned to the wide-eyed werewolf "negotiators," who had come out of the vault in time to see most of what had just happened.

"That gold werewolf," I said, with the strongest, angriest voice I had, "was your alpha. He just picked me and Green over his own mate." I looked them in the eye, one by one, letting my fuck-with-me blaze out my eyes. "If you want to die slow, you can get in the ring tomorrow with your buddy in the other room. If you want to die quick, you can fuck with me today. If you're set on choosing life? Then I suggest you do whatever the fuck I say. Are we understanding each other?"

Four heads—different heights, different hair colors, different eyes. One motion—bobbing earnestly up and down—as they all agreed with exactly what I was saying.

Mama Cory, Papa Green

THE SIDHE treasured their parents, after a fashion.

The fact was that in Bracken's family, parents and children working in concert to support a leader was the norm, probably from the race's inception. It was one reason among many that incest was not a taboo for Green's people.

The leader was the parent. The people in the parent's hill were the children. Having a taboo against "incestuous" relationships would have doomed the race.

Some sidhe broke away from their parents. Green had when he'd been only fifty years old. For much of his life, he'd preferred to flit about the world. He would find a lover, usually mortal, and settle down until his mortal died. After he'd mourned, always longer than the sidhe thought proper, he would move on.

But Green's first leaders had been compassionate and indulgent. As Green started his own faerie hill, he'd remembered them fondly. They played, broke bread together, and made love frequently and with great enjoyment. Green's childhood had been a happy one.

But he learned very quickly that not all mortals had that sort of comfort.

It had been a hard realization—and for a century or two, Green avoided the human race as a whole simply to avoid that terrible, aching pain that came with having lovers who had never been taught how to love.

Eventually he learned the joys of teaching them how to love, a discovery that made all the greatest joys—and all the greatest pains—of his long life possible.

When Cory joined the hill and became a lover to its two leaders, she had, unwittingly at first, assumed the job of the hill's mother. If he had asked Cory, Green was sure she would have said Grace, the very maternal vampire, did a fine job as hill mother, and her own services were not needed—but both Green and Grace knew that while Cory was still learning like a journeyman learns from a master, she was the true hill mama, down to her tough-love disposition.

And she had done a fine job mothering Teague. She had listened, given advice, kept him from the worst parts of himself, and, along with Green and

Bracken, stood back and prayed when it was time for Teague to confront his own demons. She had even chased him into the rain and forced him to forgive himself—a classic mother move if Green had ever seen one.

Teague went to her when he was stressed, confided in her when he was confused, and valued her beyond measure.

But boys—especially human boys—sometimes had violent human reactions that many women—including Green's beloved—were not comfortable with.

Sometimes a boy just needed his father.

Teague's heart had been screaming for a father since he was born.

Green snagged a blanket as he blurred through the house. As he outstripped the wolf streaking through the gardens to the South Placer hills beyond Green's environs, he kept it tucked under his arm.

Elves could move in what Cory called *hyperspeed*—Green thought of it as *blurring* or *moving*—but he didn't need his hyperspeed to keep up with Teague. He just needed to run, barefoot, fleet, and graceful, across the earth that sustained him. He did, for several miles across the rough grass and twiggy undergrowth of the foothills, until Teague showed signs of flagging.

Of course, Teague being Teague, it took a while. Even after his pace slowed, he still pushed himself until his body was straining, his fur was slicked against his lean wolf's body with sweat, and his breath was coming in ragged pants. Suddenly, just like a switch going out, his back end flopped to the ground as his front paws churned into the mud in front of them.

Slowly Green stepped out from behind the trees he'd been using for cover. He held the blanket spread out between his hands and waited patiently. Teague looked at him from miserable wolf's eyes—green-hazel in color, like Teague's as a man.

Teague whimpered and looked away, and Green sighed, kneeling to the forest floor to wrap him in the blanket. As Green's arms moved around him, he felt the change, and as he stood, he held a short, scrawny, exhausted man wrapped in a blanket like a child. Green walked back toward the hill and the house at an easy pace, cradling Teague like the little boy he'd never been.

"He turned away from me, Green."

Green looked at Teague. They were the first words he'd said in nearly twenty minutes. His hair was plastered to his head with sweat, the same as his fur had been when he was a wolf, and he was pale—so pale. If Teague didn't figure this out, didn't find his balance with his lovers, Green had no doubt he'd make himself sick, just as Cory had before Bracken. Unlike Cory, Teague didn't have any good memories to sustain him. As a package of flesh, he would probably catch pneumonia, get a fever, develop cancer—something physical that doctors would give a name to. As a supernatural being—even a werewolf—he would simply waste away.

"He didn't understand, mate. Give him time. He's nearly as stubborn as you, right?" It was true, Green had no doubt. Jacky had a good heart under all that jealousy and selfishness. He'd never had a reason to look beyond his own needs, that was all.

"How can he love me again?" Teague asked, and his naked, bleeding voice was all the proof needed that the man was at the end of a very short survival rope. "He thinks I turned against him… that I picked you over him. I… I'm no damned good at this." That naked voice hardened, became bitter. "You should have never put us together, Green. I'm only going to hurt them."

Green sighed, looked around, and found a nice tree to sit against. He was wearing jeans and a sweatshirt. They might get damp in the November dew, but this afternoon had some thin, butter-colored sunshine to offer—and Green, like most elves, was seldom bothered by the cold.

He settled himself in, cradling Teague close for warmth, and took advantage of his height and size in the same way he had for Jacky two days ago. His children—his lost, sad, wayward children. A good father needed to be there in the calm after the tantrum. All children would frighten themselves with the force of their emotions, even the fully grown ones.

"How could he love you?" Green asked when he was settled. "How could he *not* love you? That's the real question."

Teague harrumphed, some of his usual fight back in place. "I don't even know why I'm asking you. I'm not sure why *you* love me either!"

Green kissed his forehead, exactly as he would have kissed a five-year-old's. "I love you because you're strong, Teague Sullivan. You're brave and you're kind. I love you because you try, and because as sore as your heart is, you still haven't given up on love. I love you because you defend me and mine and because you simply are. Is that good enough?"

Teague just lay there, wrapped in his arms, weeping silently in the cold November sunshine. "Bracken would have killed him."

"Mmm-hmmm. *I* might have killed him. I love you both, mate, but that's my beloved he was threatening. You did exactly right."

"Why does he hate her so much?"

Ah, there was the brave Teague Green had been looking for. It was a ballsy, necessary question.

"Because he thinks she threatens your love for him."

"Why can't he see?" For the first time, Teague showed some animation. He sat up, adjusting his body on Green's lap, unconsciously snuggling into Green like Cory would. "I… I was nothing until I met you. I was nothing before I came to work here. Doesn't he see, I wouldn't be the thing he loves if I didn't have a… a family to fight for?"

Green smiled at him, for the first time making sure Teague could see his expression—the acceptance, the sober attention. Green wanted Teague under no misconceptions that he was loved and loved well. "You were most definitely something fine before you came here, Teague, but you're right. Your belief in yourself, your self-worth, it comes from serving us, from being a part of a larger purpose. There is no shame in that. Jacky, he's always been an island, you see? A lonely boy, up in his own head. He's never seen the world as something that could hurt him. You've seen it as chaos, Teague. You know the only way to keep your family safe from the chaos is to fight on the side of order. But maybe he'd know some of this if you spoke to him."

Teague grunted, and Green threw back his head and laughed. When he was done, he looked at the stubborn little Irishman with sincere affection and saw that Teague was blushing to the roots of his hair and couldn't meet Green's eyes.

Green abruptly sobered. His voice slid into cockney territory— Adrian territory—and he clucked reassuringly. "Aye, Teague, I know. You and words, not friends, not so much, am I right, mate?"

Teague grunted and rolled his eyes. "No. Me and words aren't friendly."

"I didn't think so. Ye see, ducks, you and words—you're afraid, aren't you? You give too many words, you give too much of your heart, and that's a bad thing, aye?"

Teague nodded and leaned his head against Green's shoulder, probably so he wouldn't have to meet Green's gaze. "Aye."

Green cupped Teague's chin in long fingers and forced him to meet Green's eyes. "The problem with that, luvie, is that this boy already has your heart. He and Katy, they hold it beating in their hands, aye?"

Teague blinked at him slowly. "Aye," he whispered despondently.

"Well, I've got news for you, mate. They're going to keep breaking off pieces of it—especially Jacky—if they don't know what it is they hold. Katy not so much. She's softer. She'll give and yield, and you need that. But ye need yer Jacky as well, aye?"

Teague swallowed. Green watched his Adam's apple bob. "Aye."

"Well then, ye need to risk your words, mate. If they don't know what it is that's beating in their hands, they're going to make some mistakes in the keeping of it, aren't they." It was a statement, in spite of the lilt at the end.

"Aye," Teague conceded, still staring at Green with wide, childlike eyes. "Green?"

"Aye?" Green tilted his lean mouth so Teague would know he was aware of his accent and the way it went from cultured British to cockney to Lake District to Wales and back.

"Where are you, when your voice goes like that?" Teague's voice throbbed with a need Green recognized.

"Under the moonlight, ducky, with Adrian by my side." Ah gods, it even hurt to say. Cory knew. It broke her heart to hear the cockney in his voice, but sometimes she all but begged him to break her heart.

Teague nodded and leaned against Green again.

"You ready to go back, mate?" Green asked, although his bottom wasn't as cold and his body wasn't as sore as all that.

"No, Green. I'd… I'd really love just to hear you talk some more."

Green looked down at him, but Teague was relaxed, his arms crossed against his chest, a look approaching peace on his usually scowling face.

"Aye, werewolf. We could sit here and talk. You up for some stories?"

"Yeah," Teague sighed dreamily. There was a space, and Green knew what was coming before he even said it. "Tell me about Adrian."

It wasn't a hardship. Green and Cory talked about him freely now—no more of that horrible, heart-steeling silence before they mentioned his name. And Teague was so earnest—and he so rarely reached for anything.

So Green started with their arrival in the foothills, and the hard, ungiving land. By the time they'd met their first werewolf, Teague was dozing serenely on his shoulder, and Green was ready to move on. He stood quietly, then kept his gait steady and his footsteps silent to give his poor werewolf a chance to heal.

BRUISES

JACK MANAGED to get his clothes back on, and for an hour he followed a grim, angry Nicky around, pretending to be useful when dealing with the Southern California werewolves. Eventually each of the "negotiators" had a room—and two roommates who would sleep in resentful shifts. By the time they were done with the logistics, Jack had the feeling the new guys would have eaten their tongues rather than do anything to further piss off one little college student and her terrible fist of death.

"You *grabbed* that chick?" said the last guy to get shoved into Nicky's grasp by Bracken—who was standing in front of Cory like a sentinel of death. "You may be dumber than the assholes who dragged me into this clusterfuck."

Jacky was starting to agree.

This house, this operation, this *place*, it was all so much *bigger* than he was. These guys he was housing, they had lost their friends trying to *kill* Cory and Bracken—and him and Teague. Jack had been so immersed in his own personal bullshit on the night the werewolves arrived and the battle went down, he hadn't comprehended how ugly the massacre had been.

Now he was starting to realize how stupid his own actions were. If he'd taken control of the carload of guys at the airport, maybe fewer people would have died. Teague was right. Teague had been right all along. Jack wasn't made for this paramilitary shit. He wasn't good at it. He could take orders, and he'd always been good at having Teague's back, but he'd never been great at the battle itself or thinking through the strategy or….

Or apparently seeing the big picture.

By the time the whole thing was sorted out, Nicky's unfriendly glare had lightened up maybe one tenth of an iota. "You have possibilities for not being a complete asshole," he said as he dropped Jack off at his own door. "Now could you stay out of the way and try not to hurt anyone today?"

Jack turned bleak eyes to the guy who had carried out his wife's orders with the crisp efficiency of an army lieutenant. "Too late. Damage done."

Nicky shook his head. "I hope you know your guy saved your life today."

Jack frowned. Sure, Cory had told him Bracken would have gotten violent, but he wasn't sure it had gotten *that* bad. "What do you mean?"

Nicky shook his head again. "You know, you really must have been riding his coattails for the last year and a half. I've seen Bracken kill before, and so have you. Do you remember the expression on his face?"

Two nights ago, Bracken had been pissed. He'd reached out his hand with a snarl of irritation and his teeth bared in fury and grabbed the blood and organs from his targets and yanked it across a vacant field.

Jack had seen that expression not an hour before, right before Teague had turned wolf and taken him down.

"Holy Christ." He almost sat down right there in the hallway.

Nicky rolled his eyes in disgust. "Yeah, Jack. You know why we love Teague? It's because he's not convinced he's the only person on the planet with problems. Katy should be home soon—maybe you should just go wait for her. I'm done babysitting."

Jack made his way into the bedroom feeling numb and used. How could he have fucked everything up so badly?

He'd been eating in the weres' common room, making tentative gestures of friendship toward some of the people there, when a sort of electricity passed through the hill. A few moments later, Green had sprinted by, moving with some serious preternatural speed. Jack wouldn't have been able to see the elf move at all if he hadn't been a werewolf.

In spite of the electricity and the group knowledge that something was decidedly up, nobody moved. The pretty, dark-haired girl who had been talking quietly at the table next to Jack caught his apprehensive look. "Word will spread," she said with certainty. "And if it pertains to us personally, someone will let us know."

The words were hardly out of her mouth when Nicky appeared and gave him a nod from the doorway. "He's fine, but you may want to see for yourself."

Jack could hardly remember shouting at Cory after that, or Teague's angry voice pulling him away. Until Nicky had brought it up, he hadn't been able to recall Bracken's murderous expression—he'd been convinced that, just like in his dream, Teague had gone and sacrificed himself for the indifferent lady of the house.

He was lying on the bed staring at the ceiling when Katy came in. He was desperately trying to recapture the smell, the touch, the transcendent moment of making love that morning, when Teague had reached up, held him so tight he couldn't breathe, and actually asked for something.

Stay. Please stay.

Jack had lived for that moment—it had been everything he'd ever dreamed about love.

In this particular moment, thinking back on it, Jack hated himself so badly that he thought not hiding under the bed like a child when Katy walked in was one of the bravest things he'd ever done.

"Heya, Jacky," she said happily, then got a good look at Jack's face and let loose a string of expletives that almost rivaled what Jack had heard out of Cory's mouth. She finished up with "What did you *do?*"

Jack looked away just as he had with Teague, and he had to admit it rankled. He had not known he was a coward, and now he couldn't seem to escape the fact.

"Don't you *do* that to me!" Katy snapped. She looked around wildly for something to throw, since she'd already dropped her purse, but their room was bare and spartan. Even with their personal things, it was still very masculine, which was very Teague. She settled for kicking the stuffed chair Jack had started to claim as his and then running up and grabbing his shoulders to shake him.

"Don't you do that! It took us weeks to put that man together, to fix him, to make his heart strong enough to not run away. I walk in here and you look like you knifed him in his damned heart. Don't look away from me, asshole—you got to fucking own up!" She was right there in his face, and he couldn't bring himself to meet her eyes.

Jack rubbed his hand across his mouth and spoke to the far side of the room. "It's just," he said quietly, taking some of the heat from Katy's angry glare, "that I don't understand why he needs the hill. When it was just the two of us, he was okay, you know? Why couldn't he have loved me then, when it was just us?"

Katy shook her head and muttered something that sounded like "I have no words." Then she sighed and flopped onto the bed next to him.

"He…. You may have thought it was just the two of you, Jacky. I know you did. But it wasn't. Who were you working for that entire time?"

Jack shrugged. "Green."

"Yeah, sure—and I know the first time you were ever at the hill was when I bit you. But Teague… he'd been here before. He knew what he was serving. He liked it that way."

Jack's eyes widened considerably. Of all the dumbshit things that had *never* occurred to him. "But why?" He was whining, and he didn't care.

Katy stood up and started to pace. Her mouth moved quickly, as though she was talking in rapid-fire Spanish, but no words came out for a minute. "Why? Jacky, you dumbass—why not?"

Jack opened his mouth in surprise, but she just kept going right over him.

"I know you think you're all anybody needs, but—damn! Jacky, here at the hill, you're never lonely. Yeah, you're never *alone*, but if I get mad at you, I run out that door and there are a hundred people who will sit and listen to my problems. I want to go shopping, I've got a pretty plastic card that makes all my dreams come true, and all I've got to do to earn it is go work at a place where people smile at me and make me feel like I do good just to show up. I don't even got to do that if I don't want to. Green doesn't *make* anybody work. We just *do*, because not one of us hasn't been helped in some way, and usually big shit too. They don't just fix your flat tire in the rain, baby—they bail you out of the car before it goes off a cliff and then they give you a new one! And it's bigger than that! You know it is. Because there I was, trapped in some asshole's silver cage, and you know, even when I was out of my mind, even when I thought you and Teague were the bad guys, I still knew that somewhere out there, help was coming. I knew help was coming for *me*."

She'd been pacing the whole time. Now she sank slowly down on the bed next to a speechless Jack, who was trying to make his brain wrap around the world she'd shown him. He'd been living in it, eating, drinking, dreaming in it, but he hadn't known he was in it, not until now, when he saw how Katy fit in.

"Even if they didn't get there on time, Jacky. Yes, even then. We all know about your sister, about Renny's first husband, about Adrian. People die—people die here. I knew that. But just the idea... just the thought... that even if that asshole killed me, *someone* was on their way to get me...." She looked at Jack, and he met her eyes for the first time since she'd come in. "Goddess, Jacky, do you have any idea what people like me and Teague would do, just to know somebody would be coming to the rescue? They don't even have to make it in time. They just have to give a shit." She shook her head and sighed, leaning against him, stroking his arm and trying to get him to understand. "That's powerful shit, Jacky. That's big fucking medicine right there, you know?"

Jack tried to imagine it. His parents had always had money. When his sister was doing drugs, they'd thrown her into rehab after rehab, not once wondering if maybe what she needed was simply to know they'd come after her because they cared and not because they had to.

For the first time since Green had come to his apartment and offered him solace, Jack thought about his sister. He'd been angry when she died. He'd thought her new people had deserted her, just as the two of them had been deserted by the people in authority for their entire lives.

Now he wondered… seriously wondered. *Were you scared, Sara? Or did you know someone would have your back? Did it matter? Did it make it easier, knowing someone had your back?*

And someone really *did* have her back, Jack realized. Jack was here in the hill, the place Sara had told him would care for her. Green had come and taken care of the things she cared about, since her backup had been too late.

The enormity of what Jack didn't know assaulted him again, and he had a sudden flash to two nights before.

They had been hijacked and ambushed, and not once had Bracken or Nicky or even Teague acted like they were alone. Bracken had been cocksure that help was coming. He'd been pissed off, because he and Cory were at odds, but he'd known she was going to save their asses.

…if we don't kill you in the next five minutes, my beloved will when she arrives. You and your friends? You just became a domestic dispute of cosmic proportions—and that alone is a reason to kill you.

Teague had been wounded, and Green had healed him. Cory's hands had been dripping with Teague's blood not because she'd been hurting him, but because she'd been tending to him. And Jack had stalked in and assumed the worst, and he'd… he'd….

He told Katy then about what had happened, what he'd done. Afterward, he never could figure out where he'd gotten the words or the bravery to do it.

When her hand cracked across his cheek, it was almost a relief.

The stillness in the room was suffocating, and he was a coward again because Katy broke it.

"Jacky!" She was in tears, and so was he. "You turned away from him? How could you make him make that choice?"

"Because I'm an asshole," he admitted. He'd never thought he was, but God… the look of betrayal on Teague's face came back to him again, and he thought he'd be sick. Before he could actually finish his thought or say anything else, there was a tentative knock on the door.

"Come in," Katy said automatically. Maybe it would be Teague, or Green, or someone to make them feel better.

But it wasn't. Jacky was beginning to learn that atonement didn't come cheap or easy.

It was Cory.

"Hi," she said, looking over her shoulder as though she was expecting someone she didn't want to see. She closed the door behind her and dumped an armload of clothes on the dresser next to her—Teague's, left on the floor of the anteroom. When she was done, she turned to face them, smiling weakly. "Look. I need to do this and then find Green before Bracken sees, okay? I just…." Her voice firmed. "Jack, I really think you need to see this. It might make dealing together easier, okay?"

Jack looked up at her, his eyes still unfriendly. God, he hated himself for everything he'd done, he really did, but he resented her. He couldn't help it. He looked at her and saw the person who put his beloved in danger. It wasn't rational or kind, but there it was.

Her mouth quirked up on one side as though she knew exactly what was going through his head.

"Right. See, here's the thing." She unzipped the hooded green sweatshirt she was wearing, revealing a plain, oversized man's blue T-shirt underneath. It was, Jacky realized, *way* oversized—it was bunched at her middle and hung nearly to her knees. It must have been Bracken's or Green's, and she looked so much younger in it.

"How old are you, Lady?" Katy asked, echoing his very thought.

Cory wrinkled her nose. "Why does everyone ask me that? I'm old enough to drink—how's that?"

Barely, Jack realized in surprise. Then she took the sleeve of the shirt—it went nearly to her elbows—and raised it up to her pale shoulders, and he forgot about how old she was.

There were bruises on the back of her arm—four swollen, red-purple, blood-filled hematomas exactly the size of his fingers. The one from his thumb on the front was especially heinous, and he moaned a little in his throat. She lowered her sleeve and pulled up the other one, and there was an identical set of marks—but he must have pinched her flesh in his hand, because the hematoma was raised in a wedge shape behind the finger marks.

Jack stared at her in horror.

"I'm not a werewolf," she said unnecessarily. "I'm not an elf. I can do some pretty cool stuff with my power, and I really do function as an excellent weapon. But there's a reason Bracken and Nicky guard me. I chafe under it, and I give them shit, but the fact is, my physical body is just not that strong. I…." She blushed and shrugged. "I'm mortal, and I'm weak. Bracken would have killed you just to keep me safe from something like this, you understand?" She quickly put her sweatshirt back on and zipped it up, then put her hands in the pockets like an ordinary street kid using all that extra fabric as defense against the world.

"Teague's spent the last month getting used to jumping between me and anything threatening. He… he saved your life today. He jumped between us to keep me safe and to keep Bracken from killing you. It was all about keeping his family from being hurt, okay? You've got to forgive him for that."

Jack's mouth was dry, and he fought against darkness in his vision and bile in his throat. He'd done that. He'd laid hands on someone weaker than he was and….

"Why didn't you defend yourself?" he rasped, knowing he sounded petulant, but God… she could have pulverized him. She could have squashed him against the wall like a bug!

Cory flushed and looked away. "Well, you're Teague's beloved, you know? I don't like to use my shit against family—not when they don't have the same shit to fight back with…."

He didn't hear her next words, because her bruises flashed in front of his eyes and her words *I'm mortal and weak* rang in his ears, and he absolutely had to go to the bathroom to be violently ill.

Not One of the Men

Katy and Cory watched him run down the little hallway and then winced at the unmistakable sounds coming from the bathroom.

Cory grimaced. "Wonderful. I'm batting oh-in-a-thousand today. Maybe I should buy a lottery ticket and see what else I can fuck up."

Katy was usually very shy around the lady of the house. Cory was smart, like Jacky, and she seemed to have her shit together in ways Katy hadn't even dreamed of when Katy had been clawing her way through the back alleys and smack houses of Angel's Camp. But this hadn't been Cory's fault—it hadn't. As much as Katy loved Jack, well, she'd slapped him across the face for a reason.

"It wasn't your fault, Lady. Jacky, he's like…." She floundered for a minute and then said the first dumb thing that came into her head. "He's like a little boy making a fort in his bedroom, you know? There he is, and he thinks, 'Hey, I got Teague in here, we have a fort together!' Then I come and play, and he thinks, 'This is it. This is the most people who can come into my fort!' But the whole time, he doesn't realize that the fort in his bedroom is also in a house, which is also on a street, which is also in a city, you know? It's not just me and Teague and Jacky in his fort. There's a whole world protecting the fort, and he just thinks that's what it does, right?" Oh God… she was fucking this all up, she was sure of it—until Cory gave her an out-and-out blinding grin. Katy, who knew she was pretty and Lady Cory was not, suddenly also knew that Lady Cory was beautiful.

"That's awesome, Katy. You're right. He doesn't know how big we are. I guess…." She looked down to the bathroom again. The sounds of barfing had stopped, but Jack was making weak little sobs that echoed from the toilet and down the hall, and she looked away again. "I guess we'll tell him some other time, you think?"

Katy nodded and sighed. "I should probably go make sure he's okay. I know, I know he hurt you and all, but…."

Cory looked up and put her hand tentatively on Katy's as it waved generally between them. "Katy, believe me—you don't ever have to apologize for loving someone in spite of their flaws. Remember me? I'm the one married to a cave man."

Katy shook her head, and suddenly Cory's grip on her hand fluttered. Cory got a look for all the world as if she was listening to music in her head. Then she blinked and gave that tentative, shy smile.

"Green's back with Teague. He, uhm, he thinks that Jacky doesn't love him anymore, so you should be prepared for, uhm, you know. Beating his stubborn Irish head in with affection, right?"

Katy grinned at her widely and gave her a quick, exuberant hug. "Right. Good point. He's not so bright when it comes to love, no?"

Cory shrugged. "None of us are, except maybe Green." She turned to leave and then turned back, her pale, freckled cheeks washed with a blush. "Oh yeah. Bracken and I don't go back to work until Tuesday, but Grace is having a sale on those samplers. The same artist as before, with the wolves. She wants to know if you want one?"

And now it was Katy's turn to blush. Lady Cory, all ninja bitch and shit, going off to fight with the men, and she was getting Katy needlepoint. This was a good place. A good place with good family. Jacky had to see it. He had to understand that you wanted these people to love you, and that it would only make your heart bigger and stronger to have them at your back.

"That'd be nice," she said, ducking her head shyly.

Cory said, "Okay, then," and made her way out.

Katy sighed and went back to help Jack, because Goddess knew he would have been pissing his own pants for the last week if someone hadn't helped him with the fly.

He had just finished brushing his teeth when the door opened and Teague stumbled in. He was wrapped in nothing but a hand-knitted blanket, which he'd secured around his waist like a bath towel.

Katy ran up to him, fully intending to hug him until he begged for mercy, but, as Cory had warned, he was too prepared for rejection to accept her.

Keeping his head down, he started rooting through his dresser for clothes. Katy took a deep breath and tried another tack.

"Uhm, whatcha doin'?"

Teague swallowed and kept his face turned away. His dark blond hair was slicked back against his head with sweat, and his hazel eyes were red-rimmed with fatigue and grief. "Figured I'd find another room."

Katy laughed and felt her spine shift into place. "No," she said gently, and taking a page from his book, simply nudged him away from the dresser.

"Now, sit down. I'll find you some clothes, and you can go shower and wash those nasty feet, but you, me, and Jacky are sleeping in here if I have to beat you, shoot him, and drag your bleeding bodies into that bed, you hear me?"

She heard a puff of air that might have been a laugh. Then his hands came out and rested on hers, warm and still a little bit muddy from a long run as a wolf.

"That's, uhm, sweet, field mouse. But you and I both know it's not going to work. I'm… I have to work here. I…." She risked a look at his face, and if anyone recognized that terrible, fruitless struggle for words to name the maelstrom inside your heart, it was Katy. But she also knew Teague would never feel right unless he found those words on his own.

"I'm too broken to love without the hill," he said at last. "I need a reason to think I deserve you. Jacky, he can't live with that. I'll just—"

"Stay," Jack said from the bathroom. "Please stay."

Teague's face crumpled like a child's, and Katy grabbed his hands hard and then moved forward to lean her head on his chest. "You don't really want me," he whispered, the voice so like a child's that Katy thought she'd just burst into tears and they wouldn't get anything done. She womaned up, though, and swallowed all that in her throat, then soothed Teague's chest with her hands.

"Of course we want you," she reassured just for form. She knew the person he needed to believe it from was Jack.

"I'm stupid," Jack said. Katy risked a look at him. He'd stopped at the end of the hallway. His hand was gripping the doorframe so hard his knuckles were white, and he looked, if anything, even worse than he had when he'd just finished puking. His face was taut and pale, and the self-directed anger burned through his blue eyes. "I didn't know what I was doing. I was like a kid playing with a hand grenade. You threw yourself on the grenade for me, and I… I didn't even know you'd saved my life."

Teague scrubbed at his face, his chin still wobbly, and Katy hoped they could get through this because, damn it, something had to come from all this pain.

"I wasn't just saving you," he said honestly. "Jacky, you were hurting someone… you were hurting *her*… and after all she's done for us…."

Jack moaned a little. "I know," he said softly, and Katy believed him. Nothing like seeing the bruises of your bad deeds to make you know you're the bad guy. "I'm aware of my complete stupidity, okay, Teague? Please—don't. Don't let this take you away from us."

"Why do you want me, Jacky?" Teague asked, his voice raw. "You don't even know me."

And of all the sounds of hurt and disillusionment she'd heard Jacky make in the last hour, this one was the worst.

"That's not *true!*" Jack rushed up to them, but Teague's bubble of hurt, of self-containment, was so perfect and inviolable that Jack stopped just outside the place of comfort for all of them.

"What do you think you know?" Teague asked, a tinge of bitterness in the sound. "You know I've been hurt. You know I'm lonely. You know I love you and Katy. That doesn't make me your ideal mate, Jack. It just makes me vulnerable."

Jack closed his eyes and swallowed. "I'd never hurt...." *Oh fuck.* Katy winced, because he had. He'd done it more than once, each time more unforgivable than the last. He must have realized it too, because he stopped midstream and changed it. "I'll *never* hurt you again."

Teague looked up at Jack, everything in his eyes naked and bleeding. "I need to be sure," he said softly. "I can't do this if I'm worried. I can't do this if I think I'll go to sleep with you next to me one day and wake up alone in the morning. I need to know you can accept everything about me—including where my loyalties are."

Restlessly he turned back toward the dresser, where his clothes lay in a bundle. He picked up the T-shirt he'd been wearing that morning, the one with the hole and the dried blood on it, and he fingered the rent thoughtfully in the silence before turning back to Jack.

"I have violence in me, Jack." It was unequivocal. They all knew it was true. "I was a stone-cold killer for a lot of years. That hasn't changed. What's changed is now that I'm fighting for love and for people I can believe in, I'm going to throw my life into the battle with a lot more passion. You know I'd die for you, for Katy. You know that. You need to know that I'd die for Green and Cory and even that sonuvabitch Bracken. Hell, I'd probably die for Nicky if I had to. Anything, you understand, to keep this place alive. You need to get behind them, Jacky, because if you're against them, that's leaving me in the middle."

Jack blinked and swallowed, his face taut and pale. He was considering Teague's words carefully, Katy could tell, measuring the rebelliousness of his own heart against what he needed to be for Teague.

After a moment he said, "I can do that," with complete certainty.

Teague nodded and pulled out some clothes, then moved toward the door.

"Where are you going?" Katy asked, because it wasn't to the shower, that was for damned sure.

"I need to sleep alone tonight," he said, his voice empty. "I want you two to watch me fight tomorrow. Cory said I could take down the fucker with the knife in a one-on-one. I need you to see me do it."

Sleep alone? Oh God. "Teague!" Katy's voice was thick and broken. "You can't sleep alone. Who's gonna make the night monsters go away? You can't sleep alone. You'll scream and scream, and no one will kiss you better...."

The thought destroyed her. They knew. They'd heard him; they'd soothed him in his sleep. That was their job. They kept him together. They patched his heart up because it had been ripped open too many times to hold together on its own.

Teague pressed the heel of his hand hard against his eye. "You can't just love me when I'm weak, Katy," he said after a moment of pulling himself together. "You can't just love me because I need you. You need to love me when I'm strong. You need to love me when I'm an evil motherfucker defending the shit I love. I may die quicker alone, but at least I'll know what's real." He put his hand on the doorknob and looked up at both of them, meeting their eyes so they'd know he was serious.

"Please come tomorrow. The hill will tell you when."

And with that he was gone, leaving Katy alone with Jack, who was sinking to his knees, sobbing like a child.

NEVER ALONE

I ADMIT it. I stood around the corner from their room and waited to see what would happen. But I was keeping Green company, so that was okay.

I'd run into Green after passing Teague down the hall. Teague had been so shell-shocked he didn't even see me, and I'd had a horrible, skeleton-fingers-up-the-spine chill of fear.

The last time I'd seen someone look that shell-shocked was when I was looking in the mirror after Adrian died. Teague felt like someone had died. You can't hold someone when you think they've died, and if anyone needed to be held, it was Teague. And since I'd been there before, since I knew that feeling of betrayal, of loss, I knew what was coming next.

So Green and I stood shoulder to shoulder, and I read the bad news on Green's face as he unabashedly used his super elf-hearing to listen in on their most intimate, most painful conversation.

About midway through, he bumped me and I winced, and he cast me a sharp look before putting his hand on my upper arm through my sweatshirt to heal me.

"Thanks, beloved."

"You should have gotten someone else to do it."

"I couldn't let Bracken see."

He caught my eyes and nodded with a grimace. We both knew this situation, as bad as it was, could have been a whole lot worse. At that moment the door opened, and we didn't need to speak in each other's heads for me to read his little shove at my shoulders.

It was my turn.

"Hey, Teague," I said, keeping my voice friendly and neutral. Didn't know anything, didn't see anything, just a friend walking down the hall.

He looked ghastly—pale, red-eyed, and dirty, with his bare shoulders drooping over his scarred chest—but he managed a roll of the eyes.

"You are so full of shit," he called. I grimaced.

"Brown eyes," I replied softly. "Can't help it. They won't let you move out for long. You know that, right?"

Teague shrugged. He wasn't so sure. "How'd you know?" he asked seriously, and I could only give him the truth.

"It's exactly what I wanted, right after Adrian died. I figured it would hurt less to be alone, you know?" I bumped his shoulder with my own and nodded him down the hall.

"No one died," he said tersely. "Where are we going?"

"I figure you can room with Mario. He's got a king-sized bed and no designs on your body. This way you can go take a shower before you come and sit down and watch movies with me in the front room. And you feel like someone died, so don't give me that shit."

"I'm watching movies with you?" he asked, genuinely surprised.

"And eating ice cream and dancing to our favorite CDs, just like girlfriends at a slumber party. Now don't change the subject." I figured it would just be the movies and the ice cream, but I added the rest to see him roll his eyes again and scowl, which was a damned sight better than his expression of bleak hopelessness, thank you very much.

"I don't know what you mean," he growled, but he was lying and we both knew it. I stopped walking and turned to him, my eyebrows raised.

"Bullshit. You feel like you lost him, like he'll never love you again. I figure you're probably planning to make him watch you off old Dumbfuck MacShitsyerpants as painfully and savagely as possible, and then you're going to turn to him and say, 'See—I told you I was a fucking monster. Now go the fuck away!' Am I right?"

Teague turned bright red from the pale flesh of his bare stomach to the roots of his hair. "It's a plan," he defended weakly.

I snorted and turned back down the hallway. "It's a sucky one. For one thing, even if you could do it—and I don't think you can—it's not going to work."

"Sure I can do it," he said, his voice hard and flat. He was trying to convince me he was a badass. I already knew he was a badass—that wasn't the point.

"Look, I know physically you can do it, and I could really give a fuck how you kill that shitbag. That's not the point. The point is, Teague, we both know you're a better man than that. You'll kill, yes, out of necessity, and in this case I'm willing to concede this guy has to die, and there has to be some theater so his buddies will go home and tell their buddies to leave us the fuck alone. It's gone that far, and I don't have to like it to see that we need it. But you're not into torture. And even if you were, just for this one time, just to drive Jacky away, you wouldn't do it, because it would be a lie. You're a better man than lying to him to get him to do the right thing. You'll let him see the real you and make his own decision, and that's why the plan won't work."

His voice was thick with all the emotion he hadn't let loose with his mates. "And why's that?"

"Because he loves you, dumbshit. You could probably eat the bad guy a piece at a time while Dumbfuck watched you and screamed for mercy, and Jacky would be there with a napkin and ketchup. So do what you have to, be all manly if you have to, but be out in the front room in forty-five minutes for dinner, movies, and fattening shit, or I'm having Green drag you out." I stopped in front of Mario's door and gave a courtesy knock.

"Did you hear that, birdman?"

The door opened, and Mario arched his eyebrows in disgust. His blue-black hair was combed back from his high forehead, and he was wearing a tight shirt and loose jeans. He was looking mostly none the worse for wear after his showdown with a rabid werewolf two nights before.

"Yeah, Princess, I got it. Don't worry about bothering Green. I'll drag wolfboy out and watch with you, 'kay?"

I smiled at him gratefully, glad he'd read my cue and admitted he'd heard the whole conversation. "Sounds like a plan. Don't be late!"

"Who says I don't want to be alone?" Teague demanded, once he'd found his tongue and his bearings there in Mario's doorway.

"Who says you get to be?" I snapped back. "As fucking *if*!" Then I turned around and kept walking, enjoying his grunts of irritation as I went.

Nobody was alone at Green's hill. Ever. That was my new goddamned law.

Solace of the Hill

Teague didn't remember that Cory and the others had school until he woke up the next morning.

Good to her word, during the evening she and a revolving throng of people Teague had gotten to know in the last couple of weeks had come and gone. They would sit down, put a new dessert in Teague's hand, actively watch television for a while, and then move on.

It didn't occur to him that he was being "handled" in the same manner he'd seen the hill "handle" Cory or Green until after the vampires had woken up.

Phillip and Marcus had walked in—they were rarely far apart from each other—and Marcus said, "Holy Goddess! I haven't seen one of these since the last time you threw me over."

They were standing behind the couch as Teague squinted at them over his shoulder, the pieces falling into place. Phillip cast the love of his life a sour look from under the black fall of hair from his widow's peak. "If you don't learn when to shut the fuck up, I may still throw you over."

Marcus caught Teague's eyes apologetically. "You wish," he returned, bumping shoulders with his beloved. "I'm like flesh-and-blood Velcro."

"There's an appealing thought. You couldn't come up with something better than that, you bastard?"

Marcus shrugged and looked wicked, then leaned over and whispered something in Phillip's ear that made him look even *more* so. Teague watched them, his heart breaking into small, bruised, dripping, bloody pieces, and Phillip saw his expression.

"Brother, we've officially become a breakup party liability." And the two of them made themselves scarce in quick time.

Teague turned back to the movie—they were watching *Mad Max: Fury Road*, because there was nothing like a good postapocalyptic adventure to put things into perspective—and saw Cory looking at him with wordless sympathy. He shrugged silently and slipped into the colorless, emotionless void that had comforted him for the last few hours. Cory was leaning against Bracken, her knitting in her hands and her feet in Teague's lap. It was a familiar, sisterly pose, and with the vampires' prompting, it occurred to him that it was very deliberate. She was touching him in a way that had nothing at all to do with sex. She was touching him like a mother or a sister—or a friend.

That was where he stayed for another half hour, conscious that Mario had tilted his head back and started to snore in the chair next to him and that Nicky was crouched at Cory's feet, pretending to play air guitar with the Dooph. That's where they were when a vaguely familiar female voice spoke up behind him.

"Oh my God! Whose breakup party?"

Teague might have smiled a little. He didn't look behind him, but he recognized a werepuma—was it Leah? Was that the name?—and someone must have elbowed her in the side and clued her in.

"Are you shitting me? Naww… really? Them? Impossible. That's like asking two asscheeks to ride home in different cars and making the sphincter drive."

Teague's eyes bugged out. Looking to his left, he saw Cory's and Bracken's eyes were pretty damned huge as well. Then they all made the mistake of meeting each other's bulged-out eyes and cracking up. Teague laughed in short breaths, little blasts of happiness in between painful moments of self-denial. He wasn't sure when the first little burst of breath went from laughter to sobs, he really wasn't. He would have sworn it couldn't happen. He'd been avoiding thinking, avoiding *feeling* ever since Jacky had burst in by the vampire vault, and it wasn't like he had a whole lot of emotional reserves anyway. By the time he'd spoken to Green, he'd already been emotionally exhausted. Green's soothing presence had been a balm, an aloe bandage on his shredded soul.

By the time he'd walked out of the room he'd been sharing with Jack and Katy for the past weeks, he hadn't thought he had any tears or pain left. He'd been relieved. He figured maybe he'd never have to cry again.

But something about laughing… God… something about letting an emotion—any emotion—register on his radar cracked his heart wide open.

Within moments the room had cleared of everybody but Cory and Bracken. Cory was holding Teague's head in her lap as he cried, and Bracken was holding her.

He wasn't sure how long it lasted. When his sobs reduced to little hiccups, he looked at the television and realized that *Captain America: Civil War* was playing. Not one of his favorite movies, but then, he'd been out of it for a while. He was glad if someone was happy with what was on TV.

He cleared his throat and made to move—God, these people were going to think he couldn't keep his shit together in a copper pot—but Cory's arms tightened around his shoulders.

"Stay, wolfman. You need to know that you'll never be alone here, okay?"

"Jacky—"

"Will love you as much tomorrow as he loved you yesterday. But in the meantime, you don't need to be alone. We've got your back, baby. It's what we do."

He didn't remember falling asleep after that. He must have, and one of the überstrong superbeings in the damned hill must have carried him back to Mario's room like a child. He knew he woke up from a dream—it didn't matter which one, they were all saturated with blood and ended with him, alone, covered in his lovers' blood—and the flannel sheets were a different color and smelled like someone else.

A light tap on his shoulder eased the scream in his throat.

"Easy, wolfman. Orders are to sleep in. You'll be doing the gladiator thing when everyone gets back from school."

"Oh Christ!" Teague scrubbed at his eyes and glowered at the thin yellow sunlight coming in through Mario's full-sized window. The room he'd shared with Jack and Katy had a small skylight, stealing sun from the only corner of the room to face outside. "They have school today. I forgot. Don't you have school too?" He glared at Mario, who was sitting up on the bed in jeans and a sweatshirt, working on what looked like a law text as it sat in his lap.

Mario held out his phone. "Yeah. LaMark's gonna send me my homework and drop off my papers. It's all good."

Teague's head felt heavy, and his neck felt too slender and no good at all for holding the damned thing up. He fell back against the pillows and fought the temptation to pull the blankets over his head. "Why didn't you go with them?"

Mario pulled the covers up over Teague's eyes for him and then went to the window and pulled the heavy curtains shut. They were green, like the sheets, Teague noted mournfully. His and Jacky's stuff was blue and red and cream.

"Exactly why you think I didn't, wolfman. I'm here to watch your back. Now go back to sleep. It's only seven in the morning."

"Jesus. What time do they leave?" Teague grumbled. Mario answered him, but Teague fell back asleep before Mario finished speaking.

He dreamed again, but it was a very different dream this time.

This time he heard Green's sharp cockney cutting through the wool in his head until he could dream the story he'd heard the previous afternoon. He saw it like a movie, like pictures, and was able to read the expressions on the faces of the players with detailed accuracy, thanks to Green's pitch-perfect narration.

"Adrian had just finished doing his bit with the other vampires to learn self-control, right? And we decided to move up to a part of the state that had as few people as possible. But you've got to remember, we were limited. The coffin wasn't as lightproof as it should have been, so we could really only move by night...."

It was night, and two men made their way across the twisted landscape of gold country in a little buckboard pulled by a single indifferent horse. The buckboard was light and carried only a few items: a store of bread and dried fruit, wooden tools—some with metal edges, carefully wrapped—woolen blankets, a few changes of clothes, and an empty coffin covered by an oilskin tarp.

The road the men were following wasn't really a road—it was more of a narrow path that followed the American River from the split with the Sacramento to hills near El Dorado. They'd slept in the valley's shadow the day before, but now it was time to take the slow, winding road up the side of the cliff to the hill where their lime trees were planted.

The lime trees had been Green's ticket from England. Salt water negated magic of any sort, and crossing the sea was usually lethal for any kind of land elf. Green had hoarded power for a hundred and fifty years while held captive in Oberon's faerie hill, and he'd fed it, driblet by orgasm, into those trees. Oberon's hill had been so saturated in power anyway that no one noticed Green's subtle power signature or caught on to his plan, at least until he had disappeared through the quarried stone walls and into the night.

When Green and Adrian arrived in San Francisco, Adrian had immediately converted. His last sunrise had been spent in Green's arms, staring at the ocean from a tiny hotel room and yearning for the moment when they could be together as equals, immortal to immortal. Adrian had spent ten years locked in the hold of a ship, being raped and abused as sort of a privilege and reward for the ship's crew. From their first touch, Green had become all the sunshine and daylight Adrian would ever need.

While they'd been in San Francisco, and it had become apparent that Adrian would need a good couple of months to become accustomed to his new life as a vampire, Green had given three lime trees to a yunwitsunsdi—the fey counterpart in this part of the world back then—to take the rest of the trees up north and plant them somewhere they might thrive with a little help from Green. They'd sworn on it, by touch, blood, and song, and a month later Green had received a map leading him to this place with the warning to be done with the "blood-eater's business" by early spring— otherwise his beloved trees might not survive long without Green's help.

Until then, Green and Adrian had only seen San Francisco. It had felt a lot like England, although Green knew enough about the taste of dirt in the air to know that there were dry grasses and dust on the wind even in the winter. He had a feeling that the world beyond the Bay City was probably more inhospitable than he'd imagined when he was coming up with a plan using nothing more than desperation and barely heard rumors of a new world.

In the five-night journey in the horse and trap, Green didn't see much to revise his opinion. The first two nights were easy enough. Once they cleared the rolling hills around the bay—Green and Adrian had pulled the damned trap more than the horse—they'd had a hell of a time finding sheltering trees beyond the long stretches of fairly flat lands. They followed the river, grateful that it was not salt, and always quit an hour or two before dawn for two reasons.

The first was that they needed to find a place for Adrian to sleep. Even in early April, the sun was fierce, and the coffin and the tarp were not enough for Green's peace of mind. More often than not, they dug out a place to put the coffin inside, making sure there was at least a foot of insulating dirt on top.

The second was that they were still honeymooning, and even if it was only bathing each other in the river shallows by the gray twilight of predawn, Green needed to touch Adrian.

Letting him die had hurt—oh Goddess. It was a subject he didn't even talk about with Cory. He had stayed to watch because Adrian had been afraid and he'd had to—and the absolute, stomach-dropping, stark, painful fear of watching the pale, lovely boy become a pale, lovely corpse was something that awakened Green for years afterward with a scream in his throat and rank sweat stinking his body. After the terrible betrayal of his last consensual lover and the mind-numbing, body-killing horridness of being Oberon's favorite concubine—oh Goddess—Green had finally found a lover who made him love, who made him feel again. And he was letting Adrian *die*?

When the stirring of Adrian's soul wind had ruffled that white-blond hair and opened those sky-spangled eyes again, Green had fallen to his knees, clasped that pulseless, cold hand to his cheek, and wept.

Adrian had blinked around Lucian's dark-suited shoulder and smiled wanly at his only true lover. "No worries, luv—didn't even hurt."

The next few months had been an education in sexual insatiability and fearsome bloodlust, but Green had clung to that sky-blue optimism, and it kept him sane.

The stolen moments by the river before dawn were lovely. On one night, after Adrian had fed chastely and minimally from an unwary—and now very happy—husband and wife they had met on the road, Green had him stand, naked and starlight white, in the ankle-deep shallows. He took a bit of cloth and, simple touch by simple touch, bathed Adrian from his wiry, muscular calves up to his groin and the crease of his thighs and his buttocks, up his concave, taut stomach, and into the hollows of his tender neck—and even behind and in his ears. Adrian stood quietly, arms raised above his head, being as marble still as a vampire could—but he couldn't sustain that sort of tranquility for long.

He started little unwilling grunts as Green bathed his thighs. He let loose a whimper as Green paid gentle attention to his privates and the sensitive places between his creases and the entrance into his body that was only used for sport now. He started panting when Green reached his chest and his pearly little nipples. By the time Green moved to his neck, Adrian was wiggling, vibrating, emitting a series of wordless words that all but begged for possession.

When Green claimed his mouth with warmth and strength and passion, Adrian groaned, clutched him close, and spent himself against Green's taut, warm thigh—and then Green truly took him, body and soul, in the waning starlight.

But that had been before the hills, before the oaks thickened to become difficult, before the land had given in to pine trees that dug into granite or slippery shale. As the two of them clawed their way up the side of the hill on some sort of joke of a path and the night raced by on a cougar's swift paws, Green was seriously wondering if either one of them would ever see a moment like that again.

Green could smell the lime trees, but he couldn't see them yet when he saw the first deadly ray of gold reach across the horizon.

"*Fuck!*" The echoes of the oath hadn't stopped dying off the hills before Green shoved Adrian into his coffin, threw the tarpaulin over the damned thing, and found a crumbling, red-dirt crusted spot in the east-facing cliff wall they had been trying to negotiate.

Then he used all the sidhe power he had in his bones and literally *vibrated* the casket into the side of the bloody hill with main force and a fucking lot of desperation. Adrian was still complaining in shock and surprise and a bit of discomfort—if it hadn't been for the quick healing of your average vampire, his brain would have splattered like an egg inside his skull from all that vibration—when the sunlight hit their mountainside and his day death shut him up.

Green was left gasping, exhausted, shell-shocked, and still quivering with fear. He'd seen Adrian die once—he wasn't sure if he could survive seeing it again. The whole reason he'd agreed with the transition to vampire was that he, oh goddammit, he didn't want to lose another lover to the merciless spiked boots of Time. In particular, he didn't want to lose Adrian.

As he stood there, leaning against the hill with rocks and stray earth falling around his shoulders, he heard a sound above his own heartbeat.

He looked up slowly and found himself face-to-face with a really angry brown bear.

He didn't know—or care—about the difference between bears back then. He didn't know that a brown bear was smaller than a grizzly, or that a black bear was bigger than a brown bear. At this precise moment, he discovered that a California bear seemed a damned sight bigger than the little buggers they'd had so long ago back in England, and this monster was far taller than he was, had mass, reach, heinous, hideous claws, and seemed to have an entire bee's nest shoved up his arse over something.

Green didn't wait for the bear to swipe first. He charged the damned thing, and together they tumbled down the cliff. Green burrowed into the bear's fur, fumbling for its skin. They rolled off a ledge, the bear thankfully on the bottom, and landed hard on the path below them. The bear was dazed, but not for long, and Green took the opportunity to plow his hands in through that dense, thick pelt and grab the loose skin with both hands.

Then he ripped it open. The bear reared his head back and roared in shock, and Green used the sidhe strength he so rarely relied on to punch his hand through the thing's ribcage and yank out its heart.

He had no idea how long he lay there, splayed over the twitching corpse of the bear, but eventually he caught his breath and his heartbeat returned to normal, and he pulled himself out of the bloody pit of the thing's chest and took stock.

Bloody hell. He didn't eat meat, Adrian didn't eat anything—and here was a life that would be wasted completely unless someone who knew something about dressing a dead animal emerged from the woodwork.

And then—oh Goddess. He was covered in blood.

He'd killed before. He was not pretty or skilled at it. He'd swung into a human regiment once, drunk on grief and a berserker's rage, and emerged dripping in viscera and completely alone. He knew it was in him and knew when to use it and for the most part was unashamed of the violence that could pulse in his veins.

But it was something Adrian had never seen.

Adrian relied on Green's compassion, his tenderness. Green had been the gentle healing for a violence-rent soul. It was irrational—Green knew he was often ruled by emotion—but suddenly it became imperative that Adrian *not* see him covered in blood.

He gave a grunt and looked below him, over the ledge of this portion of the road, and saw the river ripping its way through the canyon. He was an elf. He could move at amazing speeds, but not on terrain such as this, where every footfall was rife with the possibility of slipping on loose shale and crumbling red dirt. He gave another grunt and looked above him. Oh Holy Goddess, he'd fallen a long way. He gasped and looked at the corpse of his enemy, then gave it a vicious, irrational, and highly satisfying kick in the side. Bloody fucking thing—he was in the thick of it now, wasn't he?

And then, to make matters worse, there was a bloodthirsty monster stalking him. Hurt beyond madness, maddened by grief, it slunk in the shadows, just waiting for a moment to rip out an innocent throat, to feast on the sweet ichor of—

"Stop it." Green's voice echoed in Teague's head. *"I gave you this precious fucking memory to dream of. You'd best remember it right."*

Teague grunted, came partially awake, realized he'd allowed his own dream, his own madness, to intrude, and let out a wolf whine in shame.

"No worries." Green's voice smelled like wildflowers. Was that possible? *"Now see it through to the end, right, mate?"*

Teague's answer was to sink again into the dream, where he could smell the dust and the pine and the bright orange poppies peeking through the crevices of the rocky soil, taunting Green with a little bit of softness in this terribly hard land....

By midmorning, Green had just about decided what to do. He'd recovered his breath and sat next to the cooling body of the bear, measuring his options. His bib overalls—the steel rivets carefully treated with salt water and herbs—and thermal shirt were sopping with blood, and so was the long queue down his back. He absolutely could not face Adrian like this.

He would feel better about the kill if he knew the bear's meat would be used. He stood with a sigh and bent, getting his back and legs and shoulders into the lift, to move the body down into the coolness of the canyon, where it would be more likely to be found either by a predator or the miners who periodically ventured to the river down there. Even for a sidhe, six-hundred-plus pounds of hairy predator was something of a lift. He just about had the thing balanced, and was working up to a good trot across the scrabble path, when a wolf crossed in front of him.

Green slowed, moving smoothly. If the wolf wanted the bear, he could have it, but otherwise, Green was a wood elf. When he wasn't vibrating with desperation and panic, he was usually pretty comfortable in a rural setting. Besides, while he did not know bears, he was relatively comfortable with wolves. They were usually content to watch his kind and felt no need to interfere.

But suddenly the wolf was a naked human—his hair long, straight, and white, and his body, still muscular and sound, covered in sagging skin.

This was not just a wolf—it was an old skin-changer, a werewolf.

Green was so surprised, he dropped the bear. It landed in the dust with a heavy, bone-breaking thud, and Green and the werewolf stared at it in shock.

"It is just as well," the werewolf said after a moment. "My brothers will want to eat it, and they would rather not journey down to the river today."

Green looked up, wondering if his eyes were as big as they felt. "You speak English."

The old man blinked and sank to his haunches, as comfortable in that position nude as Green would be. Green joined him, hunkering down in the middle of the hard-scrabble trail by the corpse of the dead bear. It only seemed polite.

"I like humans," the werewolf replied mildly. His voice was canyon deep and sonorous, but not without humor. "These days, humans speak English."

After centuries of learning Gaelic, Latin, Pictish, Welsh, Old German, Old French, and a dozen Scandinavian languages that no longer existed, Green had to agree. "These days, in these ways, yes, it's true."

"So is there any other reason you were hauling a perfectly good dinner for my tribe down to the river?"

Green sighed and looked at himself. "Yes, brother. I need to wash."

The old werewolf looked at him wisely. "When you get to your trees at the top of the hill, you will be able to call water. Why not wait until then? You will need your strength, brother. Even for your kind, it will not be an easy climb if you wish to beat the dawn again."

The blush traveled from Green's chest to his cheeks—he could feel it. He did not know what it looked like through the gore and fleshy matter crusted on his face, but the werewolf sniffed the air and looked at him with some amusement.

"Surely your blood eater has no problem with violence!"

Green shrugged and looked away. "Not from me," he admitted, and the werewolf nodded as though this was not at all unusual.

"This is not the hardest land to live in," the man said after a moment of stillness. There wasn't even a breeze across the succulents and grasses to break the quiet. "There is water and game, and the snows aren't too bad, and the droughts do not last for lifetimes."

A nod, then a smile. Green was used to people speaking in poetry. It was the hallmark of the sidhe.

"But as easy as this land may be," the werewolf continued, "it is still difficult to survive. A challenge—especially for people like you, who come from an easier place."

"Yes," Green said, wondering where this was going.

"Do you not think your blood eater will be happy to know that you can defend yourself in such a place? I saw you shoving him into the earth in panic. You are afraid he cannot fend for himself. Wouldn't it be a relief if one of you could survive?"

Unexpectedly, Green felt tears. He'd been a captive for over a hundred years. How bloody good could he be at surviving if that was true? "I am not a warrior elf," he said, trying not to be wretched.

The werewolf nodded sagely. "This is good. Warriors die when they are young, or live to be naked old men having senile conversations with strangers. The world needs more men who kill from need only, not because they love it. It's good when these men can take care of themselves. It means they will survive to teach others to love."

They sat for most of the day. The werewolf brought his brothers—a motley assortment of people, every age and genetic heritage to pass over this part of the continent. They lived in a quiet pack, and after thanking Green for the meat, hoisted the monster of a creature over their backs and disappeared down the road.

The older werewolf, the pack's alpha, stayed and shared some tubers and vegetables with Green, and Green—who had been living off hardtack for more than a week—was grateful. In the late afternoon, they moved to where Adrian's coffin was buried, and Gray Flower, the werewolf chief, helped set up a sun blind using the tarp and watched over Green as he slept.

He woke Green near sunset and helped to pull the coffin out of the side of the hill. It was harder than it sounded, and more than once the old Indian remarked it was a good thing Green didn't love that blood eater too much, or they would have needed to go to the other side of the hill and pull it out that way.

At dark, Gray Flower turned wolf and faded into the wilderness. He would visit later that night and allow Adrian to feed from him, and the long tradition of werecreatures and vampires living in symbiosis would begin. But first Green lifted the lid of Adrian's resting place and waited for the soul wind to blow through him again.

Adrian's sky-spangled eyes opened, took in Green's appearance— the blood, the savagery, and his transparent, helpless relief that Adrian would survive.

"Bloody hell, mate! Whatever you fought, I'm glad it's dead!"

Green smiled, his shoulders shaking in helpless laughter, and Adrian sat up, pushed Green's crusted hair back from his face, and kissed him, gore and all.

THE DREAM ended abruptly.

Teague opened his eyes. The sun was bright enough through the drapes that it would have been impossible to go back to sleep again anyway. Teague looked to where Mario had been sitting earlier and was unsurprised to see Green instead.

Green reached out an absent hand and smoothed Teague's hair back. The gesture was sexless, genderless, and paternal, and Teague shivered and accepted it.

"I would have died," he said. "In captivity. I don't know where you were held captive, but I would have gnawed my own legs off. I couldn't have done it."

Green tilted his head back against the headboard, closed his eyes, and smiled. "You silly boy. You've lived your whole life in captivity—first in your father's grasp and then in your own mind. And you've done worse than chew your legs off. You've gnawed your heart into tiny pieces. But you've survived."

"I don't want to just survive," Teague said, shocking the hell out of himself. "I want them, Green. I want them to love me for me. I...." His chest ached. God, Goddess, whatever—it hurt just to admit. "You know, for a minute yesterday, I was happy. I...." Teague turned away from Green and buried his face in the pillows, hoping he would smother himself rather than let the words come out, but they burst free anyway. "I could be so happy with them."

Green was suddenly stretched out behind him, spooning him into a cocooning embrace Teague couldn't fight, didn't want to.

"You will be, mate. You'll see. Having them watch you fight is exactly right, and Jack's need to accept who you are is exactly right. You'll get your happy ending, mate. I cannot choose to think otherwise."

Teague had learned that elves couldn't lie, so he noticed—he noticed Green didn't say "I have no doubts."

And it was actually comforting to know that Green had doubts. Because that made two of them. But it made two of them who hoped—no, more than that. Three. No, five. No, there were more. Teague realized everybody who had sat and watched movies in the common room with him would be hoping that afternoon.

Whether he and his lovers had a hope of becoming forever or not, he would never be alone. "Captivity," Green had said. Not anymore. For the first time in his life, Teague felt free.

Passive Atonement

Jack had learned to love Katy, even though she had only showed up in the beginning to be with Teague. The fact that she didn't leave him alone after Teague left only cemented the deal.

She was the one who helped him to his feet, who sat him in his stuffed chair and stroked his face until the sobs settled in his chest. She was the one who crooned at him until he was ready to quiet and to listen. For a few moments, they sat in silence, and he appreciated her—her softness, her gentleness. He and Teague were all sharpness, rough edges, hard planes. Katy fit well with them. Fit well with *him*. The thought almost started him off again, and he couldn't do that.

"Where do you think he is?" Jack asked when the silence pressed too hard on his chest.

"In the front room having a breakup party," Katy answered promptly, without having to think, and Jack squinted at her. He'd never heard of such a thing.

"What, college boy? You never see one of those in a dorm? They're in all the movies."

Jack flushed. "I only started watching movies after I started rooming with Teague."

Katy blinked at him slowly. "Oh, Jacky! You really did think life was your own little blanket fort, didn't you? Didn't you see? The world doesn't just wait outside while you and your people make nice. You either deal with the world or it falls down and crushes your head!"

"Or your heart," Jack said softly. His face threatened to crumple again. Teague had looked… sad. Defeated. Lonely. All the things Jack had sworn Teague would never be again, and Jack had driven him to that place in his heart. And now, now Teague was out with the world, and Jack was here alone.

Katy patted his cheek. Well, not alone.

"He'll come back," she said softly. "He has a point, that's all. He is hurt, but he's not just our lover anymore. We've got to do more than kiss his boo-boos and make it better. We've got to obey him, just like a leader.

And we've got to obey the people he bows to. This isn't America anymore, Jacky. This is like the, the…." She waved her arms, looking for the word, and Jack found himself smiling. She did that a lot. As reserved as he and Teague were, it was lovely to see some animation, some excitement, in the eyes of the other member of their family.

Katy's arms stilled in a dramatic flair, and she found her words. "Like the United Peoples of Green or something! Green's the big shit, Cory's his other half, and Teague's like his cabinet or something, you know? We're not just being married to the guy who breaks our hearts. We're being married to the Secretary of Big Fucking Werewolf Shit, and if the President says our guy has to go keep the peace, baby, that's what he does!"

Jack reached out an arm and pulled gently on Katy's waist as she sat on the arm of his chair. She took the hint and allowed herself to be pulled into his lap, and he feathered his hand through her blue-black hair. "That's what he does," he echoed softly. He'd loved poetry classes in college. Sometimes the simplest grammar said the best goddamned things.

"Yeah, hon," she said into his chest. Her voice was a sad little echo, and he realized he'd done this to her too. His own stupidity—his complete lack of judgment—had not just driven Teague away from *him*, but away from *her*.

"Why didn't he take you with him?" Jack wondered aloud. "He could have stayed in your room. You didn't do anything wrong."

Katy looked up at him, her tears running her mascara, and he tenderly wiped them away with his thumbs and then wiped his thumbs on his jeans.

"Don't you get it, Jacky? He loves me. I don't doubt that. But you're the one he followed. You're the one he became a werewolf for. He can't just love one of us. He can love his family and be happy, or he can break his heart and be alone."

Jack sighed in frustration. "Damn it, that's not fair! I'm not worth all of that!"

A small, soft hand grasped his chin and forced him to meet a pair of red-rimmed brown eyes. "Now, see—that's what he's felt like these last weeks. And we finally convince him it's not true, and…."

"Yeah," Jack whispered miserably. "And I fuck it all up. And part of the reason he feels like it's not true…."

"Is that the shit he does here at the hill is important. Yeah. You're starting to get it now, aren't you, *pendejo*!"

Jack frowned. "What's *pendejo* mean?" he asked suspiciously.

Katy grinned at him tiredly. "Let's just say it's not as bad as *puta* and leave it at that, okay, Jacky?"

Jack nodded. Okay. In either language, he was an asshole. He guessed he knew that now, didn't he?

They had their own little breakup party in their room. Jack and Teague's television had been moved in, as well as their own DVD collection, and Jack put in *About Time*. Katy was about to slip away and get them some food when Grace showed up with a tray, including some desserts, and presented it to her.

Jack saw Katy blush. She cast him a surreptitious glance and looked back at Grace gratefully. "Thank you," she said, her voice soaked in shame for something Jack had done, something Katy had nothing to do with.

Grace rolled her eyes, caught Jack's miserable glance, and winked. "He's not the only one to not know what he's dealing with here. No worries, Katy. You guys are welcome in the were common room, or with the vamps...."

Katy shook her head. "No," she whispered. "It would be better if he didn't see us at all. At least not until tomorrow."

Grace took the tray back from Katy and put it on the dresser, snagged Teague's soiled, discarded clothing as she did so, and tossed it in a little pile outside the door. Then she turned to Katy and enfolded the girl in a long-limbed hug.

Jack watched as Katy went willingly. The older vampire's freckled cheeks scrunched up in sympathy, and she tucked his lover into her embrace as though Katy was her own daughter recovering from a broken heart. If nothing else in the rest of the day proved to be an education, this was. Jack might have thought they lived in a vacuum, but Teague and Katy—who had been torn so badly in their lives one would think they were almost beyond repair—had been engaged and active in a community that cared about them.

As Katy sniffled a little and Grace said soft things about how Teague wouldn't be gone for long, Jack had to wonder at his hubris. He'd wanted to be their everything. How could he be their everything when he didn't even know the world they walked in?

Eventually Grace left, taking Teague's dirty clothes with her, and Katy made plates and sat with Jack so they could eat.

"I'm a fool," Jack said quietly, taking a bite of lasagna like a chastised child.

"Yeah, Jacky, we know. What are you foolish about now?" Katy took a bite of garlic bread with relish. It occurred to Jack that Grace had a sense of humor about being a cook who couldn't eat her own food.

"This is a family. I thought… I thought I was the only family you guys had. This place, it's bigger than me."

Katy looked at him with big eyes. "You really are stupid, aren't you?"

Jack grimaced. "Let's hope I've wised up enough to do the smart thing tomorrow." He took another glum bite.

Katy reached across the arms of their chairs and took his hand to her lips and kissed it. "Oh, don't you worry about that. All you've got to do tomorrow is love him. I think it could be the only thing you're good at."

Her lips were warm and a little buttery on the back of his hand, and he turned the hand around to cup her cheek. "Now look at who's all optimistic and shit."

Katy gave him a watery grin and pressed his palm to her skin. "Grace said he fell apart like a little baby, Jack. I got to believe he'll forgive you for anything. Now you just got to make sure 'anything' doesn't happen again, right?"

Jack's food lost all appeal whatsoever, and he reclaimed his hand. Fell apart like a little baby. *God, Goddess, whoever*, he prayed. *Let me be the sort of man Teague needs. Please, let me not fuck this up again.*

They slept curled up together, in their pajamas. Jack wondered— would they make love without Teague? Would they want to? Would it be comforting?

Maybe, if they knew he'd be gone forever, they could have. Maybe.

But now they didn't want sex. They wanted their mate. Touching skin was comfort, but without their mate, it wasn't sex.

They woke up late, and as soon as they'd showered, Jack sent Katy out into the were room to get the buzz. She came back in short order, carrying some sandwiches and some milk, and with a resigned expression.

"After the students get home and the vampires wake up, in the banquet room by the dance floor. You and me get front row seats. He's downstairs now, helping to clear out the room and get it ready. We can go to the common room if we want."

"But what if he…." God, this was stupid. But it was becoming like seeing the bride before the wedding day. They didn't want to see him until he'd done this thing, until they could prove to him that they— Jacky—wouldn't let him down again.

Katy shook her head, positive. "Green told me. He said we could go to the common room or we could go outside. Green would keep him busy down there or on the running trail. Don't worry, Jacky. We won't do anything to fuck this up, okay?"

"Speak for yourself," Jack said with an air of resignation.

Katy's look was pointed. "Umm, no, Jacky. You don't get to do that. We get enough from Teague. You take your lumps, you be a little bit humble, but you don't get to hate yourself, 'kay?"

Jack had to smile. "'Kay. Katy?" He took a bite of sandwich and chewed thoughtfully.

"Yeah?"

"How come neither of us are worried that Teague will lose?"

Katy's harrumph was almost comical. "He's the meanest bastard in the pack, Jacky. I've been telling you that since we met."

The meanest bastard in the pack. Well, he had to be, didn't he? He'd been saving his own ass, saving Jack's ass, and keeping people alive and well who had no business being alive and well, and he'd been doing it for years.

For the first time, Jack felt a sense of pride in the fact. It meant he didn't have to worry. Teague wouldn't die. Not today. He was the meanest bastard in the pack.

A few hours later, Jack wasn't so sure.

The banquet room had been completely cleared. All the hand-planed banquet tables were stacked up against the far wall near the stairs, and the chairs had been shoved over there and stacked as well. The walls were a burnished combination of earth and tree roots, with occasional spots of paneling, and the far wall from the stairs opened up into a wider area. There had been a band there after everyone had eaten on Thanksgiving, but now it was roped off. Thick, wiry hemp ropes, tied to wooden rings screwed into the wood of the tree roots, blocked one end. The three rounded, asymmetrical walls on the other side of the rope marked the other boundaries of the ring.

As Jack and Katy walked through the crowd, they were ushered to the very front of the ropes. Green, Cory, Nicky, and Bracken were already there, as well as Grace and her sidhe lover, Arturo.

Cory was vibrating with tension.

"This is so fucking barbaric," she announced to no one in particular. "And unnecessary. I could have killed him yesterday."

"Teague needs this," Green said mildly.

"Yeah, well, Goddess save me from macho assholes," she snapped.

Green leaned forward to say softly, "So far, she's done a very nice job indeed, you think, beloved?"

Cory put her hands over her eyes, growl/screamed, and kicked fruitlessly at the floor under her feet.

"She doesn't look happy," Katy observed quietly, and Jack shrugged. Yeah. It looked like she was concerned for Teague. Bully for her. The guy had taken a knife for her the day before.

Katy stomped on his foot. Hard.

"Nobody wants anybody getting hurt here. That concern is for our boy. You be fucking grateful, you hear me?"

Jack sighed. So much for resolutions—it was time to pony up. "You're right," he said softly. "I'm just nervous."

At that moment the other werewolf entered the room, flanked by two vampires Jack vaguely recognized as Marcus and Phillip. The captive's hands were tied in front of him, and he was wearing a pair of brown jeans and nothing else. His hair fell in lank black strings around his face, and his expression was pure hatred. Jack started to see why the man had to be put down—there was no reason in him. It was all unadulterated animosity, and it was obviously something that couldn't be allowed to prosper here.

The werewolf stood in the corner looking angry and rabid—and alone. When his opponent walked in, he raised his head for a moment. His eyes were flat and unintelligent, and Jack thought he was more beast than man in that moment.

Teague was wearing jeans and a white T-shirt with no shoes, and for a moment Jack wondered why a guy who wore long-sleeved henleys in the summer would be that stripped down, before the reason smacked him in the face. This was as close to naked in public as Teague would get, and since Teague might have to turn wolf, he had stripped down to make it easier. Although, Jack thought sourly, Teague seemed to avoid getting tangled up in his clothes so far. It was almost like a magic superpower or something.

Teague didn't look at Jacky or Katy, but he didn't look at Green or Cory either. His attention was all business. The guy in the corner got the up, down, and sideways, and Jack had a sudden déjà vu.

"I know that look," he said softly to Katy. "That's his fighting look." The thing was, until this very moment, Jack hadn't known it was his fighting look. He'd thought of it as Teague's "game face," because Teague got it under certain tense situations. But now Jack realized something—Teague really *had* been covering his ass for a year and a half. He'd known when violence was pending; he'd known when someone was going to throw a punch. He only wore that face when he was going to have to draw blood.

Jack had never known. Fighting had always been an unpleasant surprise. To Teague it had been a violent charge in the air, like the smell of a storm on the wind.

Teague liked storms.

"He likes this," Katy said with surprise and a little awe, and Jack nodded. How could he have worked with the man for a year and a half without seeing that Teague's flat, assessing eyes and taut face hid a boundless wealth of sheer, violent joy? Teague had been born in violence. The fact that he had forged a gentle man from that material was nothing short of a miracle, but it didn't change the fact that violence was in his blood. Of course it would give him some satisfaction to turn this… this terrible gift, this blood-soaked legacy, to something productive, something he believed in.

Teague nodded to Green and Cory. Cory gave him an irritated, narrow-eyed glare that Jack was willing to concede held mostly concern, and Green nodded his head with gentle nobility. Then Teague grinned and winked at Cory, who flipped him off in turn, and that was apparently his signal to proceed.

One of the vampires had a steel knife, and he used that to cut the bonds at the werewolf's hands. Then it was just the two of them, one desperate and the other deadly, in the ring.

Bad Guy rushed Teague first.

It wasn't a gather or a charge—it was hardly a rush. The guy didn't pull in his resources or gauge his speed. He just ran, his body tilting dangerously out of balance, and Teague gave the move the attention it deserved. He sidestepped and let the guy go crashing headfirst into the wall.

He came back snapping and feral, growling even in his human form, and Teague stepped out of his way again at the next charge. The trip to the wall was a little longer this time but no less painful when he hit.

The werewolf sat back on his human haunches and shook his head, and Teague walked up to him and spoke.

"Look, man, your heart's not in this. If you just give it up and let us help—"

The fucker turned his head and sank his very human teeth into the flesh of Teague's arm. Teague grunted. He didn't even flinch. And then Teague grabbed the guy's throat with his free hand, pressed him to the floor, and changed into a wolf, leaving his clothes in a puddle on the floor.

Jack felt the change. It sizzled in the air and pulled at his skin, and he and Katy clasped their human hands to resist it. Teague's power—his personality, his personal strength—exerted enough force over the shape-changers to call their own changes. Every shape-shifter in the room felt it. Most of them simply shifted their weight from leg to leg, like a child who had to go to the bathroom, but the younger ones, the ones with less discipline, changed with their leader.

Wolves, cougars, avians, coyotes, giant cats. It would have been total chaos, but Teague—his two front paws on the throat of the mangy-looking red wolf at his feet—barked once commandingly, and every shape-shifter in the room, both those who had changed and those who hadn't, stood absolutely still.

This was Jack's mate. *This* was the man Jack loved. Jack had seen this in him from the very beginning, but now Jack could see it was a thing, a quality, that was never meant to be Jack's alone.

Teague backed off the wolf under his paws and stood warily, growling in his throat, waiting to see what the other animal would do.

The foreign werewolf stood up, snarled, and leaped at Teague, his jaws open to snap, but he never made it. Teague caught his enemy's throat in his teeth and ripped, pulling the entire thing out—larynx, jugular, everything—in midleap. The wolf's body continued its original trajectory and landed, twitching, yards away.

Teague trotted over and waited to see if the young man would heal. It looked like it. Shape-shifters in general could take an incredible amount of punishment, and this particular one appeared to be too mean to kill. He lay there, his body changing back into a frightened, angry, rabid young man, and suddenly, as though a switch had been flipped, he was in a naked fighting crouch, snarling like a wolf without a wolf's innate intelligence behind the savagery.

Teague backed up and changed quicker than breath, but not quick enough. His opponent rushed him, landing on him just as Teague's human legs started to bear his weight, and Jack clamped his teeth together in an effort not to shout at Cory to do something. He glanced at them and saw that Green had his arms wrapped securely around Cory's shoulders—she had the same idea. Jack looked back at the man he loved more than life and saw why Green was stopping her—apparently they all needed to have a little faith.

Teague grabbed his opponent's shoulders in hard human hands and shoved him back against the wall, shouting, "Give up, goddammit! You can walk away from this!" The man was struggling, but Teague had him pinned securely. The only way he was getting out of it was to yield or die.

"Fuck. You." The enemy hawked spit in Teague's face, and Teague's eyes went flat and grim. Then he used his werewolf strength to do something truly horrific.

He punched his arm under the guy's ribcage, thrusting into the flesh itself. As the man screamed blood and spittle and death in his face, Teague grabbed hold of his heart and ripped it out of his body.

The audience gave a shocked gasp, and Teague's opponent went limp, his eyes dying even as he saw his own heart beating in his enemy's hand.

Teague took a step back as the body slid to the floor. He was a little dazed—he looked at the quivering thing in his gore-soaked hands and just sort of dropped it on the body of his kill. His face was crusted with blood from ripping his enemy's throat, and his chest was heaving back and forth as though he'd sprinted for miles. His scarred chest was smeared with blood and viscera and sweat, and his body—his battered, wiry, bantam body—was bare and barbaric, naked and bloody and victorious for all the world to see.

He looked up at Green automatically and then to Cory. It was almost shocking for Jack to see the little college student suddenly appear regal and queenly, not in the way of Jack's dream, but in the way of a real person whose confidence had been hard-won. Together, in concert, they nodded back, and then Green looked over at Jack and gave a little jerk of his chin.

The message was clear—he's all yours, mate.

Teague didn't seem to think so. He managed one half-panicked, half-resigned look at Jack before he turned back toward Cory. Cory looked at him with no sympathy and actually said something out loud, which was a relief for Jack, who was getting tired of all of this tacit discussion.

"I've got cleanup, Teague. Go deal with the hard shit."

Teague looked at her miserably. "It's my mess—"

"Nope. Not gonna fly. Now get out of here. I've got to cook something, and if I don't do it quick and don't do it clean, Green's gonna make me ask Lambent, *and that would really suck!*" She pitched her voice loud on purpose just to get the fire elf's attention, and he cast a sour look her way.

"By all means, my liege, show us that your dick is as big as every other bloke's here."

Cory grinned sweetly at the ruddy-faced elf. "It's not bigger than *everyone's*, darling. Just yours." Then she turned back and met Teague's miserable expression, giving him a stern shooing with her two hands. "Go, Teague. You can't be happy if you're just good with the one and forsake the other."

Teague had no choice, and Jack was, for once, profoundly grateful for the lady of the house. Teague turned to Jack defiantly, and Jack grinned at him and advanced. Damned if he wasn't going to kiss that man within an inch of his life.

Teague put his hands behind his back, remembered he was naked and put them in front of his crotch, and then trotted to where his jeans lay in a puddle and picked them up to hold in front of his vulnerable bits. Jack made sure he was looming over his lover before Teague even stood up.

They regarded each other for a moment so fraught with tension that Jack could actually smell the blush traveling over Teague's skin. If Jack had looked, he could have seen it start at Teague's chest and then work its way across his shoulders and neck and even down to his thighs, but Jack had seen all that—if only once or twice—in bed. Right now he was more interested in what was going on behind Teague's depthless hazel eyes.

He looked horrified—probably at himself. And ashamed.

"Give it up," Jack commanded after a moment. "I'm going to kiss you. I'm going to hold you. And if you think you're ever going to spend another night in another bed, you're completely off your rocker."

Teague's lips quirked even as he ducked his head shyly. "Don't want to touch you all covered in blood and shit, Jacky."

Jack met Katy's eyes over Teague's shoulders. She grimaced because she knew what he was going to do, but she nodded anyway. Jack put his hands behind his back like a good boy. "No hands involved, I swear," he promised—and then, because he would have died if he didn't, he lowered his head as Teague just gazed at him, all starry-eyed and dumb struck, and touched lips with his beloved.

Teague gasped, and Jack used the opportunity to slip his tongue in. Teague tasted like blood, and sweat, and a little like fur, and Jack didn't care. He swept Teague's mouth with his tongue and licked at his palate and teeth and lips deliberately. He wanted no ambiguity in the kiss. *I love you, right down to the blood on your hands, you dumb Irish motherfucker.* It couldn't have been clearer if he'd used Cory's power to burn the message into the burnished, root-tangled walls.

Teague groaned at Jack's invasion, his acceptance, his benediction. Jack lifted his hands up to Teague's shoulders, pushed him up against the gnarled wooden wall, and kissed him and kissed him and kissed him until Teague broke away, panting and clutching his clothes to his groin with a little more force.

"Let me shower," he gasped, and Jack nodded with a little smile.

"As long as I can brush my teeth," Jack panted, and Teague actually grinned.

"I'll do that too in the shower. Now let's *go*...."

They made it back to the room using preternatural speed. Teague got there first and was running the shower as Jack and Katy walked in. Katy hung back by the door for a minute, and Jack turned to her with his hand extended. "What?"

She shrugged, looking embarrassed. "I don't know. This is your makeup thing. You really want me here with your makeup thing?"

Jack snorted. "He broke up with both of us, sweetheart. You get the hurt, you get the makeup sex. It's only fair."

Her slow-blooming grin was unrepentantly sexy. "There's gonna be some awesome makeup sex, isn't there?"

Jack answered the grin with one of his own. "Oh yeah. Just as soon as I—"

Katy nodded vigorously. "I know, baby. As soon as you brush your teeth. Now hurry! That man can take a damned quick shower!"

Jack managed to get in and out of the bathroom before Teague emerged. He had a thought about going into the shower and joining Teague, but the shower wouldn't fit three, and he'd meant what he said to Katy. She shared the heartbreak, she shared the joy.

When he got out to the bedroom, Katy was bouncing restlessly on the bed.

"What now?" she asked. He rolled his eyes, feeling nervous too.

"I don't know. It's like I just want to offer myself up to him. I don't want him to ever doubt that my...." Jack blushed. He was talking too much. This next part sounded great in his head but sappy and overdone out loud. But he couldn't help it. He looked at Katy slowly, still blushing. "I want him to know that my body is just like my heart. It's always his."

Katy flashed him that wood-erecting grin again. "Baby, hurry up and get naked. Man, I'm looking forward to this!"

Tender Reckonings

TEAGUE DIDN'T know what to expect when he walked into the bedroom. He was thinking more talk, which was probably necessary, but he was tired of talking. He wanted his family back. He wanted to claim them. He didn't know the relationship protocol for saying "It's all forgiven. I want you now."

Turns out he didn't need to.

He walked down the short hallway, a towel knotted around his waist, prepared to go through his drawers and find clothes and sit down and say whatever needed to be said. Instead he found Jacky on his knees on the floor, bent over the bed.

He was naked, and his backside glistened with lubricant. Katy was lying on her stomach in front of him, talking softly in his ear as she anchored his hands in front of him with her own.

"I want to touch you!" Jacky complained. She laughed softly, wickedly, and Teague's erection was instant, burgeoning, and painfully hard.

"Katy," he rasped. She looked up at him, her brown eyes innocent and challenging at the same time.

"What?"

"Take off your clothes, lie on your back, and spread your knees. He wants to touch you. Make him taste you instead."

Her smile was slow and sensuous as she wriggled out of her jeans and threw them over the bed. "It's good to have you back."

Teague growled, and his towel fell to the floor. Words. He was tired of them. His family had come and seen him be savage and violent, and they'd claimed him anyway. It was time to return the favor.

He leaned over the bed as Katy scooted down, losing her bra and sweater as she opened her bare thighs around Jack's head. Teague touched lips with her, and she arched off the bed and wrapped her arms around his shoulders—and oh *Goddess*, she was soft and silky under his hands. He pulled away and suckled a lush breast, playing the nipple with his tongue, and she knotted her hands in the hair at his neck. Then she made a little keening sound as Jacky began to taste her.

Teague pulled away long enough to ask, "You know what you're doing, Jacky?"

Jack raised a shiny face to his lover. "I'm not very good at this," he apologized. Katy laughed throatily and reached down between her thighs to push at his head.

"You know what you're doing, Jacky—just keep…." She moaned. "Yeah. Like that…."

Teague leaned over Jack's side so he could talk in his ear while Jack was busy. "Don't ever turn away from me again."

Jack tried to look at him around the plumpness of Katy's thigh. "Never," he swore. "Never."

Teague kissed him—tasting Katy, tasting *them*. Then, before he could get lost in the kiss, before the kiss became everything and he lost this fantasy of Jack pleasuring Katy as Teague fucked him into oblivion, Teague broke off the kiss and positioned himself at Jack's backside.

Jack was already stretched and prepared, and Teague had to rest his head on Jack's spine for a moment to get control of himself. The thought of Jack and Katy in here, making him ready for Teague…. God. God *damn*, that was sexy. They were his. It was that simple and that absolute.

Teague's cock probed at Jack's entrance. Jack made a muffled whimper, a begging sound, and he must have stopped what he was doing because Katy made one too. Their physical happiness literally depended on Teague, and all the triumph he'd felt and squashed in his chest when defeating his enemy surged back into him now.

He thrust deeply into Jack and grunted, "Mine!" Jack howled, the noise muffled in Katy's flesh, and she giggled a little and then gasped as Jack seemed to remember what he was doing. Teague didn't give him much of a chance.

He pounded hard and slow, and every time their bodies were flush, Katy gasped. Jack's hands, which had been on either side of Katy's thighs on the bed, suddenly disappeared as Jack grabbed for his own cock.

Teague knotted one hand in Jack's hair and dragged his head back while yanking Jack's other hand off his body.

"Her, Jacky. Play with *her!*" Because as much as he loved Jack, Teague knew his lover's greatest failing was an inability to think beyond the two of them. Loving Katy, touching her slickness, making her scream, that was a start.

Katy gasped and shrieked, and Teague rewarded Jack's good behavior with a reach-around. Jack felt long and full in his hand, and as Teague thrust hard into Jack's body, Jack's erection became slick with fluid as well. Jack groaned and rested his head on Katy's thigh, and Katy protested.

"No, you can't do that, Jacky!" Teague stopped. Just stopped moving and waited for Jack to keep going. It became a lesson. Teague wouldn't move until Jack remembered there was more to their relationship than the two of them. Jack appeared to be motivated. His busy fingers were working, and his clever tongue must have been doing something right. Katy's eyes were glazed and her mouth was parted, and Teague slowly fucked Jacky to the point where—

"Teague… I've got to come!" He was begging, but Teague wasn't giving. Not yet.

"You"—*thrust*—"know"—*thrust*—"what"—*thrust*—"to do…."

Suddenly Katy started to gibber. "Oh God… Jacky, that's my… my… not… oh… yes… right *there*…." and then her body bucked, practically coming off the bed, and her thighs clenched around Jack's head. Teague, mesmerized by the sight of her beautiful climax, had mercy on Jack and cut loose his own desires. He started pounding, hammering at Jack, stroking him quickly, and as Katy relaxed and scooted backward on the bed, Jack buried his face in the sheets and howled. His climax spurted across Teague's hand, and Teague pounded again and again and again, finally letting go of Jack's cock to put both hands on Jack's hips and thrust into him until his own orgasm ripped through his body and he poured himself into his lover's flesh.

He groaned, then louder, and then in a frenzy he hauled Jack up by the chest to bite the joining of neck and shoulders hard enough to leave a mark. Jack groaned some more, an aftershock making his body clench around Teague's tight enough to make Teague bite him again. Finally they were done and lay panting, collapsed at the side of the bed, while Katy turned herself around and came to kiss them both.

She kissed Jacky first, licking daintily at her own taste around his mouth and on his chin, and Jack grinned at her and kissed her back. Then she raised her face to Teague, and he possessed her. His body, still buried in Jack's, stirred and stiffened, and Jack groaned as Teague's hips gave another convulsive round of pistoning as he and Katy continued the ripe, passionate, lingering kiss.

But eventually the passion banked, ebbed, and left them cooling their sweat, rubbing noses to cheeks and chins and jawlines as their breathing became normal.

"Want to lie down?" Katy asked at last, and both men grunted in protest as Teague pulled out. He stood to go get a washcloth, but both Jack and Katy said, "No!" He turned back to them and shook his head.

"We like the stickiness," Katy sulked. "Not forever, but… don't wash it away when it was wonderful, okay?"

Teague nodded and crawled into the rumpled bed, not surprised when they climbed up on either side of him. He plumped the pillows and sat at the head of the bed and was truly satisfied when they joined him and snuggled. Katy tucked herself under his arm and kissed his chest, rubbing it absently as she smiled up at him.

Jack sat taller and wrapped his arm around Teague's shoulders. Teague leaned back against him and closed his eyes, allowing himself to be comforted. Allowing himself to be loved.

"Never turn away from me again," he whispered, surprised. He'd thought Jacky and Katy would do the talking. Turned out he had words in his heart too.

"I won't," Jack promised, bumping his nose along Teague's jawline. Teague closed his eyes and returned the bump, then found himself talking again.

"I mean it," he said roughly. "There's only so much of me. It all goes away when you turn your back."

"I know that now," Jack said back. He reached across Teague's body and took Katy's hand, and together they made themselves into the human safety net Teague had come to rely on. "I'll never do it again."

Teague closed his eyes and figured that was about all the talking he could stand. He'd spent the last few weeks learning how to be happy and becoming the man his lovers needed. He figured now was a good time to put all that learning into practice.

THE REMAINING werewolves were easily dealt with, but apparently Cory wasn't convinced they were the end of the matter.

They discussed it the morning she and Bracken put the remaining werewolves on a 3:00 a.m. plane out of town. They came back and caught a quick breakfast before Cory and the other students left for school.

"The thing is," she mumbled through a bite of eggs and cheese, "they're going to go back and tell everyone to leave us the fuck alone, and they're going to make pretty credible witnesses. But from what I can tell, it's sort of a big snake pit down there. A little alpha on every corner, no big alpha holding the whole thing together."

Teague grunted in agreement and took the plate of bacon she handed him. He watched in amusement as Bracken gave her sausage to replace the bacon. Cory took a bite while she was talking before she even realized what he'd done and then glared at him while she was still chewing. With a sigh, she held the sausage down next to her chair. Renny was there in cat form, and she took the meat with a clawless swipe of her paw.

"We never did figure out who's converting the homeless," Teague reminded her. She looked up in bemusement from another helping of eggs on her plate.

"Bracken Brine Granite op Crocken," she snapped, "you are trying to make me fat!"

"You lost ten pounds over Thanksgiving," the elf replied with a scowl. "Who in the fuck does that?"

Cory gave Teague a rather abashed look. "We've had this argument before," she confessed. "The weird thing is, there's not a single scale on the hill. I don't know how he thinks he knows!"

"I know," Bracken said, coming back with a bottle of chocolate milk for Teague and a chocolate muffin he put down for Cory. "Mostly I know the same way I know Teague lost weight too. Your jeans are sliding off your ass. So're his. I suggest you both eat."

Teague blushed, and Cory rolled her eyes and stuck out her tongue. "I can't believe he thinks he's more mature than we are," she hissed, and Bracken managed a smile of smug superiority before he yelped and hopped off his stool.

"Damn it, Renny!"

Cory took a napkin and dabbed at the blood on his ankle with appropriate soberness, but she cast Teague a wicked look of amusement over her shoulder, and Teague laughed.

He laughed a lot in this place. Not loudly—he might never laugh loudly—but that little chuff of amusement no longer had to force its way out of his chest. He liked it that way.

"So, the werewolves," Cory continued with a pointed look at Bracken after he sat down.

"And the homeless," Teague prompted, and Cory sighed, shoving the remains of her breakfast aside and resting her chin on her hands. She and Bracken had worked the night before, catching a few scant hours of sleep before taking the werewolves to the airport. After the stresses of Thanksgiving break and the week after that spent talking to the werewolves, well, the stress of being three or four or five people was starting to tell on her. She looked very mortal and very tired.

"The way I see it," she said quietly, "is that our boys are going to go home and put the fear of God into their boys down south, or whoever is trying to organize things down there. That'll be great. They'll kill each other in-house, make sure none of their mistakes make it up here, and for a while—I'd give it a year—we'll be blissfully unaware of how truly shitty that morass is down there while we're living up here in wolftopia, right?"

Bracken mulled the thought over. "Right," he agreed. "And whoever was making psycho wolves, well, he's going to stop just so nobody notices."

"Unless it's a glitch, like a serial-killer's thing, yeah," Cory said, looking at Teague for agreement.

"And even if it's a glitch," Teague reasoned, getting into the game, "serial killers know how to lay low. Now's the time to do it."

"Right." Cory yawned, but her murky brown eyes were still focused as they worked things through. "So for a year, they or who or whatever will leave us alone—and then they'll start forgetting. Or get their shit together and reorg. For all we know, this was just a feeler—but either way. We can't go down there—we'll be fair game. So we wait. We'll start seeing bad guys and dumbshit activity eventually. Now, if we've done our job with those four, someone will call us and warn us, especially if they last that long. That would be nice, but we can't bet the farm on it. But the first sign of anything hinky…."

"We need to be ready to kick ass," Teague concluded, and Cory agreed. She gave a sleepy, worn smile from her cupped chin on the wooden table.

"We've got a war brewing," she said softly.

"Then what was this last week about?" Teague asked, curious.

"A year of peace. We did all of that for a year of peace. Aren't you glad you signed on, Teague?" There was some bitterness in her words, some self-recrimination. Teague hated to hear it, but before he could reply, Bracken put a hand on the back of her neck, and she leaned into it as he whispered something in her ear. "This is our last week before finals," she said back softly. "We can't skip school now. You know that. I'll nap on the way there."

"Yeah," Teague said belatedly, meaning it. "I am glad I signed on."

Cory smiled up at him again, looking dreamy and happy, the bitterness gone. "Hey, you haven't seen us at our best. Wait until you see Christmas. It's gonna be a trip!"

Teague's best Christmas to date had been the last one. He and Jacky had exchanged gifts, talked excitedly about how they thought Green had gotten his gifts to them under their tiny tree, drank beer, and watched football. Low-key, but, well, it had been his only Christmas with somebody who actually gave a shit.

He privately cherished that memory, but now that he and Jacky were living at the hill, he learned that Christmas should *never* be low-key.

One day while the students were out and Katy and Jacky were at the bakery, Green came and got him from the garage—he was working on the Mustang—and said, "Wash up, mate. Come with us. We can be back before everyone gets home. It will be a grand surprise!"

Teague had no idea where he was going until they ended up in the woods surrounding the gardens behind the hill itself, past the dividing line where the oak and scrub turned into pine and undergrowth. He and Green were by no means traveling alone—they came with an entourage of fey and shifters ranging in size from flitting sprites to compact pixies to what looked like a four-foot-by-four-foot pile of rocks *holding hands* with a compact pixie. He later learned that the happy couple was actually Bracken's mother and father—a thing that about blew his mind out his left ear.

The motley assortment of walking mythology was hunting for a Christmas tree.

It had to be about twelve feet tall and perfectly proportioned, and most importantly it had to be in a position to be lifted from the ground, wrapped tenderly in cloths, and replanted into the floor of Green's home for a bit before being returned.

Apparently some of their company were wood nymphs—two-foot-tall, perfectly proportioned women with green skin and green hair everywhere. Green assured him that not only did the tiny women not feel the cold, they also grew to human size—when it suited them. Sort of like trees themselves, actually.

When they found a tree—or rather, Arturo spotted it and the littles chittered, cooed, tinkled, and generally fussed over it—Green asked Teague with a smile if it would do.

Teague blinked. "It's perfect," he said with some bemusement. "Why ask me? I'm not an expert!"

Green's smile was 100 percent tolerant affection. "It's going to be your tree too, Teague—and Jacky's and Katy's as well. Is this the tree you want?"

Teague looked at the tree again with new eyes. It looked less symmetrical than it had when Arturo first pointed it out, but it also looked personally perfect—those shoes you get from the rack and fit like you've owned them for years once they're on your feet. "It's an excellent tree," he said soberly, and the tinkling, chittering, chattering cheer from his little entourage was worth the careful consideration and sincerity.

Afterward he sat in the front room and drank white hot chocolate with Kahlúa, watching as Cory and the other students—and Jacky and Katy as well—exclaimed over the tree and decorated it with blown-glass ornaments and tiny snowflakes hand cut from translucent white paper and strung on red thread.

Cory came into the kitchen to lean into Green and thank him. "It's wonderful, beloved. I've never decorated one this big!"

Green smiled indulgently at her and rubbed noses. "You humans keep saying size doesn't matter!"

Cory laughed softly. "You're right—especially in Christmas trees, where it's all symmetry."

Bracken came up then and looped his arms over her shoulders as she leaned into Green. "Last year's was bigger," he said critically, and Green nodded.

"That one was too big for the house this year. This way we get to be acquainted with this one for a few years. He'll be happy when we put him back, you think?"

Teague blinked, trying to put their conversation together. "Why didn't you decorate last year's?" he asked Cory, and she shrugged.

"It was sort of a surprise for me—he had it all decorated when we got home from the city. Green wanted to do Christmas up really huge." Her smile was all for her beloved. "Not that size matters or anything."

Teague turned his attention to his own lovers, who were engaged in a snowflake fight. Jack was winning, and Katy was wearing a glittering rain of translucent rainbow snowflakes in her black hair, on her cheeks, and in her eyelashes. Jack bent to take one of them out of her eyelashes, and as she stood there waiting for him to finish, he snuck in a kiss that she responded to with a smile—and an open mouth. They would have a "last year's tree" in their history. They would remember this snowflake fight and try to recreate it. They were already building good memories, memories of each other, to become a family—a true family—like Cory and Green and Bracken and Nicky.

Jack and Katy surfaced from their kiss and caught him staring at them with shining eyes. They exchanged wicked glances, and Teague had the foresight to put down his cocoa before being chased around the myriad halls of the hill, being showered with translucent snowflakes and avoiding the mistletoe dripping from every doorway.

Eventually he allowed himself to be caught, to be kissed, and to be seduced and lured into their bedroom, but in the meantime he whooped laughter like a child, and another little piece of his heart was patched together and sealed with the rest of it. The damned thing was getting more and more sound, more and more capable of sustaining his life and that of his lovers, by the day.

That didn't mean that Teague wasn't still a taciturn, defensive, grumpy fucker on occasion—it just meant the payoff was bigger when he let down his guard.

One night after he'd been out patrolling with the vampires, engaging in mock fights and making sure the neighbors from the surrounding hills didn't venture too close to Green's territory, he crawled into bed with Jacky, hoping for once to fall asleep. Except....

"Where's Katy?" he asked irritably.

"In her room, planning Christmas."

"This late?" Teague blinked, threatening to sit up, but Jack wrapped a long arm around his chest and pushed.

"She's wrapping presents, Teague. Let her be. She's really psyched about this whole thing, okay? Now tell me about the job."

"Job was boring. The vampires ate, Nicky cracked bad jokes, and nobody grabbed my ass. Are we happy now? I'm ready for bed!" There was more to it than that. Fighting with the vampires was no joke, and Teague would have some bruises the next morning, werewolf healing or not. But just because Jacky had accepted who Teague was didn't mean he was okay with Teague being hurt.

"I was just wondering if we were going to go shopping for Christmas."

Teague grimaced in the darkness. "I need to see if we can leave the place unescorted, Jacky. Last night was the full moon. We'd better wait another day before we go alone, you think?"

"That's cutting it close, Teague!" Jack sounded really anxious, and Teague grinned. It was cute. Just was.

"Well, then, maybe we can get someone to take us. Cory, Brack, and Nicky are going tomorrow. Cory asked if we wanted to go." Teague had said he'd check with Jacky—and he'd planned to. *In the morning!*

"Fun. Wonderful." Jack turned over in bed and sulked, and Teague sighed. Just a little bit of goddamned sleep, was it too much to ask?

He grunted and sighed and rolled over, missing Jack's body but not wanting to give in to the sulk. "You know, there's always the internet," he said dryly.

"Yeah, great. I was looking today, and I saw a great pair of men's underwear for you. They were pink and had 'Batter Up' on the crotch!"

"Only if your pair has a catcher's mitt on the ass!"

"Teague, this is serious!"

Teague growled. "You know, Princess, unless Santa's gonna slide down the fucking chimney early this year, I'm pretty sure this could have waited until morning!"

"Unless your dick is Santa, I'm not counting on it," Jack snapped back. Jack propped himself on one elbow, and Teague tucked his hands under his armpits and glared up at him. No touchy-feely sweetness tonight. All Teague wanted was bed.

"I was just wondering what you wanted for Christmas," Jack was saying sulkily.

"I liked the model car display," Teague replied, at a loss. "You know… something like that?"

"We weren't sleeping together last year, Teague!" Jack said, using his hands to talk, which was dangerous in the dark, even for a werewolf. Teague barely ducked a grand gesture, and he sat up in bed so Jack could sort of see him with his werewolf vision.

"Do you have any idea how tired I am?"

"Not really, asshole, since you just patently lied to me about the job!" Apparently Teague hadn't been as sly about hiding the bruises as he'd thought. "I was just wondering what we're going to do for Christmas, since we're fucking each other instead of, well, whatever we were doing last year."

"We're not 'fucking each other,'" Teague grunted, not liking the phrase in this context in the least.

Jack's hand found his cheek in the dark, and although their words had been the sharp, tangy sort of banter they had perfected during the whole of their relationship, the hand on his cheek was everything they'd been in the past month.

"Not right now," Jack said with some humor.

Teague sighed and kissed his palm, adding a graze of teeth. "I'm really honestly tired, Jacky. If I promise to have people take us out tomorrow, can we go to sleep now?"

Jack took his hand back and used it to turn Teague around and spoon up behind him. "Will you tell me about the job?" he asked softly.

"I'll tell you tomorrow if you promise not to get me anything… you know…."

"Gay?" Jack supplied cheekily.

"I was gonna say 'sappy,' smartass. And you haven't told me what *you* want for Christmas."

"I thought Santa was gonna bring me a big ol' dick up my—"

"Shut up."

"Yes, sir."

Jack kissed his shoulder in the dark, and Teague relaxed against him, but he still didn't know what he was going to get Jack or Katy for Christmas. Now that the students were out of school and the excitement of Christmas—or Yule, since the fey were mostly pagans—was starting to permeate the hill like the sound of a distant waterfall, it seemed incumbent on him to make some sort of big romantic gesture or something.

He was pretty sure he was going to fall short.

"YOU WANT *my* help?" Cory looked at him oddly, and Bracken eyed the two of them with amusement.

"Well, we're all here together, aren't we?" Teague grunted. The shopping trip had been okayed—which, considering the fact that the full moon was so damned recent, was a minor miracle—but Teague took it at face value. Maybe Green had faith, right?

Not too much faith—Green was with Jack and Katy on the other side of the wood-and-glass three-story structure that was built into a hill in one of Auburn's oldest downtown streets. It was where Grace's yarn store and Katy's bakery sat, and the majority of the stores were little handcraft boutiques. It was close to Green's hill, and many of the businesses were Green's, with Green's people inside. If somebody turned furry, there were plenty of folks who would help cover.

"I just think you'd be better off asking a girl," Cory was saying doubtfully. Then she ducked as Bracken tried flicking the back of her head.

"I'm asking a friend!" Teague said with some desperation. "I've managed three gifts my entire life—real bookshelves for Jacky last Christmas, and gift certificates to Amazon for his birthdays. I'm sort of thinking they need me to do better than that!"

"That's not bad!" Cory protested, but Bracken put both hands squarely on her shoulders, gave her a shove toward Teague, and then took off. She glared at his retreating back and then looked sourly at Teague. "He thinks we'll talk better without him," she explained unnecessarily.

"He could be right," Teague told her. "He's scary as hell."

She wrinkled her nose. "You think? I don't see it."

Teague just rolled his eyes. The guy could rip out someone's viscera from a hundred yards away—Teague would hate to know what she found scary. "Whatever. Christmas presents. What do you do for them?"

Cory sighed. "I knit. It's weird. I don't know if other husbands do this, but mine get all gooey when I knit something for them—which is funny, because knitting makes me happy, so it's really like being a selfish bitch and getting praised for it." She shrugged. "What's to do?"

"So last Christmas…?" Teague asked with what he felt to be exaggerated patience.

"Last Christmas I made Green and Bracken scarves while I was in recovery," she said thoughtfully. "I barely had time to make Nicky a hat. Green and I got Bracken a chess set, because that was Adrian's gift to Bracken every year, and we got Nicky a motorcycle and made Brack pick out the helmet."

"Recovery?"

"Bad shit stories, remember, Teague? I was sick for a long time." Her voice was sober, as it hadn't been when she'd talked about Bracken's chess set.

"What did Green get you?"

And now the sadness was palpable. "The granite bench with Adrian's likeness, the one in the garden."

Teague grimaced. "How do you top that?" he asked, almost to himself, and Cory grinned. She looked just like what she was—a plain college student. And queen of the northern California fey and undead.

"You don't, sweetie. You're right. The first year's the hardest. This year I think I'm getting clothes in three sizes—at least that's what he's been threatening to get me for the last month."

Teague blinked and looked at her. Her jeans were falling off her hips, and her chin and cheeks looked sharper than they had when he'd arrived over a month ago, when he'd been sitting disconsolate in the living room waiting to hear if Jack would live or die.

"Why three sizes?"

She sighed, then took his arm and started pulling him with her. The building was designed with lots of glass looking out into the dark, and even though it was fairly crowded, there was a curious sense of isolation as they walked the white-tiled halls.

"One to fit me now, one to fit me when I gain a little weight, and one to fit me when I'm where he thinks I should be."

"If you don't have scales on the hill, where is that exactly?" Teague asked. He was starting to get on the concern bandwagon—she was easy to care about, the little queen of the hill.

She sighed and shrugged. "I think he'll be happy when I start my period. I haven't had one in a year and a half. It's sort of freaking everybody out." She gave him another grin. "And isn't that information you wish you didn't have."

Teague looked at her carefully, thought of calming Jack down about the bruises from his workouts, thought of Katy's constant pampering and the way she *always* brought him something to eat every night if he didn't eat in the common room, and came to a realization.

"People will always worry about us, won't they?" The thought was boggling. It was as though he'd been working this entire time with no idea what he was working *toward*.

Cory grinned at him. "Yeah. It'll drive you crazy sometimes, but you'll never want to change it." She tugged on his arm, and they walked into a glassblower's shop. The shelves were stocked with some of the most frighteningly lovely, exquisite things Teague had ever seen.

"This place scares the hell out of me!" he whispered. He was afraid if he spoke normally, his voice would splinter the store's wares to powder.

"Yeah," she said, looking at him carefully. "Scares me too. Shit this fragile—doesn't feel like people like us should be anywhere near it, you think?"

Teague blinked. She was speaking in metaphors, and he followed her. "But it's so pretty," he said after a moment. "Maybe the risk is worth seeing what's in here?"

"Yeah." And with that, she turned to the slightly built young man behind the counter and, to Teague's surprise, bowed. "Master Splinter—good to see you tonight."

Teague watched the guy startle up from the book of color theory he was reading and bow low at the waist. Then he realized that in spite of the longish hair cut trendily about his shoulders and the understated height, the guy had pointy ears and a faintly fuchsia cast to his skin. He was one of Green's.

"My lady! How can I help you tonight?"

Cory smiled, looking self-conscious, and dragged Teague up to the front counter. "Actually, we're here for Teague. He wants something beautiful to give his mates for Christmas. Do you have time to do something custom?"

She needn't have worried. From the way the guy was fawning over her, he probably would have gone without sleep for a week just to be who she needed. It took them a while, but Cory helped. She had a surprisingly poetic soul, and when she was done outlining what she had in mind, Teague looked at her with a little bit of awe.

"What?" she asked him irritably as they left the store, leaving Splinter in their wake making illustrations and graphics for all he was worth.

"You're just… every now and then I see why we'd follow you to hell and back," he said at last, feeling stupid.

"Shut the fuck up." She punctuated this with a slug on his arm. She put her shoulder behind it, and it might have bruised a mortal—barely— but it only served to emphasize how mortal and fragile she was.

He'd die to defend her. He'd die to defend Green too, but Green wouldn't survive without Cory. Teague would throw himself in front of anything life or death dealt out.

As he caught up to Jacky and Katy, he bumped Jack's shoulder with his own and took Katy's hand in his, rubbing her wrist softly with his thumb. She smiled up at him, and Jack slung an arm over his shoulder, and he realized he really could love both his mates and his leaders. He never would have thought his heart was big enough. Of all things, this surprised him the most.

CHRISTMAS REALLY was everything the hill had cracked it up to be. Nobody was allowed to open presents in their rooms. It was the one rule. It meant people were constantly wandering into the living room under the tree to open presents or watch their particular friends open gifts, but that was part of the excitement. Someone was *always* receiving something. Someone was *always* giving something. From around five in the morning until dinnertime, someone was *always* exclaiming with "Thank you" and "You're welcome." And after the Christmas banquet, it was the vampires' turn. It was the one time of the year that everybody came into the front room and greeted the world. In a place the size of Green's hill, it was sometimes the only time of the year people actually saw each other—and they were always happy for the honor.

But it wasn't easy on the lord and lady of the house.

It took a while for Teague to notice that what was joyful for everybody else was a joyful responsibility for Cory and Green. He'd opened his own presents—a quilt and bedding for him and Jack from Katy, who had commissioned one of the elves who worked in Grace's store to do one custom with three wolves appliquéd in the center. The whole hill had seen them as wolves—one of the animals was golden, one was dark-haired, and one had bright gold hair over black fur underneath. The colors were cleverly done with different fabrics, and the effect was breathtaking. Teague and Jack had been impressed, both with the final product and with the symbolism.

Jack had gotten Katy a little privacy screen for their room—although she was still keeping her own exclusively female sanctuary down the hall—and had gotten Teague ceramic figurines of wolves to paint. Jack had been embarrassed about his gift.

"I know it's dumb," he said, red-faced. "But you love models, and this was close to a model, and I wanted it to be, you know, important. I'll take it back. You hate it. I'm so bad at this—you'd think I could manage giving a damned gift, but…."

Teague had laughed. It was exactly how he'd felt when they'd started shopping. "It's not pink underwear, Jacky. I think you did fine."

Jack flipped his hair back and gave Teague a private and positively evil smile. "That's in the next box."

Teague blushed. "As long as you're wearing the pair that says 'catcher,' that's fine too."

And that's when Jack and Katy finally made it through the sixty-zillion layers of tissue and gold wrapping paper that had kept Teague's gift to them safe from gravity and Teague's own shaking hands. Underwear and the lack thereof were forgotten as the two of them knelt breathlessly over the colored glass sculpture that Teague—with a lot of help from Cory—had designed.

They were speechless.

Three wolves, their bodies only an abstract suggestion as they formed the base, pointed their muzzles at a distant moon and howled. One, delicate and female, was colored a rich, exotic burgundy. Another, the taller one, was a blue slightly paler than indigo. The third was a translucent forest green.

The silence went on so long that Teague got nervous. "So. Uhm. It's okay?"

Katy started squealing in some arcane pitch that made Teague's wolf cringe—but she launched herself at him with a lot of enthusiasm, so he figured it was a good thing. Jacky hugged them both, and it was pretty damned maudlin there for a minute—and satisfying. Pretty damned satisfying.

Teague looked over to where Cory was being presented with what appeared to be miles of strings of preciously formed, cut, molded, or carved beads, one bead at a time. She caught his eye over the myriad heads in the sitting room and smiled sweetly, then nodded to Green. Green looked up and excused himself. The two of them had been sitting for most of the morning, being gracious and kind and hosting Christmas with the aplomb of an Arthur and a Guinevere. Teague wasn't sure if Jack or Katy had noticed that Bracken and Nicky had been in constant, subtle attendance—with glasses of water or soda or eggnog, and small finger foods for breakfast—since Cory and Green didn't seem to have had time to sit at the table and eat. Teague figured they were too busy for a conversation, so he was surprised when Green nodded him over.

Cory was busy talking to the tiny sprites. She held a stiffened piece of string straight in front of her, and the smaller fey were coming up and presenting her with one bead at a time before placing it on the string. At her feet there were dozens of "necklaces"—she had been doing this for more than an hour.

"Thank you!" she said. Although her voice was rough, her enthusiasm was just as bright as it had been that morning when the werewolves had come out for the breakfast buffet that sat on the kitchen table *and* the breakfast nook *and* the surrounding counters. Cory nodded soberly at the latest tiny creature, who looked like a cross between a gerbil and a bluebird with surprisingly human arms under her wings. "It's beautiful. It's completely different and precisely perfect. I will think of you every time I see that bead!" The bead itself was hand carved, with tiny little loops etched into its sanded wood surface. It was truly one of a kind—but then, so was every one of what must have been thousands of beads she'd received that morning.

It didn't make her sincerity any less real, though, and Teague felt a surge of affection for her. Everyone was special. Everyone was cherished. Every gift was just that. A gift.

She stopped for a moment and looked at the next supplicant. "Hold on just a minute, okay? I want to give it my full attention. Just give me a sec." She smiled as she said it, and a very humanoid little fairy, holding a bead like a dewdrop from a spider's web, bowed patiently and waited her turn.

Cory looked at Green beseechingly. "I don't think there are many more," she said.

Green grimaced. "Don't be so sure, beloved. But don't worry. I'll spread the word that you need a break, and you can join us when the queue finishes up."

Teague felt bad. "I can come back—"

"No no no!" Cory interjected. "It's just that Katy and Jacky got clothes from us, but your gift is bigger. You need us to show it to you! I want to be there too!" She sounded distressed, and Green bent down and kissed her cheek.

"We'll wait outside for you, right, beloved? Don't worry. You'll get a chance to see his face when he 'opens' it."

Cory nodded anxiously and then grinned and flashed the charm bracelet Teague had asked Katy to pick out for her. His exact words had been "Something girly, but us." Every tinkling silver charm was either a wolf in a different pose or the moon in a different phase.

"Thank you. Make sure you let Jack and Katy know I love it!"

Teague flushed and bowed and then allowed Green to lead him quietly outside. As they were walking, Green looked significantly at Bracken's mother, a four-foot-tall, charmingly beautiful little pixie who both floated and walked with equal kittenish grace, and Blissa nodded.

"They can wait until tomorrow, Green. They're quite aware that she's getting tired." Blissa's wings were rainbow-colored when they were still enough to see, although her hair was decidedly purple, but she sounded as matter-of-fact as any mother Teague had ever heard.

"Thank you, Blissa. She'd make herself sick if we let her. Tell her we'll be outside at the old barn, okay?"

Another pixie appeared with Teague's battered denim jacket and a newer fleece-lined denim jacket for Green, along with a hand-knit scarf in green and gold. Teague looked at the scarf with his eyebrows raised. Cory had given him, Jack, and Katy fingerless mittens—the better to wear while turning into a werewolf without shredding the knitting. He was wearing his pair now—and the work was finer and far more practiced, as well as more complex, than the rough, simple scarf. Green caught the direction of his gaze and smiled fondly.

"It was the first thing she ever made."

Teague wanted to blush just looking at Green's expression. Love that clean and simple almost didn't belong on earth. "She does good work" is what he said, and as he and Green slid outside into the refreshing December cold, he was grateful for that work. It kept his hands a hell of a lot warmer than his pockets, which was what he usually used.

Green took him walking down the landing and across the drive, their feet crunching in the gravel and then crunching on the frost-ridden lawn. The property in this direction was simply short-cut grass, although Teague had heard that after Christmas, Green would let the snow that usually fell in this area gather everywhere but the crown of the hill with Adrian's garden. About two hundred yards from the house in the hill were a series of outbuildings—there were three of them—that looked like old barns or maybe converted garages. Green led Teague to the far one.

It had a big green-and-red bow and a ribbon wrapped around the entire building. A smaller plastic tube—the kind used to hold architects' plans—also wrapped in ribbons and bows, leaned against the front door.

"Merry Christmas, Teague," Green said quietly. "This is from my family to yours."

Teague looked at the old barn and saw a good foundation. Green opened the smaller door next to the big double front door, and Teague saw neat stacks of lumber, drywall, plumbing supplies, and tools, as well as buckets of clean, shiny nails, drywall screws, and the assorted paraphernalia used to convert a big barn into a family home.

"Wow." That was all he had. "Just… shit. Wow. I…."

"You don't have to move in right away!" Cory called, running across the yard in her T-shirt, sleep pants, and bare feet. The door above the landing slammed—they could hear it from where they were—and Teague watched as a formless blur that *must* have been Bracken came zooming across the yard.

"God*damn* it!" Bracken swore, materializing and slowing down in time to pick her up and run her toward them. "I swear, it's like you were sneaking out on purpose." He set her down on the frost-covered ground and wrapped her black pea coat around her, adding in a hooded scarf for good measure, and then swung her up into his arms.

Cory glared at him and, in spite of the fact that she was in his arms, ignored him, concentrating on Teague instead.

"We had a couple of floor plans drawn up," she said earnestly. "You and Jack and Katy can pick which ones you want. And everybody will help. Because you're not going to be doing werewolf shit all the time, right? It's just...."

Teague looked at Bracken for permission, and Bracken nodded so he could drop a kiss on his little sorceress's cheek. "It's just perfect," he said gruffly. "They'll love it. I love it. Thank you."

Cory grinned at him, and Green came over and took her from Bracken. She didn't protest, and Teague could detect an air of penitence in the way she raised her arms obediently in the transfer. "We're really glad you're here, Teague," she told him. "We're really really grateful for you and your family. You don't have to worry about reaching for stuff anymore. We want you to have whatever you want. We want you to be happy."

Teague nodded, not able to find any words. "I am," he said after a minute. "I am. Could you... could you send them out? I want to show them...."

He wanted to be alone for a minute, was what he wanted. He wanted to absorb and enjoy. He had a home. He had a family. He had a purpose. All the things he could have become, and he'd become this. It was almost more than he could bear.

Cory pulled him down into an awkward hug, and Green dropped a kiss on his hair, like a father. "We'll send them out in a minute," she said softly. "We're glad you like."

He gave a watery smile. "Don't like. Love. Thank you."

She grinned back. Then they turned around and left him there, wandering in the wonder of the raw materials with which to build the rest of his life. He was still there, trying to visualize how they would use the vast space of the cold barn, when Jack and Katy got out there and stood with him in the dark, smelling the raw lumber and the cold steel.

"It's better than a blanket fort, right, Jacky?" Katy said, her voice a little bit lost in the awe of the gift.

"Who's got a blanket fort?" Teague asked, sounding confused. Jack looked at Katy. He understood what she meant—Teague, thinking it could just be the three of them, not understanding that they had an entire hill of people who loved them enough to see them happy.

"Not us," Jack said. Katy leaned her head on his shoulder, Teague pulled him in against his chest, and they stood there in the Christmas quiet and planned what their home would become.

Royal Betrayals

"You want to go where? How? Why?"

Teague had pulled me aside on the morning before New Year's Eve. I'd picked up a teeny-tiny virus the day after Christmas. It was plenty easy for Green to heal me, which he did, but the resulting moratorium on me doing anything *at all* in the week between Christmas and New Year's Eve had made me a little testy. I'd get to go running the day after tomorrow, and I'd been hoping Teague could join me, and, well, his request just didn't make any sense.

"I need to leave the hill tomorrow, in the morning. I'd be back before dark. But I want to go alone, okay? Could you… I don't know. Make up a reason for me to leave? Cover for me?"

Teague looked restless and unhappy to be asking me this, and I didn't know what to tell him. He should be restless and unhappy to make a request like this. Of all the things to reach for, he wanted to reach for being alone?

"Can you give me a reason?" I asked, entertaining the thought of going along with him. It wouldn't work. For one thing, nobody would let me out of the house, and for another, Bracken would have to come. Teague liked Bracken, but Bracken wasn't Teague's best friend. I was. It was flattering—and a terrible responsibility too.

Teague paced a little and looked around, seeing who was in the living room. Nobody, that was who. They'd all bugged out discreetly when he'd seen me knitting and walked in with that "can we talk" vibe radiating from him like a child's fever. I'd actually breathed a sigh of relief. It was the closest I'd come to being alone since I'd awakened next to Bracken the day after Christmas—flushed, feverish, and coughing up a lung.

"I have this thing," he said at last, blushing up along his Irish-pale neck and into his ears. "I…. Christ, Jacky doesn't even know about this. I go up to Mokolumne Hill every year—and, well, let's just say I give the old man the send-off he deserved."

I blinked and swallowed, my throat suddenly sore and dry. "That's a horrible-assed tradition to keep," I said roughly. "That's like us celebrating the time I almost died."

"Maybe you're celebrating the time you chose to live," Teague said squarely, meeting my eyes with some resolve. I blushed and tried not to cough. Damn. *Green leaves the hill for half a day and the damned virus tries to sneak back.* I guess running in two days was right out.

"Maybe you need to start celebrating the day you leave all that behind you," I said without dropping my eyes. "They'd want to be a part of that."

Teague looked away, looked down at his battered working-man's hands. He'd started roughing out the frame in the last week. Not too much work, because it was cold and we were still doing the holiday-vacation thing, but it had made him happy.

"They have to deal with my bullshit every day, Cory. Every fucking day, something comes up. Someone has to tiptoe around me, Jacky has to worry if I'm all right, Katy has to remind me I have a family now. It would be just a fucking miracle if I didn't have to burden them with something this goddamned ugly, you know?"

I gave it up and released a cough, then glanced over my shoulder to see Bracken glaring at me from the doorway. "Tell me about it," I pouted. "Teague, I'm the poster child for letting my mortal human bullshit get in the way. You want to know what I've learned from hard experience? I've learned that once you join hands and go skipping into the wild blue future with someone, they're in it for the long haul, and they're in it for the ugly and the clean. Asking them to go with you out to Mokolumne Hill will be the best Christmas gift you could give."

I coughed again, and Bracken was suddenly at my elbow with a cup of honey tea he had apparently pulled fully heated out of his ass and put a hand on my forehead. "I'll go get Lambent," he threatened. "And then I'm calling Green."

"It's a cold, asshole," I protested, leaning into that hand on my face in spite of myself. "Even mortal old me isn't going to drop dead from a damned cold."

Bracken seized my face in his hands and forced me to look into his pond-shadow eyes. "We're in it for the ugly and the clean, beloved. You'd best learn to take what you dish out. Now, you stay here with that blanket on your lap and finish your little chat with the wolfman, and then you're done. No audiences with sprites, no planning next semester, no nothing. We're putting in movies, and you're sitting in my lap like a good little mortal, and we'll forget that you spent four hours this morning on the computer helping Grace with inventory without your slippers on, shall we? I'll get you some tomato soup for dinner, and we're done."

I closed my eyes and felt his breath on my face. It sounded lovely. "Agreed," I conceded, and he kissed me softly on the lips, because we both knew *he* wasn't coming down with a damned head cold, was he?

He left, and I met Teague's eyes ironically. "I think he just made my point," I said mildly, and Teague shrugged, looking away.

"And I think you just made mine. No. It would be best if I do this alone."

Ha! Like I was going to let that happen.

I had to sneak away from Bracken *and* Teague. I told them I was going to the bathroom and then to pick out some more yarn for a project, and managed to get down the hall and knock on the door to the werewolves' shared room.

Katy was asleep already, curled up on her side in the dark of a lamp. She worked bakers' hours—it didn't surprise me. Jack was awake, and he answered the door in his sleep pants and a T-shirt, holding a book I was pretty sure he'd borrowed from me. He frowned when he saw me, because honestly, I'd been avoiding him since he'd all but rattled my teeth from my skull. But I tried not to be a coward about these things, so I put that aside.

"Hey," I said quietly, standing in their doorway. "You need to know that Teague's taking a trip tomorrow morning. He'll probably try to sneak out after Katy goes to work and before you wake up. It's fine if he goes, right, but, well. You may want to find a way to be with him."

Jack blinked. "I'm surprised you're not going," he said. The tone of his voice made me suck on my teeth.

"I'm not his beloved, okay? You are. And if you want, I can help you sneak into his car, but only if you're not a complete bastard to me in the meantime." I masked a cough, because Green wouldn't be back until later tonight and I was still sick, and glared at Jack to force him not to make a big stinking deal about this.

Jack swallowed and blushed and made an effort not to be an asshole, then said, "What did you have in mind?"

The next morning, I made sure I was up before Teague, waiting in the breakfast nook as he came walking past the living room on his way to the stairs.

"Hey, Teague!" I kept my voice low. There was something about being up that early in the morning that made loud voices sort of obscene, especially when it was cold. It was like Mother Nature needed you to observe the sleep of the world with silence. He looked at me and pulled on the mittens I'd made him, then followed that up with the hat I'd finished for him the day before.

"There's a picnic lunch down in the car for you," I said, keeping my eyes on him and very carefully not watching as Jack ran down the stairs in his wolf skin. There was a change of clothes and Jack's coat, gloves, and hat down there too, but I didn't mention that. "And we replaced your cell phone and the charger, so don't freak out. We also have a new contact out at Angel's Camp. I put the number in your phone, so look for 'Elm' if you need to get a hold of anyone, okay?"

Teague nodded at me tersely, and I gave him an impromptu hug. Hopefully I'd given Jack enough time to get his clothes on. He'd have a better chance of staying in the car if he was fully clothed with boots and everything by the time Teague got down there.

"Don't be afraid to reach for us," I told him softly. "Don't be afraid of how you've changed. It's okay, right?"

His arms tightened around me, and I could feel the need in them. Not for me—for *somebody* while he did this. I thought maybe I'd done the right thing in sending Jacky down there. Teague *could* do this alone. He didn't have to.

Teague kissed my cheek and turned silently toward the stairs to the underground garage, and I held my breath.

In about five minutes, I saw the lights from the Mustang as it crunched its way across the icy gravel drive, and then the house was as silent as it ever got. The vampires were still awake, but they were mostly downstairs in their own common room. I gave a little sigh of relief and made my way back to bed. Green was there, looking at me reprovingly from the edge of the bed, while Bracken continued to sleep, unaware I'd even left.

"Meddling, beloved?" he asked quietly, pulling back the covers and ushering me under them. I went, shivering because being up at 4:00 a.m. in the winter did that to you. He climbed in next to me, making me the happiest filling in an elf Oreo cookie ever.

"Yes," I said through chattering teeth. I backed up against Bracken and burrowed into Green's embrace. I pulled his T-shirt out of his cotton shorts and put my hands against the blessedly warm, satiny small of his back. "Yes, I was meddling. Why do you ask?"

Green laughed and adjusted his head so his long yellow queue streamed behind him. "No reason at all," he rumbled, rubbing his hands up and down my shoulders until the shivers stopped. "Not a reason in the world."

BONDING

JACK THOUGHT Teague looked unsurprised to see him sitting in the car, lacing his boots and breathing hotly on his half-mitted hands.

"She put you up to this?" he asked gruffly as he trotted down the stairs to the driver's side of the Mustang.

"C—Lady Cory? Yeah. Did she tell you?" Jack hadn't ridden in the front seat of the Mustang since going Christmas shopping. As he belted in and smelled the cold leather and oil, he realized he'd missed it. For a year and a half, his entire reason for living had been to be right here in this car at Teague's side.

Teague shook his head and stood with the door to the 'Stang open and grunted. "Didn't tell me anything—she just can't lie for shit. I thought I got out of there a little easily."

Jack stood up out of the car and leaned on the roof with his door open. "You gonna make a big, furry-assed deal out of this, or can we get our asses in gear so we can be back in time for New Year's Eve? I understand there's one hell of a party."

"You don't like parties," Teague reminded him. Neither one of them made a move to get in the car.

"Neither do you." Jack was stonewalling. He knew it. But Teague hadn't overtly kicked him out of the car yet, and that was encouraging.

"You don't even know where I'm going," Teague reached into the car and turned the key in the ignition to warm it up inside. The garage wasn't too chilly, because it was underground and the worst of the frosty cold stopped at the door. But the car needed warming up anyway.

"You're going the same place you went last year, Teague. You left early in the morning, you came back in the afternoon, and you didn't talk for a week. You didn't eat for a week either. Our next job, *you* were the one who picked a fight. Remember that? You almost got *shot*!"

"I remember," Teague grunted, rubbing his chest uneasily.

"I'd rather not go through that again," Jack said reasonably. "How about this time, I go along?"

"I'm gonna be a grumpy asshole anyway." Jack was pretty sure Teague knew he had won. "There's no reason for you to catch that in the teeth."

"How about because I love you and I choose to. Will that do you? Can we get in the goddamned car now?"

"Fine."

"Fine."

And away they went. Teague cranked the music as soon as they cleared Green's driveway.

Jack was prepared for a long, silent run, but there was a big hamper of food behind him, and he decided to dive right in. The first thing out was one of the two big thermoses of white hot chocolate with hazelnut cream—and while it made Jack happy, he knew that once he gave Teague a big-assed mug full of it, Teague would be as pleased as a little kid. Jack found it in himself to let go of the resentment that Cory'd had to tell him about this little adventure. She'd done it for him and Teague and their little family, and it was hard to stay mad at someone for that.

"Mmmmm…," Teague all but groaned. "Damn, Jacky. It'd be worth becoming a werewolf just to get this in your coffee mug every morning."

Jack grunted an agreement and then found his balls and asked, "So. Where are we going?"

Teague sighed. "Angel's Camp. But we have to stop somewhere first."

The stop was at a liquor store for a bottle of Jose Cuervo Gold. Jack was surprised—Teague drank nothing but beer. But as the car drove around the lake and then took the rolling back roads toward Mokolumne Hill, he started to have an inkling of what this was about.

Mokolumne Hill was one of those places that had become an icon for bad roads and possible vehicular death. The road wound closely along the hill, switchbacks abounded, and railings were thin and often falling off the crumbling scrabble of soil. By the time they arrived at the hill, the sun was up, and Jack was supremely grateful. Werewolf or no werewolf, he didn't want to become a highway statistic, no matter *how* carefully Teague was driving.

Near the crown of the hill was a pullout, where slower traffic could pull over and allow faster traffic to pass, and Teague was nothing if not cautious as he pulled the car onto the muddy shoulder and parked. He should be cautious. Not too far from this spot was where his father had gone off the road and died.

He got out, grabbed the tequila, and walked to the front of the car, looking out over the mist-shrouded, ice-coated valley in the thin orange sunlight of morning.

Jack sat, torn. Teague was so good at isolating himself, at creating an impenetrable force field of space around his body, that it was hard to know if he was being stoic or truly wanted to be left alone. But watching Teague's shoulders slump as he stood alone and shivering, Jack didn't think he could stand to watch him be alone for another moment.

Jack stepped quietly out into the dawn.

Teague was muttering. Two months ago, Jack wouldn't have been able to make out real words, but he heard them now.

"I'm more than you ever said I would be, and I've got more than you ever said I could have. Nobody beats me, nobody hurts me—just your ghost, you ass-ripping motherfucker. I've let you eat up most of my life up to now, but I'll tell you something. This is the last thing you'll ever get from me, Sean Sullivan. It's the last drop of Cuervo you'll ever drink. It's the last thing your kid is ever gonna do for you.

It's more than you deserve, you sonuvabitch."

Teague pulled his shoulder back and hurled the Cuervo out into the desolate valley below. It sailed far, far from where they stood before plummeting down, and Jack realized Teague had probably picked this exact spot because there wasn't a soul in sight for miles on this side of the road.

The distant tinkle of glass reached them, and Jack watched Teague dumbly, feeling useless. Teague turned, making sure his face was averted. "We'd best be going, Jacky. We've got a party."

"Yeah, wait a minute," Jack said. He didn't have anything to throw, he thought wretchedly, so he picked up a rock because that's all he had. If he was going to make a grand gesture, a rock would have to do.

"*He's mine, motherfucker! You can't hurt him anymore!*" He really put his diaphragm into it, shouting loud enough to echo off the valley, to make his throat burn with the anger.

He turned a defiant face to Teague, realizing his face was freezing and wet. It was enough for Teague to come and comfort *him*, squaring that bantam little body protectively in front of him. Jack looked down and framed Teague's scowling, freckled cheeks in his slender hands.

"He can't hurt you anymore, beloved," Jack told his lover softly. "You're ours, okay?"

Teague nodded mutely, and when Jack wrapped long arms around his shoulders, Teague leaned against his chest willingly.

"You're ours," Jack repeated. "Ours."

They stood quietly then. If Jack expected Teague to fall apart, he was mistaken. Maybe all of that had been cleansed, purged in their tumultuous first days at Green's hill. Maybe the only place it would ever come out was Green's hill. One set of arms alone was not enough to keep Teague safe from the bloody monster of his dreams. But it didn't matter. Jack was his comfort, his harbor, his beloved, and while the scary dreams might never be gone completely, Jack and Katy would be there to quiet him in the night. It would be enough.

The drive home was quiet too, at least until Mokolumne Hill was safely in their rearview mirror.

"We need a ceremony," Teague said into the blue. "Something… permanent. I know we're supposed to, like, physically bond—"

"I have," Jack said, surprised. "So has Katy."

Teague's eyes got big.

"How do you know?" he asked, surprised.

Jack shrugged. "Because we were watching a show on TV that used to get me hot because the actor looks just like you, but I didn't get hot until you walked into the room. I said something to Katy, and she realized the same thing. Katy and I turn each other on, but otherwise it's you and no one else."

Teague blushed. "Oh."

Uh-oh. "What?" Jack turned to him, surprised. Of all things, he didn't expect this to be a problem.

"Uhm… you know that thing that happens when the vampires feed?"

Jack frowned. "Not anymore."

"Oh."

Jack shook his head, not sure what to say. And then he realized it didn't matter. "It's no big deal," he said, meaning it. Teague had said he was damaged. If this was the extent of the damage, well, so what?

"Well, it's another reason for the thing," Teague said. "A big thing—a… ceremony, like what we just did, only not horrible."

Jack felt his chest grow tight. "Like, you know, a wedding?"

Teague nodded. "Yeah. Like, in front of the hill. Like us, and the hill, and… you know."

"Like a wedding."

Teague grunted. "Whatever."

Jack smiled to himself. Like the opposite of what Teague had planned for himself two months ago. Like Jack and Katy loving him for a very long life. Like announcing "forever" to the world. Like Teague never being alone, ever ever again.

"Like a wedding," he repeated.

"Forget I said anything," Teague grumbled. Jack, comfortable that they were on a straightaway, reached over and took Teague's hand as it rested on the steering wheel and brought it to his lips.

"Katy and I would be happy to marry you."

"That sounds so…."

"Gay?"

"Shut up."

Jack laughed. "So who's going to officiate?" he asked playfully, starting to like the idea.

"Who else?"

"Green." Jack was trying not to be *that* dumb about things. "Will Cory be in it?"

Teague shrugged. "I'm sure she'll stand up there with him. They're sort of a team."

Yeah. A team. "They do a good job of it," Jack agreed, no rancor in his voice at all. "Do you think the three of us will be like that—Cory and Green and the rest?"

Teague squeezed Jack's hand tight. "Yeah, Jacky. We'll be like… like a werewolf version, you think? It'll be good." He hesitated for a minute. "You think we could ask her how she did it when it was her turn?"

Jack had to smile. Yeah, he'd been dumb about things, but the hill— the hill was magical for a reason. Part of that reason was its leaders. He'd respect that. He *had* to respect that. The hill had given him Teague and Katy, and if nothing else, he should be grateful.

"Yeah, we can ask her. But you know what we should do *first*?"

Teague's smile went soft, the way it *only* did when he was thinking about her. "Ask Katy."

"Yeah. Are we going to get down on one knee?"

Teague's nose wrinkled. "Hell, no. But we should do it sweet. With dinner, and private, and maybe the ring and everything. Make her feel cherished. Make her feel special."

Jack swallowed. "*You* are cherished. *You* are special," he said quietly and kissed Teague's hand. "And we will spend our lives making you feel that."

Teague flushed and scowled. "Oh *Jesus*, Jacky," he complained. "Save the sweet stuff for *her*."

But Jack knew he was pleased. Jack planned to do a whole lot of pleasing, for both his lovers, for the rest of his life. He figured this moment, this icy, funny, happy moment at the death of an eventful year, was probably a good start.

Epilogue—
Putting the Past to Bed

"Absolutely," Cory was saying. "February 11 would be perfect."

Green fought the urge to goggle, and Bracken's wide eyes met his as they shared the same thought. But neither of them put a voice to it, and Cory continued to talk to Teague, animation in every line of her still healing body. Green thought privately that the next time she decided to run across the yard in her bare feet in December, he'd actually spank her bare pink bottom himself.

"I thought you hated being in public," Bracken interrupted. Tact and Bracken were still virtual strangers, after all.

Teague blushed. "You guys… the hill. You got to see all the bad shit. Maybe it's time for you to see the good shit, you know?"

Cory nodded at Teague at the same time she rolled her eyes at Bracken. Bracken shrugged, but she soldiered on. "I get it, Teague. I think it's perfect. The day is great. You guys get an idea of what you want, and we'll do the rest, okay?"

Teague gave an actual smile, and Cory launched herself at him for a hug. "I'm so glad you came here," she said softly, and he mumbled a thank-you before he went to tell his mates the wedding was a go.

"February 11?" Green asked, as soon as he was out of earshot. "Isn't that the day—"

"Yeah," she allowed. "It's the day I looked up." Cory and Adrian had possessed, when all was said and done, just a handful of days as lovers. Cory had been so sure someone as beautiful as Adrian could never love someone as plain as she was that she hadn't even looked him in the eyes for their first year of acquaintance. She'd worked her nowhere job in one of Green's gas stations, and Adrian had come and gone, checking on Green's people who inhabited the place, and only at the end had she looked up, met his eyes, allowed herself to fall in love.

"Beloved," Green said quietly. They'd been sitting on the couch together, Cory leaning on Bracken and knitting while Green caressed her calf absently as he worked. Now he put the laptop down entirely and held out his arms. She went to him, rubbing her face on his shoulder.

"I'm tired of bad-shit anniversaries, Green." She said it softly, but Green had no doubt she meant it sincerely. "I've got so few good memories of Adrian. I'm throwing that one—or at least the regret in it—under the bus. Is that okay?"

"That's fine," he told her. He met Bracken's eyes over her shoulders, and Bracken looked stricken for a moment. Anything that threatened Adrian's memory would hurt him. But after a considering silence, he patted her shoulder and leaned in for the group hug.

"Adrian would probably rather you forgive yourself for that one," he said, and she lifted her arm and held Bracken to her chest as Green was holding her.

"Do you think he'd be with us?" she asked hesitantly. "If he'd stayed with us, do you think…. This thing we've become, we all would have done it together, right?"

"I have no doubts, beloved." And Green didn't. Not a single one.

Jack and Teague and Katy were proof of all a group of people could become if they opened their hearts to love. His beloved, with her enormous heart and her unlimited capacity for bravery? There was nothing she couldn't be, no family she couldn't forge. Together there was nothing they couldn't become.

BEING

Prologue—Falling

Katy dreamed in red when she was a wolf. This nightmare was black, edged in red, and in it she watched Teague falling through the sky, a black form against the old-blood dark. He didn't flail, he didn't fight, he just fell.

For a moment he stalled, fell slower, and while he was doing that, he adjusted his body, slowed his motion, prepared to land in such a way that his thigh bones wouldn't be driven through his brain; and then, just when her heart stopped screaming in despair, when he was still near enough the treetops of the horizon to be seen, the plummet began again.

She'd been running toward his still form before it was even him.

But in the dream, in the way of dreams, she was back with her mother, back when she was tiny, before the drugs had devoured Mommy whole, and Mommy was throwing her up in the air.

"Up, up, up!"

"Wheee!"

But Mommy threw her too high, too high, higher than—smack! Katy went high as the trees, and then there she was, holding her heart, plummeting to the ground to shatter on top of Teague's still form.

She woke up and woofed, then howled when she looked around the alien house with the alien sea smell and the alien sea view from the windows.

Jack tackled her before she could get to all fours and really throw her throat into the howl, and suddenly she was pinned to the floor by a tender, exhausted man.

"Shh… baby. Shh…. He's okay. He's going to be okay. C'mon, baby, you need to snap out of it. Please, for me?"

Jack was speaking at a whisper, and his voice sounded… funny. Strange. Broken.

Then another voice rasped across the alien space, and Katy's heart actually beat so loud she almost couldn't hear it.

"Jesus Christ, Jacky! What in the fuck is all that noise?"

Katy whimpered in Jack's arms, and something broke, something that had been holding her to this wolf's body when she was just as happy as a curvy human.

Abruptly she was soft and naked in her lover's arms, and she was sobbing.

Catching

Even though Jack had to tackle Katy, his relief when she turned human was gut-churning and profound.

Teague had been wounded in the heat of battle with a kiss of rogue vampires in a way that had been terrifying. Excruciating. Every fear Jack had ever had for the three of them. But Katy's refusal to return to her human form had been frightening too. Jack… Jack was the weakest member of their little group, in spite of his size and apparent strength. He was the emotional one; he was the one who lost his everlovin' mind in any given situation.

Teague was the leader. Katy was the anchor. Jack was the emotional drama queen who could fuck up a wet dream if someone didn't throw a rein over his shoulders and pull hard, but he'd been the one giving all the orders and doing all the thinking since the three of them had been shoved on the medevac helicopter and taken to the hospital where Teague had been plastered and then—oddly and surrealistically enough—taken here to a house on a cliff, overlooking the redwoods and gray-blue surf of Monterey.

And for the last twelve hours or so, he'd… he'd sat, here in this spacious, darkened room, looking out at the ocean below them. He'd petted Katy, kept her calm, and listened above the sound of his own heartbeat for Teague's breathing and the occasional grunt as he tried to turn sideways and curl up in a ball, only to be thwarted by the gazillion layers of plaster and fiberglass that covered him from the balls of his feet to the top of his balls and above.

Somewhere above Teague's breathing, Jack could hear the sea.

Teague didn't whimper—not even in his sleep—although the pain must have been breath-stopping. He just lay there and twitched, the weight of the plaster and all the pulleys and things keeping him from curling into that psychologically necessary self-protective ball. Jack had been torn between going to lie down with him, bed be damned, and staying with Katy. But Teague was unconscious, and Katy was holding on to herself by a thread, so he'd made the hard choice and stayed where he was needed instead of going where he wanted to be.

About an hour before Katy fell asleep—and two hours before she woke up so spectacularly—the phone had rung, and that proved a welcome distraction. It was Green.

"Hullo, Jacky. You lot settling in?" Green sounded… tired, Jack thought. Weary and a little bit ragged.

"He hasn't woken up yet," Jack said plaintively, and Green was not so weary and so ragged that he couldn't soothe an emotional wingnut werewolf's frazzled nerves.

"He will. Lambent said the push he gave to send Teague under would have sent a mortal into a coma for a week." Jacky remembered that moment, and how the push had seemed gentle and effortless. Apparently Lambent—a fire-haired elf with a wicked-evil tongue—had a soft spot for Teague as well. "Teague will wake up eventually," Green continued, "when his body's not working quite so hard at putting itself together, yeah?"

"Yeah," Jack said with some relief. It was nothing he hadn't thought of himself, but… but he was a beta wolf. He had been his whole life and had known it from the moment he met Teague Sullivan in a bar and wanted his first man. He needed confirmation that it was going to be all right. Good beta wolf, right?

But then, even Jacky could grow a little beyond being a beta wolf.

"How is Lady Cory?" he asked reverently. The leader he'd resented for taking so much of Teague's time. The woman he'd been jealous of, because so many men seemed to fall at her feet. The little, smart-mouthed college student who could barely hold on to her patience most days when Jack was being his queenie, possessive worst. She'd almost killed herself to save Teague's life.

There were not enough ways to show his loyalty after that.

"She's…." Green sighed. "She scared us. Is still scaring us. Her clambake wasn't over by a long shot when you three left. She's sleeping now, but she's got some more grim business to do in a bit."

Jack sighed. So here he'd been, freaking out and resentful because he had to be the head of his werewolf household for half a day, and the kid—she was younger than he was, goddammit, she was nearly three years younger than he was, she was younger than Katy!—the *woman* who'd slit her own throat on her enemy's knife to keep Teague from falling from the sky without even a little bit of a net, *she'd* been saving the world during that time. And now she was going to wake up from a little nap and do it all again.

"Tell her...." He breathed out hard, knowing no words were enough. "Tell her I'm grateful. Tell her that. Jacky's grateful."

For once, Green didn't ask if Jacky was going to be okay. It would hit Jack later—and hit him hard—that this was as close as Green ever came to being self-centered, and that what had happened with the little sorceress beloved by so many had shaken the tall, self-contained, and joyous sidhe to his sound and wholesome core.

"I'm glad you're grateful, brother" is what Green did say. "I'm profoundly glad that the lot of you will be okay. But don't get me wrong. What she did for your mate, she can't do again. Ever. There's more here than you know, Jacky, and her life is much bigger than her life. Teague won't let her do it again—he'll likely be hard-pressed to forgive her for it now, ye ken?"

"I'm sorry?" Jack didn't understand the expression.

Green sighed. His accent had slipped. It did that sometimes, took a little memory surf around England, depending on the mood he was in. When he spoke of Adrian, it was damned near cockney. Jack had once heard him speak of the old ruling structure, and then it had been pure aristocrat.

"Do you understand in your bones, Jacky boy?" Green said softly. "Do you feel with all your breath that what she did was wrong?"

Jack tried hard to remember. It had all been so confused. He and Katy had been on the fringes of the battle, picking off vampires and shape-shifters who had entered ground zero for the fight. And then Cory had screamed, "Teague, get him!" and something *huge* pursuing Jack had disintegrated— with a little help from several silver rounds out of Teague's shotgun.

Then Cory had been tackled. Jack had seen that part. He had been watching in slow motion, along with everybody else, to make sure she made it to her feet, fought her attacker off, and lived to lead them some more, when she looked up in the air and screamed Teague's name.

Jack saw Teague lifted into the air by the vampire. Jack changed into a human to stand on two legs and squint at the sky to see his beloved—the tough, bandy-legged little dumb motherfucker of an Irishman who had been so sure he wasn't worth loving. Teague was hauled up… up… two tree lengths, three tree lengths beyond the treetops at their high horizon, and Jack thought he would simply drop dead when Teague was released to fall back down.

He looked helplessly at Cory, who had been seized while she was distracted by Teague's capture and was standing with a knife to her throat, watching with the same horror Jack was feeling. Jack cringed as he remembered how he'd begged her silently to do something, anything, to save his beloved.

What she'd done had been spectacular—and spectacularly stupid. She shot the guy. Nobody knew she had a gun still clenched in her hand, and he was a vampire. Even if she'd gotten him with silver shot—which she did—he would still live plenty long enough to jerk the knife at her throat.

Which he did.

Jack hardly saw the blood gushing from her pale, freckled skin as she stepped forward, bleeding mortally, and used her sorcery to slow Teague's descent, but Jack sure as hell took note of it when she collapsed from blood loss and Teague dropped the last tree length to shatter the bottom half of his body.

He remembered rushing to Teague's side, although others got there first. He *barely* remembered Bracken ripping the dripping hearts through the flesh of anyone who still opposed them on the gore-spattered, bloody battlefield. Jack could barely pinpoint the moment he glanced behind him to see how Cory was doing, assuming she would be fine. He had finally gotten over his unfounded jealousy. Teague wasn't her lover; he was merely her friend and self-appointed protector. Who risked their life, truly, for a friend?

Apparently a girl with more lovers than friends. Or a leader who needed badly to believe she deserved to lead.

Teague was trying not to scream in agony, and Jack was forced to look away. What he saw had nearly made him nauseated, and it had definitely made him rethink his entire place in the scheme of Green's hill.

Bracken had slashed his own wrist and, using that spectacular power he had, was *feeding* her his blood through the wound in her throat. For a moment even Jack could see that she'd stopped breathing.

Oh Christ. Oh Christ. Jack couldn't look. He couldn't watch that tableau—he was too busy watching Teague bite his own lip until it bled, trying so hard to be stoic and hardy and all the things he'd had to be just to survive childhood. Jack was too busy watching Katy turn into a girl and beg, beg with every fiber of her being, for Teague to be all right.

Both of them had flinched, absolutely *cringed*, when Cory came to, screaming in pain because Bracken was a sidhe and his blood did *not* belong in her body, and because she was armed to the teeth and now all that cold iron burned her too.

Jack remembered her staggering over to see if Teague was alive. He remembered she had been coated in her own blood, and she had been the one to convince Teague to let Lambent put him under so he might sleep beyond the overwhelming pain.

He remembered her mental conversation with Green, the one that had led to them being flown far away—far away from rogue vampire kisses, far away from battle, someplace sweet and isolated, someplace where they could have a little peace.

Monterey, of all places. It seemed like such an odd choice. But Teague, rolling around in pain, trying hard not to scream or pass out, had mentioned that he'd never seen the sea. Green would give his people anything he possibly could, and apparently a mansion on a cliff overlooking the Monterey coast had been one of his gifts to give.

Cory gave them Teague's life. Green gave them their peace. At this point, Jack would follow them into hell.

But that didn't mean he understood any of it, not Cory's sacrifice and not Green's weary, simmering anger.

"No," Jack said roughly. "I don't understand. I don't. I wish I did, Green. If I understood why it was wrong, I'd understand why Teague follows her the way he does. If I understood why it was wrong, I would have been a better mate these last months, because right now my mate has a part of him that I barely understand. So I don't. Teague is here. Teague's all right. I'm just a beta wolf, Green. All I understand…." Jack's breath caught, and his hands clenched. "All I understand is that he's alive."

Jack was sitting on a couch. He and Katy had slept and eaten there since they'd arrived. Teague was on one of those hospital beds you can rent for the short term. They'd set him up with a view to the sea. As the orderlies and paramedics had hustled about getting his plastered, immobilized body set up in one of those complicated getups that held his healing limbs exactly in place, that had been the one thing clear in Jack's head.

Let him see the ocean. He'll feel trapped. It'll give him a place to run in his head.

Now, as he spoke to Green, he looked hungrily over at Teague to see if he was close to consciousness yet. He just… just….

Jack interrupted what Green was saying. "I'd just understand better if he was awake."

Green's indulgent, weary chuckle was enough to pull Jack back to the present and away from that twitching figure with the unnaturally still, bulky hips and legs. "There will be time to get it, Jacky. It sounds like you're done in. You need to sleep too, boyo. Do me a favor and just… that's it. Put your head down on the pillow…." How Green knew he was following orders, Jack would never know. "That's right. Katy's still a wolf, you said?"

Jack grunted. Hurt too much for real words.

"Well, make sure your hands are in her fur, right? You can touch, she can touch… you both need it. Now here, mate. I'm just going to hum to myself for a minute, yeah?"

"Yeah…," Jack mumbled. "You do that." Green had a lovely singing voice. Every now and then, he and Cory would sing with Bracken as backup, and the entire hill would resonate with joy. Jack lay back with the rough silk of Katy's fur and the panting rhythm of her breath under his fingers, and when he woke up, it was early afternoon.

He stood and stretched. Someone had brought out sandwiches, and he realized he was *starving*. He wolfed (literally) down a couple of submarine sandwiches—lots of meat and cheese, only a little bit of veggies—as he stood and watched Teague sleep.

Teague had never been big.

He looked even smaller in the big white bed. His skin looked stretched thin over his sharp cheekbones, and his mouth was pressed with worry even though he'd been rendered unconscious by a first-class healing elf.

Jack shuddered.

Teague had always been a little shorter than tall and a little skinnier than broad. He had never eaten enough to let all those painful workouts bulk him up, and that hadn't changed since he and Jack had started sharing the same bed. It hadn't even changed since the wedding ceremony in February, the one where he'd surprised everybody with the indelible mark on his back to show his love for his mates.

No—Teague was still, would always be, a man with demons.

But living with Jacky and Katy, being their mate, their lover—those things had given him a measure of peace. Jack swallowed painfully; so had being Cory's knight protector and friend.

Jack had barely come to acknowledge that when they were up in Redding facing the rogue kiss. He'd barely brought himself to thank Cory for saving Teague's life, and….

He remembered more clearly what she had looked like covered in the gore of her enemies and her own blood. She had looked… grim. Like a soldier who'd seen twenty years of war. And she had looked defensive, like a girl who had accidentally injured her lover and did not know how to make it right. It had taken Jack twelve hours to realize that she looked like hell because she'd just been scolded by a lover who had been dead for over two years. By the time Adrian's name had permeated his brain through the chaos and the haze, Jack had learned for sure that Teague would live and his relief had drowned out the world.

Staring at his beloved's face in the gray light of the wraparound window, Jack felt the terrible wonder of that knowledge resurface.

He'd seen Adrian's ghost—he and Katy both. They'd seen the transparent presence wandering Green's garden disconsolately looking for his beloved while Cory had been out putting herself at risk for Green's people. Jack's throat closed, and he laced his fingers with Teague's, gratified when Teague's cool, dry fingers gave a squeeze. Green and Adrian had done the same, although Adrian's fingers had been made only of moonlight.

That, he thought helplessly, *that is what it would be like to live without Teague.*

Teague's fingers tightened, and Jack felt a sob, a leftover of a night of fear, bubble up from somewhere around his groin.

And that was when Katy sat up and started howling.

"*Shit!*" Jack snarled and launched himself at her with a full body slam.

They were *not* the only ones in the house. Jack had dim memories of two exceedingly… odd elves who had answered the door and welcomed them into their home. One of them had probably brought the sandwiches, and both of them….

The closest Jack could come to was an analogy about old hippies, though he knew elves weren't susceptible to chemicals the way humans were. But… something? Blood/sugar/sex/magic, whatever! Somewhere along the way, these two had done too much of something, and he wasn't sure they could deal with Katy when Katy couldn't deal with the world.

Katy howled in Jack's arms and squirmed and fought, and Jack held on to her and tried his best to be soothing, tried his best to be… to be strong.

But he was going to lose her. Holy God, merciful Goddess, she was going to become more wolf than girl….

"Katy?" The voice was weak and confused, but it was still the voice of an alpha wolf. "Jesus Christ, Jacky, what in the fuck is all that noise?"

Katy changed just that quickly, sobbing in Jack's arms, and Jack folded her up on his lap and wrapped his overlong arms around her, rubbing his wet face against her tangled hair.

"Don't mind us," Jack laughed/cried against her. "We're just a puddle of goo over here."

There was a grunt of pain as Teague put his elbows under his body and tried to push himself up. It wasn't going to happen—the hip cast and catheter made sure of that.

"What's got you two so worked up?" Teague grunted. "What in the fuck is this thing?"

Jack choked on a sob and wiped the back of his hand across his eyes. In his arms, Katy gave a small, convulsive shiver.

"Jesus, Teague, you dumb motherfucker! That's a cast, and we're just fucking glad you're going to live, that's all!"

Teague grunted again, and Jack hauled himself to his feet. Looking around a little dazedly, he found an afghan on the couch and wrapped it around Katy's shoulders so she wouldn't feel exposed or, heaven forbid, cold in the chill of the beach in late afternoon. She didn't say anything, though. She just hid her face in Jack's side as the two of them made their way to the bed.

Fretting

THEY WERE crying and he couldn't reach them, and that fucking pissed him off.

"I'm fine," he grunted, looking at the horrible blocky thing that immobilized his lower body. "Seriously, didn't anybody think this was overboard?"

Jack was there, looming over the side of his bed with a face crumpled and red and swollen eyes the same color. "No," Jack snapped, wiping a hand across his face. "No, asshole, we did not think it was overboard. We thought it was just the right amount of board. We thought it was superior judgment in board, and fuck you for asking about it."

Teague scowled at him and stretched out a hand to cup Katy's face. She didn't say anything, and the look in her eyes was still… wolfish.

"Jesus, Katy, how long were you under?" he asked tenderly. He felt… muddled. Muddled and incapable of dealing with Jacky's hysterics and… oh yeah. There it was. Apparently a freight train was still plowing over his body, in the damned cast and everything.

"'Bout as long as you," she said gruffly. Her voice was still wolfish too.

"Oh Christ." Teague scrubbed his face with his hands, felt the stubble against his palm. "Okay, you two. I give. What day is it? How'd we get here…?" And the sudden thought of what had happened, of what they'd been doing when he'd fallen from the sky, tried to drive him upright. He howled, actually howled, because he'd only *thought* a freight train hurt when it was destroying your lower body. Turns out that trying to move all of a sudden while the freight train was carrying plutonium-lead weight from your spine to your toes was where the *real* pain was at.

"No, no… sh-sh-sh…." All Jacky's attitude fell away, and he took Teague's weight before he could slam it back down on the bed. His arm around Teague's shoulders was firm and strong and all the things Teague knew Jack could be when he tried.

"Look, you dumb Mick," Jack snapped, once Teague was settled back on the bed and spots had stopped swimming around his eyes, "here's the deal. You fell out of the fucking sky. There you were, taking out a big motherfucking werewhale or something…."

"I remember that," Teague mumbled. "Weretiger. Fucker was huge."

"Yeah, well, thank you," Jack snapped. "I'm glad I wasn't kitty kibble, because that would have been fucking humiliating."

"Cory gave me the shot," Teague said modestly. Then his eyes *really* opened. "Oh shit, Jack! Cory! She was covered in blood!"

Jack sighed, and his grip tightened on Teague's. "She's going to be fine" were the words he said.

Teague squinted at him. "What aren't you telling me?"

Jack shrugged uncomfortably. "A whole lot I don't know myself," he said with some honesty. "Green didn't want to talk about it. He just said she'd be okay, and that you'd have to get the rest from her."

Teague grunted, about ready to ask for the phone. His hand shook. His wide-palmed, big-knuckled, working-man's hand actually *shook* as he stretched. He pulled his hand back to his side, trying not to let them see. Christ, he felt like crap.

"Later!" Jack snapped, so maybe Teague hadn't been so sly hiding that tremor.

Teague frowned. "What's the matter, Jacky?" he asked, both puzzled and frustrated. He couldn't even keep his eyes open all the way, he was fighting the healing elf's compulsion so hard. "You two… you're *really* freaked out…."

The word that lashed out of Katy's mouth was Spanish, but not the kind you learned in school. Teague gaped.

"You haven't called me that since we were courting," he said, shocked. As a reply, she growled at him, a real wolf growl from her human throat.

Then she crawled onto the big white space beside him and laid her head on his shoulder, whimpering and stroking his bare chest with gentle little pats.

"Katy," he whispered, looking at Jack helplessly. "Katy, darlin', where are your words?"

Jack groaned a little and sank his ass onto the foot of the bed where there was still room. "You fell out of the sky, asshole," he said, his voice strained. "Teague… man, we watched you fall. You saw me unconscious once and thought I was dead, and you…." His voice was hanging by a thread, and Teague fought against the irritation of immobility.

"Jacky. Here." Teague used the hand that wasn't stroking Katy's back to pat the space on the other side of him. "Here. Du…." Dude?

Two years of partnership, eight months of sharing the same bed, and five months of marriage, and that was the best he could do?

"Beloved," he whispered hoarsely, the endearment rusty on his tongue. "Beloved, come here. Lay down with me. Let me touch you. I swear… nothing will feel as bad as your voice if you just let me touch you."

Jack swallowed and nodded. The next two minutes were horrible, hot, and tearfully awkward as he pushed the bed far enough from the window to make his way between them and then clambered into the space between Teague and the wall.

He tucked his head gingerly on Teague's shoulder, and Teague stroked that long dark hair back from his hot face. "I'm fine, Jacky. No worries, right? Job hazard, right? You knew that going out?"

That winter Teague had suffered a complete tectonic plate separation of a nuclear emotional meltdown. It had been a ten plus a billion on the Richter scale, and his scream of desolation had shaken the entire hill.

He shouldn't have been surprised that Jacky came unglued on his shoulder and sobbed. He shouldn't have been. It was just that… well, hell. All this time Jacky and Katy had been trying to convince him that he was worthy of their love, and he had never understood that he was as vital to them as they were to him.

"I was fine," he told them, lying. The last few moments of slowing through the air… oh, oh Christ. He remembered the slowdown with perfect clarity. He'd had enough time to miss them in his arms in those drifty, gauzy seconds of being lowered with the roughness of an airplane in turbulence. He'd had a heartbeat to pray for more time, for more moments of touching the two of them, for the right thing to say to make Jacky know Teague loved him first, would always love him, and the exact words to tell Katy she was the princess of his dreams.

"I'm fine now," he lied again. Jack groaned and his big body was wracked with more sobs. Teague could do nothing but lie there, feeling his bones and tissues knitting together like steel needles and glass fiber grating along his nerves. He patted them both, stroked them both, but they were disconsolate, terrified, and shaking in delayed aftermath.

Jesus, it was like they hadn't let themselves feel *anything* until they could feel relief.

He was uncomfortable. He was in pain. He didn't want to move, didn't want to shift the two of them off even though they were hurting him. Damn, they seemed to need him so badly, but… he'd spent his formative years learning that pain weren't no big thing. He wasn't going to hurt the two of them now by letting it rule him.

Turned out he didn't have to.

Abruptly Jack and Katy were asleep, and a midsized woman—no, scratch that, a tiny elf—was bustling in, a redwood tree of an elf behind her. The woman was, well, odd. Her hair was cinnamon red, and she was dressed—well, "old hippie" would have been the most appropriate description. She had a brightly flowered bandana tied around her forehead, and a loose dress that went to midthigh made of the same floaty material. Teague would have bet his *car*, far more valuable than money, that she had nothing on underneath it, but in spite of that, her air was so medical-personnel-meets-earth-mama that he had a hard time thinking of her as a sexual creature at all. She wore a pair of round-lensed glasses just to prove it. They must have been for show—elves didn't have problems with pesky things like bad vision.

"Joshua," the woman ordered—no doubt it was an order—"get the girl first and take her to the guest room. You have their sleep spell covered?"

Joshua—as in *tree*, Teague presumed—grunted and scooped Katy into his arms just that easily.

"She was comfortable," Teague objected.

Joshua was taller than Bracken and probably taller than Green, and he really was built like one of those redwood trees you could drive a car through. His skin was even tinged faintly red, and his hair was a thick, glossy greenish black. He looked at Teague curiously and grunted, then walked away with Katy in his arms.

"She was," said the elf woman briskly, "but you were suffering, and that won't do." She moved to his side, and Teague tightened his grip on Jacky instinctively. They'd already taken Katy away.

The woman clucked. "No need to get all protective, sir knight. We're just putting him in the guest room so you can sleep yourself. It's late afternoon, and those two... well, they've practically worried themselves onto the crazy wheel. Neither of them have slept since they got here, and they got here at eight in the morning. It's time."

Teague scowled. "Yeah? You put them out pretty neatly. Why not do it while I was asleep?"

The woman looked at him sternly. "We both know they wouldn't have slept right until they knew you were fine. Green managed to spell them both a little when the big one was on the phone, but that was at my request. He just sat here and stared at you. It made me twitchy. I think it made the she-wolf twitchy too, tell the truth. Honestly? I've never met you, but I'm just as glad you survived. I *wouldn't* want to be in charge of the healing of those two if you left this mortal coil without them."

Teague grunted, but she rested a hand on the hard fiberglass of his hip casing and the discomfort eased a bit. Then she moved her hand to a bare spot on his stomach, and in a blissfully cool sweep from his back to his legs, it went away entirely. His shoulders relaxed from a tension he hadn't been aware he'd been holding. The feeling was almost euphoric, and when Joshua Tree came back into the room to get Jacky, Teague didn't have the backbone he should have had to argue. The most he could manage was a little whimper of protest, but the woman held the tree man back with a clearing of her throat.

"Let him kiss the man's cheek, Joshua. They're werefolk—touch is very important, right?"

Jack was swung around, his head vulnerable in sleep and resting against a clay-colored bicep. Teague could turn his head enough to nuzzle the longish dark hair at Jack's temple. His narrow, lean-lipped, high-cheekboned face didn't even stir, but Teague hoped his dreams would be less blood-tinted for that little touch. Oh… God. Teague wanted to touch him some more.

A completely irrational surge of desire swept him, and he shifted uncomfortably and glared at the elf woman who had touched him in healing.

She raised her eyebrows at him mildly, and he blushed.

"Interesting," she said quietly, and he blushed some more. "They're mated to you, but you're not mated to them."

Teague grunted and then realized she expected more explanation than that. "Cory and Bracken think it's because I'm sort of—" What was the word? Was there a word? "—pledged," he came up with weakly. "I'm pledged to my…." Oh God. Did he really have to say this? He longed for Cory just then, in a completely nonsexual way, because she could say this shit in her college student voice and it just sounded right. He swallowed. "I'm pledged to my lord and my lady," he said at last, lamely. "I owe, you know. Loyalty. Fealty. Allegiance. What-the-fuck-ever. And that's until death too, so I don't get the mating bond."

The thought process was almost as uncomfortable as the knitting of bones and flesh, and he'd gone to massage the bridge of his nose with his thumb and forefinger when he realized his hand was heavy… so heavy… so weighty….

He scowled a little and shook off the lassitude. "Stop that," he ordered. "Nobody has told me how she is yet. I'll sleep then."

The woman—what was her name?—looked unhappy.

"Cinnamon," she replied sweetly, although Teague hadn't voiced the question. "Just like the Neil Young song. And Lady Cory is, well, she is fine, but it is going to take some time for her to be right with her lovers again. Is that what you wanted to hear?"

"No," Teague acknowledged, knowing this was the truth and feeling like shit. "She should have let me die."

"There are two exhausted werewolves in the other room who disagree," Cinnamon said sharply. "And one exhausted sorceress in another part of the state who does as well. She saved you because you are worth saving, sir knight, and that is what it comes down to, isn't it? It wasn't for love, not the way she loves her mates, or you love yours. It wasn't for glory—as if! It was possibly for friendship, because that is who she is. But mostly it was because your life was worth saving to her, and that was worth fighting for, and not just when it cost her most of her blood either."

Teague suppressed a groan. He didn't remember much after he'd fallen, but he did remember her covered in her own blood. He remembered her plaintive voice—*Bracken, don't be mad*, or something close. He knew the tone she took when her big, frightening beloved was angry. Sometimes she fought him, but sometimes… sometimes she just begged him to understand.

He thought maybe the reason the two of them got along so well was that Teague understood that too.

"Bracken will never forgive me." His statement was met by a raised, red-tinted eyebrow over that pair of round moon lenses, and a pillow under his shoulders that helped to displace some of the pressure on his lower extremities.

"Bracken is not even close to mad at you. It is his beloved he needs to forgive. And you need to forget it for now. You need to heal. You may not be able to bond for your mates, but the whole reason they sent you here in seclusion is so that you could heal for them. And with them. They are considerably damaged, same as you."

Teague startled up, and the cool veil of elf magic gave way. He collapsed back onto the bed in serious agony, choking a whimper. "You said they were hurt!" he accused. Cinnamon rewarded him with a clucking sound. Her voice was high and gravelly and oddly accented. She almost reminded him of a redheaded Yoda, and in spite of the fact that the sidhe traditionally had flawless skin, he kept expecting to see freckles across her nose.

He also expected to see gray in her hair. But then, sidhe didn't really age like that, did they?

"I said *damaged*, werewolf. They saw their mate fall from the sky. Don't think you're the only one who's going to need to knit back together. The little she-wolf, especially. She could fracture easily, forgetting she's a girl most of the time, if you're not careful. You'll need to reassure her a lot before she heals."

Teague grunted, thinking about Renny the werecat. Renny's husband had died horribly, right before her eyes. Cory had told Teague that Renny had been more cat than girl for nearly six months—and even now, more than two years later and happily mated to another werekitty, it was clear that Renny would never be completely human again.

The thought of Katy that far from herself hurt Teague on a whole new level.

"Here." Cinnamon's voice grew kind, and Teague realized she'd pushed a moveable tray with some soup on it up near him. "You need to eat. You need to rest. There will be time to make peace with your mates when that is done."

Teague grunted. "Not hungry." Although, truth be told, he was not really in touch with his stomach enough to know. His reward for the lie was a stinging smack across the top of his head. "Ouch!"

"You will eat, damn it!" the elf woman snapped. "You will eat and you will ask for more, even if it's just for a cookie and some chocolate milk!"

Teague looked up in naked hope. Who had told her?

"After you eat your soup," Cinnamon grumbled, seemingly mollified by his weakness for sweets. She glared at him until he took a taste of soup, and then another. It was good—tomatoes and beef, and very hearty. She shook her head. "Damn it, werewolf! Don't you see? No matter what else results from last night's confluence, the fact remains that our little Goddess almost died for you. If nothing else, that makes you important enough to be cared for. We won't lose you now, not even from your own neglect."

Teague's sudden desire for cookies and chocolate milk deserted him, and he plowed silently through the rest of his soup until he was too weary to lift the spoon. He fell back against his pillows, suddenly too tired to keep his eyes open—almost.

"Can they come sleep with me now?" he asked, his own voice faint and far away.

"Next time" came that oddly accented woman's voice. It was accompanied by a soothing hand on his brow and a kiss on his cheek. "Let them sleep without worry, sir werewolf knight. With you in their life, it's not like they'll get a lot of chances, now is it?"

"They shouldn't worry. Not 'bout me." Sleep was like a giant cat purring on his head, just one rumble from pushing him under. "Can do better."

He was not so far gone that Cinnamon's mutter under her breath didn't reach his ears.

"Jackass."

But he was too tired to tell her that "jackass" was Jacky's nickname, and his was "dumb Irish motherfucker." He didn't think she'd find it very funny anyway.

WAKING

Katy was always so soft and sweet in his arms.

Jack had vague memories of the girls he'd slept with in college—and the one in high school. He remembered there being inconvenient bones—elbows, clavicles, shoulders, knees, hips and ankles—very often his, but more often theirs.

The first night he'd slept in Teague's bed, it had been all about the compact, sleek, tightly wound packet of muscles in his arms. It should have made Teague into insomnia waiting to happen, but Jack found that when he wrapped his arms around Teague's shoulders and powered the man into being sweet, it was a little like powering a feral cat into settling down for a nap—a little bit dangerous, very addicting, and surprisingly somnolent.

Katy had been a surprise in the opposite direction.

They usually slept on either side of Teague, partly because he was their focus. Katy had loved him first, and Jack had loved him hardest, and together they kept Teague anchored and kept his skittish, damaged heart taped together with love, good wishes, and as much Psych 101 as they could cram into his thick, stubborn head to try to make him see that he was worth their love.

Occasionally, when Teague was out on a run, Jack and Katy slept next to each other, and Jack was always surprised at what a sweet-smelling, beloved armful she was. Her breasts were full, fuller than any of Jack's college girlfriends, and her hips were wide and lush. Her thighs were soft, and so were her arms, and all in all, there was a sort of velvet ice-cream delicacy to her. Jack adored all of her, from taste to smell to texture. In fact, he thought if any of his college girlfriends had been like Katy, it might have taken him a little longer—like, say, a week instead of a day—to figure out he was in love with Teague Sullivan.

As it was, he was truly in love with both of them.

And waking up with Katy in his arms was a revelation.

She groaned, and he tightened his embrace around her shoulders, his palm sliding silkily over the smooth skin of her stomach. She arched against his palm, shifting her hips and parting her thighs, and he teased his fingertips along the crease of her mound and into the sweet little apex of her body, but he wasn't quite ready to go there.

"Mmm… Jacky…," she complained, and he chuckled.

"But I like your breasts," he whispered, nuzzling the back of her neck and her ear. *Actions*, he thought muzzily. Actions always spoke louder than words. Her breasts were large and plump, and one of them felt decadent in his palm. Her nipple teased the tender flesh at the center, so he teased it with his fingertips until it stood up, sharp and hard.

Katy moaned again and wiggled against him, and he returned the favor by grunting and pressing his groin against her.

"Hmm…," she complained. "Too many clothes, Jacky."

It was true. He didn't remember how he'd ended up in this bed in the guest bedroom, but he was still in his jeans and T-shirt and the flannel shirt he'd been wearing while he'd waited for Teague to wake up. He pulled away impatiently and started to fumble with his jeans, but then Katy was there pushing his hands out of the way and undoing the buttons herself. He palmed the smooth skin of her shoulders, and she looked at him with exasperation in her warm brown eyes.

"Get your shirt, damn it!"

It was a relief to chuckle in sex play. He did what she demanded, pulling the whole works over his head, getting free just when his jeans and underwear hit the floor with a thump and…

"Gawwww*wwwwddd*… damn it, Katy, that's not… oh shit…*fair*…."

Katy was a direct lover. No teasing, no skating her fingers on sensitized skin, no nuzzling. She had Jack's shaft in her palm and his cockhead in her mouth and was sucking on him hard enough to turn him inside out.

He was sort of thinking she might succeed.

He growled and dug his fingers into her thick black hair. "Please, Katy… please let me…."

Her response was to glower at him and move her hand so she could take him all the way into her throat and suck harder.

"Aaaauuughhh…." Jack threw his head against the pillow and saw stars. He got it. Katy had seen Teague fall out of the sky and could do nothing about it. She needed control, and here was Jack, all ready to be driven by his dumbstick. He wanted to pleasure her—oh Goddess, he *needed* to pleasure her—but… but… she dug her tongue into him and snuck her hand back underneath to toy with the place that was usually exclusively Teague's….

"You think?" he asked, part sarcasm and part desperate arousal. She responded by letting some saliva trickle out of her mouth so she could use it as lubricant.

Oh God, Goddess, what-the-fuck-ever. She really did mean to control him, to *be* the one in control, and he was torn, because he was used to being… well, not *in charge* when they were making love, but at least on the leadership team, because he was usually working in concert with Teague.

We'll do this, Jacky, but we've got to treat her like a princess, right?

Teague had insisted. Jack had been the first person to ever unlock the battered steel vault that held Teague's heart, and Teague hadn't wanted Katy—who had loved him since childhood—to feel like she was getting a guest pass inside. He'd wanted her to feel welcome.

A princess. Well, right now that princess was swallowing Jack's cock and fingering his asshole like she had a goddamned right to be there, and Jack was left with one alternative.

"Katy…," he groaned, trying to be a gentleman. "Katy…."

For a reply she sucked harder and scissored her fingers inside him, and he had no goddamned choice but to—

"*Gaaaawwwwddd….*"

He curled around her, and she swallowed ravenously as he convulsed and came until his gut clenched and his eyes rolled back in his head and the pressure of her mouth was exquisitely painful.

At last there was nothing left—nothing but Katy sobbing into his groin, and Jack tingling from the nape of his neck to his toes and gasping like a fish.

He recovered first and hauled her up by main strength, where she continued to sob on his chest with great gulping breaths. He *shh*ed her and soothed her, kissing her cheeks and ears and down her rounded jawline, and that was when she turned her head and captured his next kiss.

He tried to keep it simple, keep it warm but not hot, but she opened her mouth and shuddered against him, and he realized her body was still revving, hot and unsatisfied, and she truly needed to climax or this horrible pain/worry/sex/death spiral would never be over for her.

This time he took over. It was a stretch, but he was bigger and stronger, and he had all the tender purpose in the world. He flipped her to her back and lay on top of her, knowing she was a werewolf and stronger than she looked. She groaned and spread her thighs for him, and he kissed his way down her soft, soft body, tasting it, finding it salty and sweet.

He stopped at her breasts and the tightly pearled plum-colored nipples, and he suckled on her, finding comfort and—surprise!—arousal in having her flesh in his mouth and drawing passion from the way she writhed beneath him and clenched her fingers in his hair.

When she was crying out wordlessly, making pleading whimpers into the cool air of the alien room around them, he kissed his way down to her mound and spread her thighs even farther. Her labia, puffy and swollen, were spread slightly and glistening, and he blew on her softly because he knew it would tease.

"*Jacky!*" she pleaded. Her hands were clenching in his hair, and he felt a little of that power back. Very gently he took her hands in his and placed them over her own breasts. She gasped because there were usually three bodies writhing in their bed. Katy usually had no chance to pleasure herself—Jack and Teague had made it their jobs to pleasure her.

Jack grinned at her from the apex of her thighs. She smelled like woman's musk, and it hit something visceral in his stomach. Teague's musk did the same thing, but Teague had to be coerced into being pleasured.

Katy spread her thighs wider, and one of her hands snuck under her bottom, her fingers dark against her pink flesh as she spread herself for Jack and begged some more.

Who could resist such a pretty offer?

He tasted her, slid his tongue inside her and listened to her breathy gasps keen and squeal. He parted her with his thumbs and licked her from core to tiny hooded nerve bundle, and then back again. She groaned, low in her stomach, the sound seemingly ripped from the hard-beating heart under her ribs.

He was good at this. Teague had once whispered instructions to him while sheathed so tightly inside Jack's ass that Jack could almost taste him. Jack had licked and sucked, probed and plumbed, stroked and rubbed and teased until Katy had screamed and Teague had shot until he was shaking, and then Jack had climbed up on top of Katy and buried himself so deeply inside her that *she* could probably have tasted Teague.

He imagined Teague's harsh breathing in his ear as he pleasured Katy, as she arched and screamed, her hands tightening on her own nipples to the point of pain. He felt Teague's hands on his shoulders, damn near felt his ass tingle with Teague's thick invasion as he placed his palm under Katy's ass and licked her some more. His own cock hardened again, grew thick and aching, and his hands shook with the need to pound inside her as she begged him to fuck her, *oh, please, Jacky, please, please please she needed needed needed*—

"*Goddess, yes!*"

Jack lunged up and into her, feeling her flesh wrap around his body and rocking into it with all his power. Katy was a wolf, they had done this as wolves, and her body was as strong as their passion. He had no fears about hurting her. The only way he'd hurt her would be by holding back.

His hips rocked back and forth, driven by the piston of his fear and his anger and his love, and she took all that into her body and shaped it into strength. She reached that ultimate climax women can achieve, the kind that rocks and trembles their bodies and their wombs for long minutes after it erupts from their very cores, and Jack was sucked into it with her. She came off the bed into his arms and screamed, sinking her teeth into his shoulder in an effort to anchor her crazed emotions, and Jack howled back and clutched her to him as he convulsed within her.

They lay there panting, shaking, groaning softly into the cooling quiet of an early morning, and Jack's dazed, wandering vision took in the room in which they'd awakened.

The paneling was dark mahogany, as was the hardwood of the floors. The bed they were sleeping on was as big as their bed in Green's hill— king-sized to fit the three of them, of course—and covered in a dramatically colored black-and-yellow comforter. The furniture all matched the paneling—chairs, a desk, a chest of drawers—and there were bags of what looked to be new clothes set on the built-in window seat that overlooked the same view as the big window in the front room.

"Jesus," Jack breathed. "We just made all that noise and we don't even know where we are!"

Katy laughed—a little hysterically, it was true—but she laughed into his ear and tightened her arms around his shoulders, and they shivered together for another few moments.

He was the one who pulled the comforter up and shifted so he was no longer inside her. They had left the bed sloppy with their sex. He didn't mind doing that at home, but now he felt acutely embarrassed.

"Jacky," Katy said as he grimaced at their mess, "you know these peoples have to be tight with Green. If they're tight with Green, they know Green's people, right?"

Jack blushed and buried his face into the hollow of her neck. "We're certainly Green's people now," he said soberly.

She looked back at him. "I always was."

It was true. She had accepted Teague's place in Green's hill far more easily than had Jack himself. "Well, now I am too," he said softly, watching the emotions shift over her heart-shaped face. He knew the moment she settled on a topic and braced himself for the pain he saw in her dark eyes.

"I...." She grimaced and chewed on a full pink lip. "I don't know if I can be enough for you, Jacky," she said softly. "If next time no one catches him, it's gonna be you and me. What if I can't hold you down here, and you just fly away?"

Her voice broke completely, and Jack swallowed tightly and rubbed his wet face on a fold of the comforter that rested on her shoulder.

"You think I don't worry that too?" he choked. "That if it's just you and me, it's not going to be just nothing? Just pain and a big gaping hole where Teague should go?"

Katy nodded and covered her eyes with her free hand. He pulled her hand away and kissed her cheeks, and she kissed him back. Then they were locked together, comforting, weeping out their fear and the horrible, horrible pain of knowing the one they loved best had a calling that might pull him away at any moment.

Eventually they were still, their faces wiped clean on the comforter, their eyes red and their throats aching with the aftermath of the tears.

"You know what?" Jack whispered, thinking of something, anything, that could comfort Katy.

"What, Jacky?" Very delicately, she traced his high cheekbone and jaw with the tips of her fingers.

"If you think we're alone in this bed, I think you're wrong."

She closed her wide brown eyes and swallowed hard. "I could almost smell him," she confessed, and he settled his head on the pillow beside hers.

"I could feel his touch."

"We gotta take faith from that, don't we, Jacky?"

"It's what we've got, beloved. It's the only promise we have."

Katy shook her head. "Naw, beloved. We all said promises, right? In front of Goddess and Green and everybody? You're right. He's...." She swallowed and tried to say the words and make them true. "Even if he leaves us, he's not leaving us, right?"

Jack nodded. He had a sudden vision of Green and Cory's Adrian wandering the garden looking for his lovers, and his throat closed again. He had to force his next words through it.

"I'll try to be enough," he told her, feeling broken. For perhaps the first time in the two years since he'd first laid eyes on Teague Sullivan and *yearned*, he understood how Teague would be afraid to love, based on this fear alone.

"Me too. I promise. Me too."

They stopped for a moment, took stock, and looked around the room again.

"Jacky?"

"Yeah?"

"I'm so hungry, I could probably eat the feathers in this pillow and call it a duck. How about you?"

Jack couldn't help it. He giggled. "Maybe we should go see about making Teague a sandwich, yeah?"

Katy tried a little damaged grin on her full mouth. "And dream about the days when he can *be* our sandwich, right?"

"Absolutely."

They both got up and started rooting for clothes that looked like theirs, then looked for the shower.

MENDING

TEAGUE WAS not feeling wonderful when the two of them wandered in from wherever they'd been taken, but seeing them helped.

He closed his eyes against the gold light bouncing off the big blue sea out his window and breathed in. He'd heard them. Their sex noises had woken him up as the first bit of sun brightened the heaving seascape. It had soothed him, given him some peace after one of the worst nights he'd had since he'd been a kid, surviving from beating to beating.

His body... *ached* was not the word. Every throb of his heart seemed to rip asunder nerves that were still raw and stretched from being knitted up again. He was good at pain, had always been good at pain—he wouldn't have survived his first few years if he wasn't.

This was a new sort of pain, and it had awakened him in the black hours of the night with shortened breaths and clammy skin and a chest screaming for oxygen.

And then he'd looked on either side of him, and they'd been gone.

He knew what they would have looked like if they'd been there.

If he'd turned his head left, he would have seen Jacky—shaggy dark bangs falling across his forehead as he slept, dark lashes fanning across his pale cheeks. If Jacky was awake, he'd see those deep blue eyes peering at him and the hopeful, expectant look that said Jack was waiting to see if Teague would greet him sweetly, but that he was ready if the night terrors had left his lover shaky and needing.

If he'd turned his head right, he would have seen Katy—dark cloud of hair tumbling over her soft brown face, full lips curving into a smile even as she slept. Even if he woke up like a sprinter gasping for breath, the smile would be there. *No scary monsters here,* papi, *only us.*

But he'd awakened in pain, frightened, and alone in this alien place, looking out at a cloud-lit ocean. He'd had to work like a marathon runner to still his breathing, to ease the tightness in his chest, to consciously will the pain to a place where he could endure the next heartbeat, and the next one, and then the—

"Oh *Goddess*, sir werewolf! Why don't you just cry out or something? Your psychic screaming almost had me sending Joshua outside to see what sort of broken thing had stumbled into our protective geas!"

"I'll be fine!" he snapped, too focused on pain control to be diplomatic, and Cinnamon scowled at him as she put her hand on his forehead and closed her eyes.

More of that blissful, cool elfin magic stole down his body, and the whole of him sagged into the sweat-soaked sheets at his back.

"Shit," she swore as Joshua appeared at her elbow like a ginormous wraith. "We need to change the bedding. *Someone* thought he'd be a hero and power through the worst of it, and now he's going to stink up the place."

Teague suffered through the sheet changing in silence—and it *was* suffering, since every movement jarred the shattered bones in his spine, hips, and legs.

By the time they were done and Cinnamon had soothed his pain one more time, he was shamed into asking through gritted teeth, "So how long's this gonna last?"

Cinnamon smoothed her hand on his forehead again and touched the faint dimple in his cheek. "Another day or two, and the worst of it should subside," she said gently. "You're sturdy, werewolf, but not invincible. You need to remember that the next time you feel like you should swallow down on all that pain, right?"

Teague grunted. She looked away, the darkness shadowing her pale skin, and she gleamed faintly from the moonlight bouncing off the sea.

"That's not going to happen," she sighed. "I'll tell you what. You try your hardest to ask for help in the next two days, and I'll give the okay for your mates to sleep with you as soon as the worst of it has passed, yes?"

It hurt to feel so much naked hope, and she patted his cheek. "Green told me," she said. "He told me you'd break my heart, and here I am, the damned thing bleeding at my feet. Give them a full night's rest, sir werewolf, talk with them honestly tomorrow, and I'm sure at least one of them will sleep on the couch if you ask…." She trailed off and grunted in frustration. "What am I saying? *I'll* ask them to sleep on the couch tomorrow. Of course I will. You won't. What am I thinking?"

Teague's breathing evened out another notch, and she sighed and shook her head.

"Is there one person on this planet *besides* your mates that you talk to?"

"Cory," he grunted immediately. Cory knew him. She'd known him since he'd first shown up at the hill, distraught about Jacky and worried shitless. "And Green."

Cinnamon blew out a breath and absent-mindedly pleated the gauzy skirt of the brown Victorian night thing she was wearing. "Well, Cory's going to need a friend in the next week. I'll have to make sure you have a phone nearby when nobody else is around. If you won't talk to me, and you won't talk to your mates, somebody has to hear your pain, or it will fester inside you and blow like a boil!"

"Ewww." Teague's grimace of distaste was enough to make the curious woman pat his cheek again.

"You don't like the imagery, don't be the boil! Next time your body hurts, say my name twice in the dark—or the light, I guess, but I won't be sleeping in the light, so it will be easier to get a hold of me."

She left him then, and he'd been able to sleep, at least, but he'd awakened with the first sounds of Jacky and Katy making love.

There should have been something torturous about it, since he couldn't be there, but there wasn't. In fact it had been… soothing. He knew those sounds. He could picture what they were doing as they made those sounds. His cock wasn't in the mood to play, but his brain… his brain could imagine it, could imagine his mates naked, their bodies lunging in the dim dawn light, and it made him feel…

Relieved. He didn't have to be there. They would be fine without him.

It should have been a lonely feeling, a moment of uselessness in the life of a man who had striven so hard to be useful, but it wasn't. He loved them. He loved them with everything he had. The pain that still echoed through his body with every heartbeat was worth it—for them. Stripping himself emotionally naked this last winter, just so he could learn to trust them to cloak him in the cold, had been worth it—for them. Dying in the service of his queen to prove his value would be worth it—for them.

But if he was living a life that might lead to its ending sooner than later, he was relieved they would survive if that happened. He was pretty sure he wouldn't if it were the other way around.

So when they emerged from their room smelling like herbal soap and looking fresh and awake, he didn't have to fake the tired smile that twitched at his mouth. They really were the best and most beautiful thing about a painful morning.

Jack all but leaped for the bed, jostling it softly as he put his hands on the rails. "You're awake!" he said excitedly, and Teague twitched his grin up a notch.

"Half the county's awake—and horny. Next time hire a skywriter, Jacky. That way only people outside will know."

Jack rolled his eyes and darted glances around the big, echoing, wood-paneled house. "It would help if this thing didn't have acoustics like a concert hall," he said grimly. "But it's so damned beautiful, I don't think I can argue."

Teague tried to take in his surroundings—besides the dark wood, he had the impression of a lot of furniture with long, uncovered legs in the same color and dark blue or red tapestry cushions. While he was doing this, Jack took his hand and started to study him in the same way. Except with Jack, there was a lot more intensity.

"You look like shit. I'd say you were as pale as a sheet, but someone changed yours and now they're blue. What happened?"

Teague grimaced. "Got hot," he lied. He was starting to sweat again, and it was as cool in the house as it looked outside.

"It's seventy degrees in here," Jack snapped. From behind them they heard some rustling in what sounded like a kitchen, and then Katy said, "Sandwiches! Jacky, steak sandwiches! Someone loves us!" And Teague smiled a little.

"Bring 'em in here, Katy, darlin'," he said. "Come check out this view while you eat."

"The only view she wants to check out is you. Were you bleeding?"

Teague snapped his attention back to Jack and moved when he did it. Then grimaced when he moved. "No. No blood. No worries."

"Then why?"

"Why what?"

Jack scowled. "Goddammit, Teague! You're a werewolf in a body cast. Don't blow this off like it's no big deal. I got attacked by a wolf, and I was ready to fuck in less than twelve hours. What happened to you was bad. Big fucking bad. You're stuck here in a hospital bed and you look like shit and…."

Jack's voice was getting… wonky. Creaky. Sad.

Teague grasped the hand holding his a little tighter. "Shhh… shh. It's okay, Jacky. I'm fine."

Jack hooked a really expensive-looking chair behind him and sank down on it, kissing Teague's hand in a way that Teague would have shaken off if he'd been feeling better. Katy came in behind him, a big tray of sandwiches and cookies and chocolate milk in front of her, and Teague had to work hard to make eye contact as she set that down on the coffee table in front of the couch.

"Katy, darlin', come here, would you?"

"Yeah, sure. Let me just set this down. You hungry? There's steak. That's got to be a good thing for you, healing and all. And chocolate milk. I know you like that. Here, let me just…"

"Katy, stop!" There. He'd *made* her look up at him, and sure enough, her eyes were red. "Aww, damn it! You two are acting like I'm dead. I'm not. I'm here, and I'm just as much a pain in the ass as I've always been."

"You don't get to act like this is nothing," Katy snapped, her voice raw. "You don't get to just lay here and look like shit—"

"Really, do you both have to keep saying that?"

"It's *true*. And I hear you and Jacky talking. You still not give us straight answers." Uh-oh, Katy's English was slipping badly. Usually she had a little lilt, or some inverted syntax, but it only got really, really mangled when she was really, really upset.

Teague felt his face twist up into something truly unpleasant. He had flinched from her words, and there went all that pain Cinnamon had warned him about. Oh shit. Cinnamon.

"You guys, I'm fine. Look, why don't you just ask Cinnamon—"

"*Who?*" They both looked at him with big eyes, and he peered back.

"The nice elf woman who runs the place? You've seen her. Long red hair? Hippy glasses? Flower-child clothes?"

Jack and Katy both looked at him as though he was completely deluded, and he, being the complete dumbshit he was, tried to prop himself up on his elbows to look them in the eyes and convince them he was not.

The sound that wrenched out of his throat was not entirely human, and it would have frightened most wolves.

"*Fuck…*," he panted. His vision went white, then red, then black with white spots, then sort of a greenish gray, and he fought against the urge to vomit. When he'd conquered that, Cinnamon was there, and Jack and Katy were looking at her as though she'd just sprung up out of the floor.

"Now, really," the woman snapped. "I thought we'd come to an agreement."

"Sorry…," he hissed.

"Sure you're sorry! You're sorry because you were forced to call my name, weren't you?"

"I was just… ah… shit. Oh Christ. I'm sorry."

Jack had never let go of his hand. "Is there anything you can do for the pain?"

Not even Teague missed the impatient look she sent him. "We could start by making him admit he has any! Great Sheba's cat, werewolf, what's it going to take for you start asking for a little bit of help?"

"An act of the Goddess," Jack snarled. "But I'm asking now. Can you help him?"

Her hand on his brow felt so good that Teague actually sighed. "She is, princess. Just back offfff…." He sighed, feeling exhausted and sweat-ridden now that the pain was gone. "Back off," he managed dreamily, "and let her work, 'kay?"

"I've worked," Cinnamon said dryly. "And I think you should let your woman feed you. That's part of my work done, right there."

Teague grunted and tried to look like food wasn't going to make him hurl. If it would take the panicked, miserable look off Katy's face, he'd brave an entire refrigerator full of food, but Katy was looking at Cinnamon doubtfully, so he figured a sandwich would do it.

"C'mere, Katy," he said. "Gonna need your help." Raising his hand from his waist to his mouth seemed *so* out of the question right now.

Katy was there, wiggling past the other woman with an unfriendly glance. Cinnamon returned the glare with only a lifting of rust-colored eyebrows and sighed, shaking her head.

"You three are going to kill me. I need a joint, and I need to talk to Green."

With that, she stalked off in a swirl of paisley skirts, leaving the three of them staring at each other in honest surprise.

"Did she say what I thought she said?" Jack sounded stunned.

Teague finally knew better than to try to shrug. "Sure sounded like it."

Katy wrinkled her nose even as she gave Teague a bite of sandwich. To his surprise it didn't taste half-bad. "I didn't think we did that. No high, no reason to smoke that shit."

"Arturo smokes," Jack said, seemingly out of the blue, and Teague had to work very carefully at not jerking his head to look at Jacky.

"I think I knew that," Teague mused. He seemed to recall seeing the big South American sidhe leaning on the porch railing at the hill, smoking quietly on a summer's evening. "Maybe it's the same reason some humans do," he said thoughtfully. "The motion, the taste… it's just soothing."

At that thought a half laugh shook him, but not enough to hurt. "Nice to know we unsettle her that much." Then he laughed. "Must be you two having sex like monkeys, you think?"

"You sound jealous," Katy said, giving him a drink of chocolate milk. He noticed her hands were shaking and suddenly wished he could take them into his own. "We were thinking of you the whole time."

Teague grunted. "I hope not. I'd rather you were having some fun."

Jack's attention, which for a while had been focused down the corridor where the elf woman had disappeared, was suddenly 100 percent laser-beamed on Teague.

"Not funny. And I noticed you got out of telling us anything useful at all."

Gods. Teague let out a sound like an old dog getting kicked in the ribs. "Jacky, it hurts, okay?" And so did the admission, but then, they all knew that. "It hurt enough to wake me up last night in a sweat. That's why the sheets are different. It hurts enough to make me glad you guys got busy this morning and to make me wish you'd go outside or something after this. I'm just going to lie here and be miserable and fucking hurt for two days, and I'd just as soon you not have to see that, okay?"

His voice was breaking, and he would have taken a moment to wonder at that—because it must have been a combination of pain and exhaustion and maybe, just maybe, learning to finally trust his mates with his heart the same way he'd asked them to trust him with their lives. Before he could finish the thought, though, Jack had gently taken his hand again and sat down in the neglected chair, pushing a kiss into his palm.

"No," he said softly. Katy shoved another bite into Teague's mouth before he could ask "No, what?"

"Nnn mmmmt?" he tried instead, then forced the sandwich down with a glare at Katy, who raised her eyebrows in return.

"We're not leaving you," she said, wiping the corner of his mouth. "Even if all we do here is piss you off, we're not going. You think we're gonna go out and be all happy skippy walking on the beach when you can't even stare out after us without looking like you sucked lemons? No, you're stuck with us. That's what the whole wedding thing in February was all about. You think that 'sickness and health' stuff was bullshit?"

Teague tried to glare at her, but he never could be mad at Katy. "It wasn't a traditional ceremony," he said with dignity. Jack smirked against his rough palm.

"Wasn't a traditional honeymoon."

He smiled tiredly and suddenly was too weary to even be brave. "It hurts," he confessed again and swallowed. "Hurts like a sonuvabitch. I don't want you guys here for that. It… I can't…." He was scrunching up his face and trying to stay stoic, but Katy's hands were suddenly cupping his cheeks and Jack had brought Teague's hand up to smooth against Jacky's stubble and lips.

"It's okay," Katy whispered. "You think it hurts? I think nothing hurts worse than watching you fall out of the sky and—" Her voice caught. "—and not know if I'll ever see you again. So you go ahead and hurt, 'kay?"

Teague closed his eyes tightly and felt tears slip out the corners. "I was pretty fucking scared," he admitted.

"Oh thank God," Jack choked against his hand. "I was wondering if you had any sense at all."

The tears seemed to keep slipping, and there was nothing Teague could do to stop them. He remembered the terrible, painful sobs that had shaken him so very badly when he'd thought he'd lost Jacky and decided that maybe, right now, when he felt like six- to ten-grade horseshit, letting a little weakness slide by was the way to go.

CINNAMON CAME back in an hour and talked them through a sponge bath. It was fair to partly humiliating to lie there while his mates tended to him, and he tried not to snap their heads off when they jostled him.

Finally he was fed, clean, and ready for a little kindergarten nappy-poo. They had settled down with him, and he hated that they had to deal with just… just *sitting* with him, and that was how he managed to convince them to go outside.

"Look, guys, it's gorgeous here. It's beautiful. I told Green I'd never seen the ocean, and he sent us here. Go out and enjoy it for a little." His eyelids drooped. He felt himself falling asleep and resorted to his only weapon. "Please?" he asked quietly. "It would mean a lot if I could look out there and see you two on the beach. Please?"

Katy looked up from where she was doing needlepoint on the couch, and Jack set down his book. Jack was still holding Teague's hand as he read, and Teague hated to admit that the physical contact would be missed.

"That's playing dirty," she accused. Jack rolled his eyes.

"I think that's the point, field mouse," Jack told her. He looked back at Teague and seemed to come to a compromise. "I'll tell you what, beloved. You let us sit here and bask in the peace of knowing you're not gonna go tits up—"

"Who talks like that?" Teague snapped.

"Cory. And now me. Now let me finish. You let us sit here until you fall asleep. I see you nodding off, so you just let it happen, and then when you're asleep, we'll go out and walk. How's that?"

Teague chuffed some air. "Fair enough." He wasn't going to last long anyway; he knew it. "But you guys take the car to town too. Go… go forget about being afraid and about me being hurt. I want to smell the ocean on you when you come back. Deal?"

Their eyes met, and he almost knew what they were saying.

"Deal," they came back, and he sighed gratefully.

Then he gave them something for their consideration.

"I love you," he said softly. "You're both so worth it, okay? Don't ever doubt that."

Jack kissed his hand again. "You neither."

They lapsed into quiet again, and he fell asleep to the sound of their breathing and the muted roar of the ocean.

WHEN HE woke up, a couple of hours into the afternoon, judging by the sun, they were gone. He was in enough pain to call for Cinnamon, now that there was no one to be stoic for, and she relieved his pain and brought him some lunch. Then, when that was done, she did him a solid he'd never forget.

She brought him the phone. Cory's cell number was already on speed dial.

REPENTING

TEAGUE SOUNDED like he'd just broken every bone in his body.

Lambent had assured me that he had—most of them in more than one place.

"So you're going to be okay?" I asked for what was probably the gazillionth time, and repetition must have worked, because *finally* I got a little honesty.

"It doesn't feel like it, but that's what Cinnamon keeps telling me."

"Green promised me you'd have a healer. Is that her?"

"How'd you know it was a girl?"

"I like Neil Young. So she says you're going to be okay? Does it hurt?"

He made a negative grunt, and I called bullshit. "Bullshit."

"Fine. Does the whole world need to know it hurts?"

"Yes," I said, pulling my knees up to my chest and setting my knitting down on the coffee table. It was hard to knit and talk on the phone anyway, and I wondered where my hands-free was. I would have asked Bracken, but he was in a dark-hearted snit, and I didn't want to poke it with a stick. Of course, with Bracken right now, just sitting in the same room and breathing amounted to poking his snit with a stick—and stirring up shit, ha ha ha *help*.

"Why?" Teague demanded, and I sighed.

"Because you scared the shit out of me, for one—"

"I know what I'm doing when I go out with you—"

"—and it was my fault you were in that position, for another—"

"I just *told* you—"

"—and I feel like shit because you got hurt and I should have stopped it!" I finished, raising my voice over his. Teague didn't yell a lot, and I did. And I was sort of his leader. It gave me an unfair advantage, but there you go.

"You *did* stop it!" he yelled. I was surprised. He must *really* be hurting, and that didn't make me feel any better either.

"Not in time," I reminded him. "Man, I'm so sorry. I got clear of that guy, and one second I had you, and you were slowing down, and the next second...." I trailed off.

Teague grunted. "Yeah… what happened?" he asked.

I closed my eyes. "Nobody told you?"

I could imagine Teague shaking his head. It was a characteristic gesture, and if his dark blond hair was long enough, it would fall in his eyes when he did it. Then I heard him wince, and then I winced, because apparently even shaking his head hurt.

"Well, I sort of got hurt getting away from the guy," I said. My fingers went up to the spanking new scar I had at my throat and pressed against the thick tissue. I'd asked Grace if she could maybe help me macramé a choker or something to hide it, but she'd been so mad at me that she said if she was speaking to me by the time I went back to school, *then* she'd do it.

Another classic Teague grunt. "That *was* your blood," he reasoned. "I *thought* so. *Jesus*, Cory, what in the fuck did you do?"

I sighed. "I don't want to talk about it," I said honestly—but Teague was one of the few people on earth who wouldn't take that.

"I don't give a fuck," he said back smartly. "I'm sorry, Cory, but I'm lying here when I should have been dead. That was a long-assed fall. I had plenty of time to get used to the idea of being dead, and I was at peace with it. Now I don't mind—" Ouch. He must have done something, because he cringed over the phone. "Okay, I can *live with* the pain, but I've gotta know… what sort of price did you pay to keep me here?"

Oh shit. I leaned my forehead on my knees. Teague would *so* not appreciate this. But… but I had such a short list of people I could save, really. Bracken, Green, maybe Nicky in a pinch. Everyone else had made it perfectly clear that I was supposed to make *my* life a priority. I hated it. I had all this shit I could do, all this amazing, wonderful, *perfectly useless* shit. If I couldn't save a guy like Teague, a guy who reminded us all of Adrian, a guy who deserved a happy ending like nobody fucking else, I should turn in my queenship card, and that was just all there was to it.

"Cory?" He sounded like hell. He deserved to know why I had failed, and how I had succeeded.

"He had a knife against my throat," I said roughly. "And he didn't know I had a gun against his side. I shot him, he slit my throat, and before I bled out, that's when I caught you."

There was a silence on the other end of the line, and I shivered.

"Teague, buddy, you still with me?"

"You fucking bitch," he hissed. I winced. Teague was a gentleman down to his bones. He must really be pissed to pull out the bad word.

"I'm sorry." I'd been saying that since we got back. Green and Bracken seemed to accept it, but… but there was something… something they weren't telling me. Something that was getting in the way of forgiveness.

"I'm sorry I let you down," I said, miserable. "I'm sorry I let that guy take you and I couldn't hold on long enough to keep you from getting hurt." I didn't remember the rest of the fall. I'd been visiting Adrian at the time. He'd been pissed too.

"*That's* what you're sorry about?" he demanded, his voice crooked. "What you should be sorry about is that you didn't let me die!"

"That's the one thing I'm *not* sorry about!" I snapped back, pissed. "How many friends do you think I've got?"

"How did you survive that, Cory? Jesus fucking Christ! If you were bleeding enough to pass out—"

"Green knit me back up," I interrupted, not wanting to relive those aching nonheartbeats in Adrian's arms. "And Bracken gave me his blood." Ouch. Pain. Yes, my bones were intact, but I remembered pain.

"Is that even possible?" he asked, all interest.

"Apparently so," I told him dryly. And then, because he deserved it—"But not really comfortable."

"Explain?" Teague's voice was guarded.

"I broke Nicky's jaw when I came to, because I sat up screaming and he was right over me."

Teague's low whistle sounded a little forgiving. Maybe it was the idea that I hadn't done this foolhardy thing without consequences. It was like—if I'd suffered for my dumbshit decision already, he didn't have to hold it against me.

"When Bracken's angry at me, I shiver. You know, like a fever? We thought it would go away, but apparently not. It hasn't faded at all in the last two days. I may be stuck with it." Well, hell. If knowing I suffered made him less mad at me, I'd roll with it.

Teague grunted.

"So, uhm, you gonna forgive me?" I hated the plaintive note in my voice.

"What's wrong?" he asked bluntly. He'd seen me in the middle of my worst spats with Bracken—he could probably read that note in my voice from three hundred miles away.

"Nothing," I lied, my throat dry. I'd told him all that so he could be not mad at me, but I didn't want to unload my bullshit on him either.

"Look," he said. "Just *talk* to me."

"He's still mad at me," I whispered. "It comes and goes. We'll be in the same room, and I'll be happy, and he'll look at me all soft, like he does sometimes, and then his look will change, and I start shivering, and he's got to leave the fucking room."

Teague blew out a breath. "He'll forgive you," he said after a moment.

"How do you know?"

"Because I think I just did."

"Thanks," I told him, relieved because it mattered.

"You're welcome. Thanks for saving my life. Please don't do it again."

"Save your life?" This was *not* the first time I'd saved his life.

"Risk your own," he said bluntly. "Look, *Lady* Cory. You play chess. You suck at it, but you play it. I'm a knight. I'm not a bishop or a king. I go in, I bump people off the board, and sometimes I get sacrificed. It's my job. My job doesn't mean shit if my queen falls, you hear me?"

"I fucking hate fucking chess," I told him sharply. "Okay? Lesson learned, but don't fucking throw chess metaphors at me. I fucking hate them right now."

He sighed, and I kicked myself mentally. He was hurt and tired, and I was being… difficult. All my lovers knew I could be difficult, and now all my friends knew too.

"Man, I'll let you off the pho—"

"No," he said quietly. "Look… they're outside and I'm in here, and…." Oh, his heart broke to say it.

"I'm lonely too," I whispered. I was. Green was with someone, and Bracken was outside working on Teague's home so the werewolves could come home and move in. It was a joint venture with Bracken and all the other avians, werecreatures, and even vampires I'd irritated with my little act of dumbassery—it was like they all went out there and sanded drywall and got out their issues so they could come inside and be overly sweet and solicitous to me. Quite frankly, it was making me a little bit batshit.

"Where are all your people?"

"Working on a surprise for you," I told him. I didn't tell him they were avoiding me, but he figured it out.

"They're still really mad, aren't they?"

I blew out a breath and looked around. A giant chocolate-brown cat was sleeping in a sunny spot in the corner. "Charlie still likes me," I said wryly. Charlie looked up lazily and twitched an ear.

"Who's Charlie?"

"Whim's beloved, remember? The high school counselor turned werecat?"

Teague grunted. Whim—a sidhe Bracken had once described as more flutterbrained than a drunken grasshopper—had apparently been carrying on a twelve-year affair with a human whom nobody had known about. When Whim realized Charlie was dying of cancer, we'd all heard about it right quick, and the group rescue operation had been fairly impressive and resulted in Charlie's new werecat status to make healing him easier. In the end, though, it had all come down to Whim, pulling power he hadn't known he had to heal the boy he thought of as his. Well, not so much a boy now, but apparently Charlie had been barely eighteen when they'd met.

"I remember. I'm surprised Whim let him out of his sight."

I looked over at Charlie. Surprised out of his nap, Charlie was now doing that cleaning thing cats do where they stretch out their hind legs and lick their own privates.

"I don't know. Maybe Whim got lost in his workshop. He does that sometimes."

Charlie, hearing his lover's name, shifted abruptly to human form, in a position most human men would have to do a *lot* of yoga to achieve. My eyes got *huge*, and Charlie made an *urk-snork* sound that defied description, promptly let go of that thing in his mouth—thank *Goddess*—and shifted back into a cat. His fur was sticking up all over, and he danced on his toes and hissed at me before disappearing down the fucking hallway like a streak of furry lightning. Leaving me, all big eyes on the couch, trying not to swallow my own tongue.

"Holy shit."

"What? Cory, remember, I can't see what in the fuck is going on there."

"You know that thing cats can do with their tongues that men can't?"

"Lick their own balls?"

"Yeah. Well, Charlie just tried it as a human. It was an accident. I don't think it will happen again."

Teague didn't laugh often, but when he did it was a dry, chuckling, rumbling sound, and now it was pained. "Oh Jesus," he gasped, but he didn't stop laughing. "Oh fuck—"

"Teague?"

"Christ…." He kept making that sound. "Goddess, do you have *any idea* how much it hurts to laugh?"

I started to giggle helplessly. I mean… oh Goddess. Here we were, surfing the after-tsunami of life and death, and, well, there were some things in this world that were still hysterically funny. That's what made it worth it to stay.

The giggles eventually faded, and I think the endorphins did Teague some good, because when we could talk again, he sounded a little happier and in a little less pain.

"Hey, Cory…."

"Yeah?"

"How did it all turn out? The pedophile, the baby vampires, the kiss in Redding, hell, even the blackmailer? I mean… I got taken out in the first half. How did we win the game?"

He was tired—I could hear it. He didn't need the total recap. Hell, just thinking about all of it made me both queasy and exhausted. I'd been in that state pretty much since we got back from Redding—I didn't need any help feeling that way now!

"Same way it always does," I told him. "One play at a time."

"Cory…."

I smiled. "You're whining, wolfman. I think if you're whining like a big girl, then it's time for this big girl to get off the phone and let you sleep."

"I deserve to know!" Whine, whine, whine.

"Of course you do. And when you feel better, I'll give you a play-by-play." Well, I'd leave off the part where Bracken, Green, and I had apparently realigned our own personal lovers' politics in the passion of the marriage bed, because I still didn't understand that part. "But right now? Right now you really need to sleep, and—" I half giggled. "—I need to make sure Charlie doesn't run away and get hit by a truck, and—" Shit. "—and I really need to go make nice with Bracken." I'd just make sure to put on a sweater before I went.

Teague sighed, and the sound made me ache. "Cory?"

"Yeah?"

"If I said I loved you, you'd know it's not how… you know."

"I love you too, wolfman. And nobody is happier that it's totally platonic than I am."

"Talk to you tomorrow." I wondered if he was dropping the phone as he said it.

"Damned straight."

I clicked End and put the phone in my pocket. I'd started to get up when Whim wandered by. His ever-changing cloak of hair was a muted raspberry color at the moment. I assumed that meant he was amused. And he was wearing a shirt, which was something he'd never done the first year I'd met him.

"Charlie is still very human," he said apologetically, without any more explanation.

"No worries," I told him.

He looked at me happily, but of course the only thing it really took to make Whim happy was knowing that Charlie would be happy. "He is afraid you were offended. He was also worried that he had hurt something, but I rubbed it, and it was all better."

Once again my eyes got big as bowling balls. Whim blinked and then smiled wickedly.

"His *leg*, Lady Cory. That other thing is just fine. I'll probably rub it later, but we weren't worried about that."

My relief must have been palpable, and the other shit weighing on my shoulders must have been too, because he reached to the table, picked up my knitting, and put it gently in my hands.

"It's never as bad as we think," he said softly, and I looked into his pretty, color-changing eyes and smiled. "You taught me that," he said to my smile. Then he kissed my forehead and wandered out, hopefully to rub that other thing. He and Charlie were still making up for twelve years of only seeing each other once a year, and they seemed to be doing it with style.

In the meantime, I picked up my knitting—a sock for Bracken that I'd started the day we got back—and went back to knitting my fragile nerves together with sticks and string. I'd been listening to music as I worked before Teague's call, but I didn't go through the pain of swapping out the iPod for the phone and putting on the earbuds. I needed the silence of my own head for a while.

I must have buried myself in my own thoughts, because as I was turning the heel for the sock, I felt hot tears on the backs of my hands. I wiped my face, and again, and again, and kept knitting blindly until suddenly there was a set of hot, sweaty arms wrapped around my shoulder and a distinct earthy smell surrounding me as I sat on the couch.

"Don't cry, beloved," Bracken whispered in my ear, and I turned a wet cheek to him. He kissed the tears away, and my shoulders started to shake.

"I don't want you to be mad at me," I cried. "Not anymore."

"Shhh…."

"Please, Bracken," I begged. "Please, Bracken, please?"

I normally saved this sort of begging for bed, for pleading to be ravished—and not gently. For something that felt urgent and dire and pressing. How could I explain that finding peace with him when it came to deciding on my own safety, *that* was urgent and dire and pressing?

He took my chin in his fingers and tilted my mouth to meet his. I opened for him completely, wanting nothing between us—not his anger, not the strange, constrained thing that had fluttered uneasily between us since I'd forced his capitulation during lovemaking—nothing. I gave in. I surrendered. I gave up. Anything, I'd give anything for him to give me his love without reservations.

"I'm not mad," he murmured. "Not anymore." He pulled back, and I turned in the corner of the couch and looked at him, waiting.

"I'm terrified," he said at last, baldly. "I'm so scared, beloved. You are fearless, and honorable… and if you won't let our love keep you safe, I don't know if there's a force on the planet that will!"

I closed my eyes and nodded. "I'll try not to scare you," I promised. I would have promised him anything at this point. Two days—two days feeling cold and at odds with him. Two days of wondering if it would ever be right between us. Two days was a lifetime when Bracken couldn't hold me. Two days was a lifetime when Green was mad at me too.

"That will have to be enough," he conceded. I'd expected an argument, a fight, something, but as I met his murky, pond-shadow eyes, I saw an awareness there. He loved me, but he would never again try to control me, not even when I was out of control. I had broken something—a figurative rein or brain-matter control chip or something. Whatever there had been in our relationship that meant he could at some point shout me down or beg me and I would *have* to concede, it had been vaporized, and the only thing left to keep me from violating his trust was my more than questionable good judgment.

"Whatever I did," I said after a moment, "whatever happened in our hearts between the two of us, it scares me too."

With that, I buried my face in his neck and started to sob. His big hands came to cup the back of my head and span the space between my shoulder blades, and his massive biceps surrounded me on either side. Suddenly I wasn't *caged*, I was *protected*, and even while I sobbed myself stupid into his chest, I gloried in the difference.

Suspecting

"Jacky, you smell them, right?"

Jack nodded. They'd caught the scent the day before, when Teague had first sent them out to walk the beach and enjoy the sunshine for him. It smelled like wolf and man and… alcohol.

"I thought we couldn't get drunk," he said, wrinkling his nose expressively, and Katy shrugged. They were walking up a hill to the parking lot. They'd just spent the day in the aquarium, which had been amazing and colorful and deep—and not something they thought Teague would particularly enjoy.

"Maybe it makes them feel tough," she said, trying not to sound uncertain. She turned around as they neared the car. She could see the ocean from this spot in the small tourist section of town, and she loved it. All that fathomless blue. "You think maybe we should take Teague to the aquarium, just in case?"

Jack grunted a negative and swiveled around to where she stood, walking up behind her to put his hands on her shoulders and pull her backward into his body.

"What are you thinking?" he asked into her ear. A group of tourists came up the walk and surged around them like the tide. Jack held her tight, and they stayed there, gazing into the overcast sky over the bay.

"I'm thinking that they've known we're here. They knew we were here when we were out at the beach yesterday. They know we're here now. But no one's come to make an introduction. No one's even let us see a tail, or let us know where that smell is coming from. It's like they want us to know they're here, but they don't want to get friendly."

Jack *hmm*ed and then sighed into her hair. "Think we should tell Teague?"

Katy cringed. Teague had been trying very hard to be a good boy and a good patient, but good boys admitted when they hurt and ate when they were supposed to and didn't ask their healers if maybe, just in case they needed to, they could change their form in order to facilitate healing.

I don't know, werewolf—only if you want the pain to stop your heart.

I'm tough. Don't assume it would.

Katy had put a stop to that conversation right quick. She'd burst into tears and screamed at Teague about how he'd rather die than be still with his own goddamned self for more than a couple of days, and he'd promised her, after making her lie down beside him so he could stroke her hair, that he wouldn't do anything desperate.

That night a pair of knitting needles and a skein of sea-gray yarn had appeared on Teague's lap, dropped there by tiny creatures with bodies that appeared to be flickering lights. They came with an instruction book too, which included a few hastily scrawled lines from everybody's favorite queen.

It's just like following a model diagram. You'll do fine. Now stay still and stop freaking out your mates. If we have to come down there and sit on you, it will only piss Bracken off, and he's finally over being mad at me and that would suck. So sit still. I mean it!

Jack and Katy had spent the next hour sitting very still and pretending to needlepoint or read while listening to Teague growl to himself over the sticks and string.

He'd won at the end, and when they'd left, he'd put in a request for more yarn. He'd written the specs out painfully: *Worsted. Plain. Some color I don't hate.*

Jack had looked at the tight writing on the little piece of paper and figured that they'd have to see if there was a colorway called khaki. Katy had wrinkled her nose at Teague and shrugged.

"You put it to another man most every night," she said plainly to her beloved. "It's not like getting something with color is going to make you any more gay."

Teague had smirked. "Since I also put it to you, darlin', I'm thinking that makes me bi—and since you're the one who's getting some of that, I don't know how far over into the other territory you want me to shift."

Katy had smiled at him, the full-wattage kind she knew melted his knees just a little, whether he loved Jacky more or no. "I don't think I'll be getting any less if I have you make me something in purple, you think?" She'd been rewarded by a quiet, smoldering smile.

"I think you could be right, field mouse. How 'bout you get any color you want, and some more for Jacky, and I'll knit you all up whatever I can manage while I'm laid up here. How's that?"

Katy had smiled at him and rubbed noses, charmed at his sweet and slightly besotted smile back.

Now she said to Jack, "I don't want to tell him. I don't want to tell him *anything*. I want him to sit there and knit for a week. Hell, I want a fucking blanket, and we bought enough yarn for it, didn't we?"

And then, together, they both said, "Fuck."

"Which we forgot at the restaurant," Jack swore, burying his face in her back. She rolled her eyes.

"Yeah, we need to go get that." She sighed, and Jack sighed with her.

"Because sometimes you don't want to do shit that's necessary."

They weren't talking about running back for the yarn, and they both knew it.

"Maybe we could just tell Cinnamon and Joshua," Jack said hopefully—and Katy, who had been living with two taciturn men for nearly eight months now, actually grunted in response.

"And maybe he could break himself all over again in the tantrum he'll throw when he finds out we didn't tell him. And then maybe Cory could scold us like a disappointed mommy, and Green could look all sorrowful and shit because, damn, don't we know by now how this family thing works? And then, just for fun, maybe Bracken could pull all our blood out from a paper cut, and that would be the best part of our night!"

Jack chuckled behind her. Every now and then he made that height thing really work for him, and in spite of the fact that he wasn't a fighter and he wasn't Teague, he could really make her feel loved and protected. She thought that, in another life, where she wasn't a werewolf and didn't have to depend on a pack to keep her safe, she and Jacky might make a nice, stable, two-point-four-kids-picket-fence couple.

Of course if they ever met Teague Sullivan in that life, he'd rock their world, and then where would they be?

"Here," Jack said, still laughing. "How about I run back and get the bags, and you get the car and meet me down there. And then we go back and tell Teague and Cinnamon and even bite the bullet and call up Green."

"I'll go down there," she said thoughtfully. "The rest of the plan is good, but I think maybe I should go down." She turned to him and kissed the corner of his mouth, because she could. "I just think that maybe they'll show themselves when they think I'm alone and helpless."

Jacky growled. It was satisfying that he would get all protective and shit, but they'd both been in the same fight the night Teague had been wounded, and she had held her own. It hadn't been any little werewolf fight either. It had been a full-out battle, with vampires and shape-shifters and everything but elves—on the enemy's side, at least. Cory had brought enough elves for Green's people to be well represented. Katy was not particularly reckless, but she did have some confidence now. She could fight.

She could certainly hold her own with some assholes who didn't have the balls to walk up and introduce themselves to a couple of werewolves from out of town.

Teague would have said "Hell to the fuck no!"—but Teague had got himself broken, and Jacky was not Teague. He went to fetch the car while she trotted down to Bubba Gump Shrimp Company, where they'd eaten after their visit to the aquarium.

She liked the restaurant. It was pricey, but Green didn't mind when they ate on his dime, and they'd sat out on an enclosed porch, perched on pylons that were literally sunk into the ocean. Their view had been nothing but pretty blue sea under the gray sky. Why was it that at the ocean, even a gray sky wasn't a hardship?

They were in luck! When Katy dodged into the crowded foyer, she spotted the bag they'd left behind immediately, and the door hostess had seen her and simply handed it over. The restaurant was crowded and full of food and alcohol smells, which had made it a little disconcerting to sit down and eat in.

Now it also made it easier for the werewolf to hide and wait.

But that didn't mean Katy didn't smell him, and it didn't mean she didn't have her hand on the little switchblade she'd carried with her since she'd been a teenager living on the streets. She didn't need it, though. The asshole brought his own knife.

She was alert enough to expect the grab as she walked out of the restaurant, and was hauled around the gift shop to the side of the building with the dumpsters, and she was strong enough to have the guy's hunting knife at her attacker's throat before he had a chance to do more than breathe in her ear.

"You all they got, fucker?" she hissed into her new friend's surprised face. He looked to be in his thirties, which meant in werewolf years he was probably much older, but he was missing some of his teeth, and he had the bad skin and bone structure that usually came with a lot of poor nutrition as a child and growing adolescent.

If he didn't smell like drunken werewolf, he'd be just another homely white man with hair the color of dirt on a sidewalk.

"I'm not much, but there's a lot of me," the guy said, laughing without humor. Katy grunted. Obviously more than one. She wondered how long she had before Jacky brought the car around.

"Why not come up and say hello, army of one?" she asked seriously. She saw him flush and duck his head.

"I don't know." He scowled. "You didn't come introduce yourself to the area alpha. What's up with that?"

"This is Green's territory," Katy said, a little surprised. "How long's your alpha been here?"

The guy shrugged. "We been here about a year," he admitted. "Cujo and his woman came up from SoCal back then, said SoCal was waging a werewolf war, said they wanted to just have their own territory and hang here and be cool. So we did. And we ain't smelled no other werewolves until you and your man here. We figured we'd scare you off, we don't have to deal with you. Who the fuck is Green?"

Katy grimaced and wished for Cory. Cory did this shit better. "Green's the guy you're gonna have to answer to if you keep lying to me. You put a knife in my side and haul me around a building to scare me? You're so full of shit I'm surprised your shorts aren't full. You want to try again?"

The guy grimaced. "Well, scare you, get myself a piece of ass. You know. Whatever."

Katy found herself growling. "Is this knife silver, asshole?" She held it up against the guy's stubbled throat. When he didn't flinch back from it, she assumed not and contemplated her next move. But first: "Why do you guys smell funky, like sour beer? There's no reason you should be drunk."

The guy shrugged. "Man, that's not us, that's Cujo's mate. She's crazier than a shithouse rat, but she's got some serious magic mojo. Fucking crazy redheaded bitch with pointed ears. She's the one tells Cujo how to handle strangers." Suddenly he leered, and with his baggy, stubbled face and bad teeth, the expression did a lot to make Katy wish she hadn't eaten quite so much at Bubba Gump's. "I'm the one who thought your ass looked pretty tight in those jeans."

"Fucker, I got me two men, and either one of them could kill you for free and not remember the stink of your breath the minute after." Well, Teague could, but he had enough fierceness for both him and Jacky, even laid up like he was. "But good men like that, they don't pick some weak princessy bitch to be theirs, do you hear me? You tell this Cujo"—and wasn't that the *dumbest* name on the planet? Really? Cujo?—"that if he wants to introduce himself, he'd better go back to Mommy and learn him some manners. And you tell him, he messes with us, he pisses off Green. Green's worst guy, he's still better'n you. He's got a whole army of people with pointed ears that'll fuck you up unless you leave me and my men the fuck alone, and maybe even then, you hear me?"

The guy grimaced and tried to be tough. "You don't scare me, cunt. You're just waiting to bend over and take it from a man that's not afraid of you."

Katy laughed and thought maybe Lady Cory'd rubbed off on her. "That's not you, asshole! You're just lucky this knife's not silver." And with that, she used it to sever his carotid artery.

She managed to jump back and avoid most of the blood spray, which was good because she didn't want to attract any attention walking back. She'd dropped the shopping bag with the souvenirs and yarn when she'd been grabbed, and she dodged around the building to get that. When she got to the road in front of the restaurant, with the exception of some questionable stains on her pants, she looked like any other tourist in a pair of flared-leg jeans and a sporty little black leather jacket.

She hopped in the car—a very old Volvo, apparently Cinnamon's personal vehicle—and Jack's nostrils flared.

"What in the fuck? I smell blood!" He sniffed again. "Gross blood."

Katy grunted. It smelled… off. Like elf blood mixed with werewolf blood and fermented in a blender with lots and lots of pot. "Yeah. Too bad the guy will live," she told him. She'd seen his throat knitting back together as she'd left him crouched, bleeding, and swearing to himself in the dumpster lot behind the restaurant.

"He approached you?"

Katy looked at him and shrugged. "You sound all surprised and shit, Jacky. You knew that's why I wanted to go back alone, right? They wouldn't come around when you were there. They think you're a hot shit alpha. Me? To them I'm harmless. They don't know I'm Lady Cory's girl. No girl who hangs out with Lady Cory is gonna walk away without some ninja shit rubbing off, right?"

Jack made a weird sound—a whimper or a grunt or a whine or all three—and then sighed. "Holy shit. I really am the wife. Teague's the warrior, you're the ninja, and I'm the helpless asshole who gets Teague hurt because he's so busy worrying about me that he lets some fucker just scoop him up into midair!"

Katy couldn't help it. She rolled her eyes. "You think that's why Teague got hurt? That's not why Teague got hurt. Teague got hurt because we were in a battle, idiot. Teague got hurt because that's his *job*. We need to face that, Jacky, and we need to face that right now. Cory saved him, sure, but she shouldn't have done that—"

"Why does everybody keep *saying that*!" Jack swore. "I'm *tired* of hearing how she should have just let him die! Doesn't everybody realize that it was *Teague* falling from the sky there?"

"You think I don't know that?" Katy snapped. "I know it, Jacky. I know it. Green knows it. The whole damned hill knows it. And don't think people wouldn't have just choked up and cried if Teague died. But you know this nice little vacation we've got here? The house and the people make us good food and give us our car? The way we got to wake up and take care of each other when Teague was busy being hurt and in pain in the next room? You think we'd get any of that if Cory died? Do you know what would have happened if she had died a couple of nights ago? We'd have no Teague, because no one would have the heart or the skill or the love to make him better."

Katy sighed and wished she had something to kick, and Jack sighed in the exact same way with the exact same expression on his face. They caught each other's eyes and laughed.

"So you went all ninja and shit on him?" Jack asked after a moment, and Katy harrumphed into the gray of the late afternoon.

"What do you suppose they want?" Jack asked. Katy knew she had to get coherent.

"They wanted to tell us their dicks were bigger, but there's more to it than that." She squinted a little, wondering what it would be like to be out on the beach this time of the afternoon. The tide was probably full and noisy, and the swells would be terrifying and huge. She hadn't told Jacky, but she was dying to go wolf and swim in that madness. The idea of it seemed absolutely thrilling.

"What more?" Jack asked with half his brain. He was, to his credit, trying to find a way out of downtown Monterey. The famed Cannery Row might have become a tourist trap since John Steinbeck wrote about it, but that didn't make the frontage road any less congested and vital to the city's economy.

"They've got some sort of freaky leader dynamic," she said sourly. "There's an elf in there, and this assumption that they're here in a power vacuum. That and the cowardice… you know, the way they wouldn't come at me with you there." She snorted. "That and they're stupid! How they could think they'd take one of us out with a knife? Dumbest fucking criminal I've ever met, and I used to know a lot of them. Honestly, Jacky. I don't know what their game is, but it's bad. We've got to tell Teague, and we've got to tell Green or Cory. We may be stubborn here, but we've got to try hard not to be too stupid, you know?"

Jack grunted. "We were already going to tell him. How was it not stupid to tip our hand and then let them know we're not weak?"

Katy blinked. Well, shit. She hadn't thought of that.

"Maybe they'll stay the fuck away from us?" she said hopefully, but she wasn't buying it, and Jacky's shake of the head wasn't either.

"Nope. Mostly I think it means we've got to be cagier than ever. And I'll place bets that someone's going to have to come down here and kick some ass before Teague's well enough to leave."

Katy pouted. She knew it was childish, but, well, damn it. "I was sort of hoping I could scare them away until we left," she confessed. "I didn't want Teague to have to worry. You're right, it wasn't a smart thing to do. No wonder Teague loves you best."

Jack stopped short at a yellow light, and a passel of cars almost piled up behind him.

"Teague *what*?" he asked, ignoring the cacophony of horns and phalanx of dance figures behind them.

"Jacky, there's traffic—"

"What did you just say?"

"There's traffic!"

"The light's red!"

"Well there's gonna be traffic when the light goes green, and I don't want to talk about it," she told him rationally. He squinted at her. The light went green, and he pulled out like a sane person and wound his way along the coastline before going inland for 17-Mile Drive to the homes in Pebble Beach.

There was a pullout parking lot with beach access right before the road went right. Jack pulled in there and turned toward her with something approaching a stern expression on his face.

"I don't want to talk about it," Katy told him, sorry she'd ever put it into words. It was the truth. She knew it. She'd known it since she'd wormed her way into their lives. It didn't bother her—it had never bothered her. Some girls, she knew, would be all princessy, would demand to be the queen or the crown jewel in an arrangement like this. But those girls thought like humans, and Katy hadn't thought like a human even when she was one. The more she thought about it, the more she remembered those hazy, bitter days in the piles of bodies at the shooting galleries as a quest for a pack. The only pack she'd found as a human was the warped and twisted kind. But healthy Katy had found herself a healthy pack. She didn't need to be the pack princess with a diamond tiara. She just needed her men. She needed them healthy and happy, and if that meant they needed each other a little more than they needed her, well, women had been keeping quiet parts of themselves, covert desires, and secret gardens thriving and weeded in their bosoms since they first looked at their male counterparts and wondered "Where in the hell is he gonna put *that*?"

"We are too going to talk about it!" Jacky groused. She just looked at him, her mouth twisted and one eyebrow higher than the other, until he started to shift uncomfortably in his seat.

"Jacky, do you think Teague would throw himself in front of a bullet for you?" she asked after a moment. Jack's face scrunched up sourly.

"Yeah," he said softly. "Do you think he wouldn't take one for you?"

"I know he would," Katy told him with absolute assurance. "But it wouldn't leave him any less dead. You'd take a bullet for me. I'd take one for both of you. If that man had us dangling off a cliff and could only save one of us, he'd save us both if it crushed his heart. I'm not going to complain that he loved you first. That you're the one who makes him all soft before I go in and make him strong. I'm not going to complain that you followed him like a puppy dog, even into a life you're not good at. You love me. You both love me."

"But to say he loves me more—"

"Who you think Lady Cory loves more? Green or Bracken?"

Jack swallowed and thought hard. "I think it's tight," he said at last. "I think it's damned tight. But I'd probably have to say Green, just a little. Maybe because he was first, or maybe because he was part of her life with Adrian. Maybe it's just because he's her leader, and he's got the double whammy." He looked out to the sea, where jumbo breakers were swelling up almost to where the dunes dropped down to the beach.

High tide, indeed. "I think she probably hates to think about it. Probably worse, even, than me or Teague do."

He turned to look at her then, his pretty blue eyes direct and clear, which they weren't often. "But not you."

Katy looked back and smiled. It wasn't a sad smile or a resigned one. She tried very hard to put every bit of contentment and happiness she had felt in the past months into her smile so he would know what was truth and what was guilt, and why guilt should be allowed to wash out to sea.

"Have I ever told you how grateful I am? Yeah, I'm afraid for Teague. I think you and me, we're going to be worrying about that boy forever. I'm just so damned happy to have a friend—a mate—to help me, you know?"

Jack reached out and took her hand. She brought it to her lips and kissed it, smiling faintly. Then she finished the thought, the terrible one they'd both been terrified to complete the morning before when they'd awakened in each other's arms and devoured each other in lust and fear.

"And I'm glad that if he ever falls from the sky again, it won't be just me alone. I couldn't live if it was just me alone. But I could live for you, Jacky, you know?"

Jack nodded and pulled their twined hands back to his chest. "I could live for you too. But you know the hardest truth, don't you?"

Katy closed her eyes. "Yeah. Do we have to say it?"

His voice was choked, and there was something hot on the back of her hand as he held it to his cheek. "We have to. You and me—if he's going to be the front line, the guardian of the kingdom or some shit, we've got to look at it square and know it's the truth. You're the one who started telling the hard stuff today, Katy. We need to see it to the end."

"'Kay," she whispered. They both turned away, looking at the almost barren sky before them. They had to. Looking at each other when they said this would just hurt too much.

"We'll make it without him," she said quietly, hoping it was mostly true.

"But he won't…." Jack's voice stalled.

Katy picked it up, because she could and that's what they did for each other. "He won't make it without us. Or without Cory." She could feel him shudder with that last hard admission. It was something he hadn't wanted to hear and hadn't wanted to admit, but it needed to be said. Teague had enough damage to need certain things to live. One of those things was apparently an extended list of people to die for.

They sat in the quiet, with the sea whooshing beyond their little car, long enough for the tide to recede a little and for some late-afternoon cool to seep through the windows.

"We need to tell Green," Jack said tonelessly.

"Yeah. All right. Can I tell Cory I kicked ass? I think she'll be proud of me."

Jack disengaged his hand from the tangle theirs had become and lifted it to her cheek. "I think we're all proud of you. Always."

It was the sort of thing Teague would have said, but it didn't sound forced at all coming out of his mouth, and Katy gave him a grin.

"You're growing up, aren't you?"

She got a quick smile as a reward, and a faint glint of his blue eyes behind dark lashes. "I'll try to keep up with you."

She laughed. "It'll never happen. I'm just glad we're in it together is all."

He nodded and then leaned over the seat to give her a quick, warm, breathy kiss on the lips. She closed her eyes for it and soaked in his smell. Jacky had always smelled like dessert to her, cookies and innocence. He still smelled that way, but now the cookies were a little darker. No more sugar-cookie Jacky—he was all chocolate chip now.

Good. It was her second-favorite kind.

Sadder now, but content, they pulled out of the parking lot and toward the house on the cliff where their beloved awaited.

KNITTING

TEAGUE REMEMBERED Cory telling him about when she learned to knit. She told him she'd just come out of a coma in which she'd spent a week having a conversation with Adrian—about six months after he'd died.

Teague had seen her cling to the sticks and string when she was angry and holding on to her temper by a strand of sock yarn. He'd seen her knitting furiously when she was frustrated or thinking hard or trying not to strangle Bracken with her bare hands.

He'd seen her knitting meditatively when she was sitting in front of the television or reading, each tiny stitch as perfect as the last.

Finally, after spending a day stuck with daytime television and his knitting needles, he began to see the magic.

Normally, in the rare moments he let himself sit still, he was a model cars sort of guy, but he couldn't right now. For one thing, he couldn't hunch over the minute details, and for another, all the strong paints and solvents would be bad for him to inhale and to spill on the sheets. Knitting was Cory's solution for him because it had been for her, and now he knew why.

He would have been tempted—terribly tempted—to try that shape-shifting thing if he hadn't been making a scarf the color of Jacky's eyes when Jacky was mad. He just kept touching the yarn—it was soft but substantial—and making stitch after stitch, and before he knew it, an hour had passed and he hadn't looked longingly out the window, his wolf's heart fluttering like a rabbit's to get out of the trap of healing.

The needles Cory had sent were bamboo, and something about them was warm in his hands. He liked that too.

But that didn't mean he didn't have to set them down when Jack and Katy came in with their story about crazy-assed elf-werewolf motherfuckers. He was, in fact, half a breath away from breaking the damned things, when they'd all but saved his life.

Fortunately Jack and Katy had thought ahead. Green and Cory were on speakerphone when they told their story, and Cinnamon was standing by the bed with a firm hand on his shoulder. He thought darkly that *this* was what it was like to be 'handled,' and he finally understood why Cory hated it worse than brussels sprouts.

"You what?" he asked Katy again.

"I slit his throat and got away." Katy looked a little defensive. "I didn't kill him. You know—I just made it hard for him to get up and come get me, that's all."

Cory's disembodied voice crackled over the speakerphone, dripping with admiration. "Nice move, by the way."

Teague grunted. "It would have been better if one of us had *ripped his throat out for touching her*!" Someone had touched her. Someone had touched *his mate*. He didn't need the preternatural bonding bullshit for that to boil a fever under his fur.

Cory's snort on the other end of the speaker was reassuring, though. "Oh, cool your jets, wolfman. If Bracken had killed every joker who laid a hand on me, the pile of bodies would be seen from space."

"And mine would be one of them," Jack pointed out, his chin locked on stubborn. "Bracken, if you're listening, thanks for not killing me, by the way."

There was an uncomfortable pause after Jack dredged up that old business from the difficult early days of Jack and Teague's relationship. Then Bracken's disembodied voice came through clearly on the speaker.

"No problems, Jacky. You earned your keep eventually."

"Charming," Green said dryly, then got back to the matter at hand. "And I think Katy did exactly right. She sent a message not to fuck with us, and I think that's exactly what we needed."

"It's not enough," Teague growled, his body screaming with tension. Sweat was popping out on his brow, and it wasn't until Cinnamon put a warning—and soothing—hand on his shoulder that he realized he was hurting himself with his drive to go kill something.

"I agree." Green's voice had a similar soothing effect. "I'm going to send some vampires out at sunset. They'll have to drive quickly to get there. Cinnamon?"

"Yes, sir?" Cinnamon's deference to Green, when she seemed to have no deference to pretty much anybody else, was not as surprising as it was moving—true love and true service from a rather prickly individual.

"You have a basement, I trust?"

"Yes, sir. Joshua and I will have it set up for them before they get here."

"We can help," Katy offered. Cinnamon rolled her eyes.

"Please. You need to stay up here and make sure your man doesn't burst a bone through his skin out of worry."

"Teague!" Cory's voice crackled through the speakerphone. "Damn it! We will take care of them! No worries, you hear me?"

Teague had to work not to jump. "Cory, it *touched her*...."

"Yeah, Teague, and she walked away. They're strong, they're smart, they can handle themselves in a fight, and you need to work at not freaking the fuck out, do you hear me?"

Katy folded her arms and glared at him. He sighed and held out his hand, and she took it and came in to kiss him on the forehead. She smelled good; Katy always smelled good. She smelled like vanilla and bread and wolf—his wolf—and he realized he missed the smell of his mates against his skin.

"I hear you."

At the same time, Cory said, "And we're going to need some dayfolk over there too. Bracken and I can—"

"No!" Everybody jumped a little. Nobody there had ever heard Green speak sharply to his beloved. Until now.

"Not you," Green snapped, his voice implacable, and Bracken was right behind him with "You promised."

"Guys...." Cory sounded hurt and uncertain. "Guys! It's not a war. Not yet. I just thought—"

"Not so soon." Green's voice was taut. Jack's and Katy's eyes met. Then Jack flushed and nodded, and Teague wondered what his own beloved had just realized. "The scar is still red on your throat, beloved, and you're still exhausted. If something goes down, you and Bracken can fly out. I'll have a helicopter on standby. In the meantime...." There was a terrible silence in two living rooms as they listened to their leader, the man Teague had sworn to die for, pull himself together. "In the meantime, beloved, I would appreciate your presence here."

It was so quiet, they could all hear Cory swallow. "Okay, Green," she said softly. "Absolutely. You and Bracken are right. I promised."

Green cleared his throat. "I'll send Mario and LaMark, then. Mario will be an asset, and they work well together. They should be there sometime tomorrow morning, and you all can go out as a group and scent the wind. That good for you, Teague?"

Teague closed his eyes, suddenly overwhelmed with gratitude. "That's great for me, Green. I appreciate it. Cory, you stay where you are and get strong, you hear me?"

Cory's voice on the other end of the phone was lost and hurt. "Backatcha, wolfman. I'm, uhm, going to go knit, 'kay?"

"Yeah. Me too."

It seemed they both had some things to put together in their heads.

Green rang off, and Cinnamon left to go prepare for more guests in her tiny personal faerie hill. Jack came up to sit by the window, and Katy stayed where she was, holding Teague's hand.

"We're fine," she said gently. "No worries."

He smiled tightly. "I'll always worry."

They were quiet for a moment, until Katy picked up the two-foot length of scarf on his lap and put it back in his hands with the needles. He smiled a little, but oddly enough, he felt neither like a girl nor a grandmother as he started making one painful stitch after another. He simply felt at peace.

Surprisingly it was Jacky who broke the quiet. "They're still really mad at her."

Nobody had to ask who "she" was. "Yeah," Teague grunted.

Jack sighed. "I can't be," he said after a moment. He stretched out full length on the bed next to Teague and kissed his bare shoulder. Teague put down his knitting and turned his head to drop a kiss in Jacky's hair. Jack raised his pretty, open child's face to meet Teague's lips, and Teague breathed him in like air. Jack pulled back, though, and finished the thought.

"I can't be mad at her," he said again. "I can't. But I'm starting to see why they are." His mouth quirked up. "See? Jack can learn. Somebody throw a parade."

Katy reached over to the coffee table and grabbed Jack's book, handing it over Teague's body as though she'd read his mind. "Later. When Teague can walk again, we'll have our very own 'Jacky Grows Up' celebration. How's that?"

"I'd rather just have a 'Teague Can Walk Again' parade," Jack said, and Teague kissed him again. Then he turned and kissed Katy's temple and, settling in with his knitting, was content.

He was not used to being still for long periods of time. Although he was dozing off around ten when Jacky and Katy got up and wandered off to bed—where they made noisy, sweetly scented love that warmed Teague to his toes—he was wide awake at 3:00 a.m. when Kyle and another vampire he didn't know walked quietly in the door.

Kyle came up almost shyly and extended a hand to shake. It was a little too firm, and Teague had to suppress a wince. Kyle was a fierce fighter and apparently as loyal as a retriever, but he'd lost his beloved a year and a half earlier and was not the most outgoing of vampires.

Teague was surprised to see the honest relief in Kyle's eyes as Kyle assessed his still-warm body where it lay in the clean sheets and healed.

"You're warm. Everywhere." That red, slightly whirling, vampire superpower glare was a little unnerving, and Kyle had the deep-set eyes and Neanderthal brow to make it even creepier. But the sandy-haired vampire had been solid and dependable and a fellow warrior, and he'd survived a loss Teague knew he couldn't. Teague admired the hell out of the guy.

"I hope so," Teague rasped. "Good to see you." He didn't say he was *surprised* to see Kyle, but Kyle knew anyway.

"I know. Marcus and Phillip usually take the big shit, don't they?"

Teague twitched his shoulder. It was as close as he could get to a shrug. "I *was* wondering why they sat this one out."

Kyle looked over his shoulder. "Ellis, you fed before you came, right?"

Ellis looked at him and nodded. "Do you think Jack and Katy might be up for a little snack tomorrow night?" he asked Teague hopefully. Ellis was young—young for a vampire and young for a human—and the grooves of Teague's mouth deepened. It was as close as he got to a smile most days.

"Yeah, one of them will be good for you. Cinnamon said you guys are staying in the basement, if you want to stow your gear."

"Could you get mine too?" Kyle asked casually as he tossed the keys to what was probably the converted SUV with the secret vampire compartment underneath. Ellis disappeared to go shift their gear, and Kyle pulled up the bedside chair.

"They're not doing great," he said quietly. "I think they might make it through, but Phillip needs to blood from Lady Cory every night or he's just going to lose his fucking mind. That kid… that vampire Phillip blooded with? Man, when she went, she took a chunk of his soul with her."

Teague blinked. "Wait a minute—when did Gretchen die?"

Kyle looked at him with undisguised pity. "Has no one filled you in on what happened after you checked out?"

Teague shook his head. "It's like living with the eggshell brigade. Hell, even Cory won't give it to me straight."

Kyle grunted, and Teague liked him even more. "I'm not surprised," Kyle said bitterly. "Had to be one of the worst fucking nights of her life, and I've seen some of the bad ones."

Then he gave Teague the details. Teague started to feel physically nauseated as Kyle neared the end of the story, and he realized his whole body was tense again and that was exacerbating the pain. He took a deep breath and consciously relaxed himself so Cinnamon wouldn't come bustling in and interrupt the one person willing to give him the whole unvarnished truth.

Kyle was right. The story of the night Teague was hurt didn't get any prettier.

When Teague had been dropped from the sky, Green's people had been engaged in a battle with a vampire kiss up in Redding. The Redding vampires had been protecting the worst sort of predator—a vampire who molested children and then turned them.

Child vampires were truly frightening creatures. Unlike their adult brethren, there was no human left inside them, just frightening, all-consuming need. Teague had fallen from the sky—and that had been the end of *his* night. But after that Cory had subdued the vampire kiss, mind-raped the predator before killing him—messily, because her powers weren't up to par—and discovered his hidden cache of four other children, gnawing their own wrists in cages that kept them from loosing their hunger on mankind.

"She had to ask Lambent to kill them," Kyle said unhappily. Cory could pretty much fry off a gnat's testicles—or a jet plane—from two miles away. If she'd had to ask Lambent, a fire elf, to take care of that job, it was because her power had been more off from Bracken's blood transfusion than she cared to admit.

"And after all that...." Teague trailed off. Oh Christ. The entire altercation had started because they'd found a child vampire in the woods near Green's hill. And after all that pain, she and Green had taken the girl up to the crown of Green's world and let the girl conflagrate under the sun while she still *was* a girl and her death could be peaceful and not violent.

"That's horrible," he said at last. "That's just...." He shook his head. "Jesus. No wonder Green and Bracken won't let her out of their sight."

Kyle went very still.

"What?"

He got a shrug and evasion, and after just hearing what nobody else would tell him, Teague was tired of that shit.

"C'mon, man, what gives?"

Kyle looked over his shoulder to make sure Teague was truly the only one in the room. "Look, you know what she spent the next day doing, right?"

Teague blinked, then flushed. "Crying? Sleeping?"

"Getting her brains fucked out!" Kyle interrupted, and Teague blushed harder.

"It's not nice to gossip about friends," Teague grumbled. But yeah, he'd assumed.

"Well, you know how, for a while, that time of the month, we all"—the vampires—"thought she smelled like candy?"

Teague nodded, embarrassed. He'd caught the other end of that with Jacky as well. Apparently not being able to touch Bracken—as well as a horrible case of allergies—had almost leveled the little girl with the indomitable will. "I remember."

"Well, she doesn't smell like candy anymore." Kyle's voice was intense, as though he was trying to tell Teague something, and Teague felt very thick.

"So, isn't that a good thing?"

Kyle shook his head violently. "No, man, now she smells like flowers."

Teague squinted up at the vampire and blinked. "So?" Really. He wasn't getting this.

"So…." Kyle moved his hands while Teague continued to look at him blankly. Kyle finally gave it up. "So she smells like something good, right? But like something you're not supposed to eat. It's like a human protective measure… you know… to keep the species going?"

Teague was starting to wonder if he'd fallen on his head instead of his feet. "So why don't all humans or sorceresses smell like that?"

Kyle just stared at him, and something in Teague clicked.

"Fuck. Oh fuck. Oh *fuuuuuuuuuuuuuckkkkkk*…." Teague shook his head. "No! No! Man, the elves use their will as their birth control! Why would they let that happen?"

The scowl Kyle leveled was truly a terrifying thing. "Because, asshole! She broke their will when she risked her life to save you."

Fuck. Fuck. "*Fuuuuuuuuuucccccckkkkk…,*" Teague said again. "Jesus God, no! Whose? Which one of them let that happen?"

Kyle shook his head. "I'm betting it's both. But think about it. It's only been a couple of days. Odds are she doesn't know."

Teague frowned. "Do Green and Bracken know?"

"I'd put money on it. Man, Bracken has been building your fucking house like you could not believe. There are gardens in England that belong to some duke or shit that are less cared for than Green's front yard. The two of them are doing everything they can to not take this to her and just ream her for it, and she's all but stepping in time not to piss them off again. It's *awful*. The whole hill feels the pressure. And to make matters worse, the whole place smells like patchouli, cedar, chamomile, and lavender." Kyle shuddered. "It's downright *girlie*!"

In spite of the fact that this was the last thing they should be worrying about, Teague had to laugh. And then he looked outside to the ocean, which was growing steadily grayer.

"Brother, as much fun as this has been...." He trailed off meaningfully, and Kyle nodded.

"Good thought. I'll run down to the darkling, 'kay? Ellis is...." Kyle blushed. "Man, this vampire thing is so weird. I mean, I *enjoy* women, you know? My whole life I've never wanted a man. But Ellis's *blood* just turns me on." Kyle shrugged. "No shame, right? Besides...." He sobered. "It's been so long since I've wanted anything. Anyone. I'm just grateful for him, that's all."

Teague watched him go with a faint smile. Then he collapsed back into the deep pillow behind him, and the smile disappeared. His body released all his tension in one big throb, and Cinnamon was right there before he could even say her name.

"Are you two done gossiping yet? Because, you know, I could make some popcorn, we could put in a movie. I've even got some makeup you could share, how's that?"

"Fucking groovy," Teague mumbled. "If I asked you nice, could I skip that part and just get the healing?"

Cinnamon's disgusted sniff said that maybe, yes, she would relieve his pain, but he didn't think he was going to avoid the lecture. She surprised him, though. Apparently peasants all had one common worry—what was going on in the big house?

"It's probably true," she said calmly. "You know that, right?"

Teague sighed and allowed the lack of pain to wash over him and ease his breathing and his sweat. "That girl sure knows how to make things hard on herself," he said at last.

Cinnamon's clucking sound seemed to concur. "No wonder the two of you are friends. The good news is, you've both managed to find mates who will move heaven and earth to make things easy. Now, I'm going to put you under for a few hours—just long enough so you don't get your days and nights completely flip-flopped, because that will bore everyone to tears, yes? Now, give me the knitting…. Good." She smiled gently as Teague handed over the mostly finished scarf made in perfect sea-blue garter stitch.

"Now sleep, werewolf. Don't worry about your friend. There will be plenty of us to do that for the next year."

Teague's brain was getting fuzzy. He had just enough clarity to say, "Year?"

"Do you think the work ends with birth? I don't think so."

"Fuuuuuuuuccccckkkk…."

It was the last thing he could remember before Jack and Katy woke him in the morning.

BELIEVING

SHE TRIED to remember all the things we could do and she could not—but sometimes she forgot how good our hearing really was.

That was fine. It allowed me to sit behind her and hold her against my chest while she had a conversation with Teague that she forgot I could hear.

"The vampires got there okay? Good." Cory laughed a little. "Kyle talked? With more than one syllable? Really? *Ellis?* You know, we have *got* to get more women around here. We just do. I'm making it a priority."

Teague pointed out something unflattering but probably very true about his gender in general, and Cory had to concede.

"Yeah, well, young men *do* fuck up that way in bigger numbers. But there *must* be some girls out there that want to join up, you think?"

I did not point out that for young women, finding out that turning into a vampire eliminated the chance of having children—and that turning into a werecreature severely limited it—was often a deal breaker. It had been Adrian who told me that on the heels of a disappointing attempt to talk a girl out of the life he tended to recruit from.

And then Teague asked her something that made my whole body come to alert.

"No, I'm fine. Why do you ask? Yeah, still tired. Probably the transfusion or something. And I've always had a hair-trigger stomach.... Oh, sorry." She turned around to me apologetically. "Sorry, beloved. Was I squashing you?"

"I was just getting up to get a soda." It wasn't a lie—I'd planned to shortly. But a sprite appeared above her head, looking at me questioningly—they tended to wait on me that way, even if Cory liked to do that shit herself. I shook him off with a meaningful look, and he winked out of sight.

Cory hopped up off my lap and said, "I'll get it for you."

"Thank you!" I told her pleasantly. "Can I talk to Teague for a minute while you do?"

So I had the phone while she wandered into the kitchen, and I spoke so quietly *I* could barely hear myself—but I knew Teague could pick up on it just fine.

"Stop asking her how she feels," I growled, "or she's going to figure it out."

"Well, why don't you tell her?" Teague snapped, and I sighed. Green and I had held this exact conversation, and until this moment, when I was forced to defend Green's stand, I hadn't really understood it.

"Because it's been four days, moron, and she's not going to believe it," I said, frustrated. "And she hasn't hardly found her feet. Seriously, could we let her recover first?"

Teague blew out a breath, and I looked across the room to the refrigerator. Renny was in the kitchen, naked and eating pie, and Cory was talking quietly to her, so I relaxed just a smidge. Nicky came in— he'd arrived from Austin this morning, and he and Cory were still making a point of touching every so many moments to make up for the absence. We hadn't told him about… about what had happened, yet. Avians have an excellent sense of smell, but the other werecreatures and vampires have better. Renny was starting to sneeze around her. How soon would Nicky start asking questions?

"She's got to know—"

"She's human. Humans expect a month for their minds to catch up with what their bodies already know." Green had told me this. I had not been aware. "And besides—" I looked over my shoulder again. She was putting ice in a glass for me, although I hadn't asked and hadn't expected it, and my chest swelled so tight I almost couldn't speak. "—she's still not… she's not okay. All right? All of the things we love about her, and she's afraid she let us down, and she's not okay."

As though sensing my regard, she flashed me an uncertain smile over her shoulder, and I returned it reassuringly. She was pregnant with sidhe twins, and she was still not certain of her own worth. I had to breathe hard through my nose in order to keep my anger from bubbling over and into her blood.

Teague sighed. "She needs to be okay," he said gruffly. "That's your job, hoss. You need to make sure she's okay."

"Goddess… fuck. I'm trying, right?"

That was all I could do. It was all I had.

She came back with a soda for me and one for herself, and I fought with the desire to tell her to sit down and stay off her feet and all those ridiculous things men tell women when they've always been the stronger sex and always been able to deal with the stresses the Goddess gave their bodies. *Except she has the body God gave her, with its terrible curses and its frailties and its susceptibilities.* And then, because my mother had told me this the night before—*And fey women die in childbirth as well. It's one of our few weaknesses, my darling boy. It's why we needed Green's help to birth you.*

I handed her the phone without a word, but I made sure to brush her wrist with my thumb as I did it. She smiled at me and made herself comfortable against my chest. I busied myself pretending to watch television so I could listen in on her conversation without shame.

Teague clicked off for a minute, and Cory sighed. I made a questioning sound, and she looked behind her and mumbled, "Call waiting—it's Jacky," at me.

"What's he doing away from the house?" I thought the whole reason for sending the vampires and putting Mario and LaMark in the car was to keep them safe.

"I don't know." She shrugged. "I think Cinnamon needed food. Teague said something about the grocery store."

Strange, isn't it? How the most mundane of things can be our undoing?

The phone clicked again, and Teague's frantic near hysteria buzzed through the phone. I didn't even need to hear the panicked words to know what was wrong.

Jacky and Katy were in trouble, Teague was stuck in bed, and no one who could help was nearby.

"Teague, don't!" Cory begged suddenly. Oh shit. "Don't! Please, damn it. Mario and LaMark are already on their way. We'll be there, Green will get us there. Don't…. you heard what she said. Oh fuck… please…. *Bracken, go get Green!*"

I was already up as she said it, pounding down the hallway with every intention of breaking into Green's room, appointment or no, when Cory screamed, anguish in every note, *"Goddammit, Teague Sullivan, don't you go wolf on me!"*

Over the phone and two hundred miles away, we could all hear his scream as he disobeyed that order.

RUNNING

WHEN CINNAMON sent them to the grocery store for some food "to feed all these damned shape-shifters with their love for meat!" neither Jacky or Katy actually gave much thought to the wolves who had been following them in and about Monterey and Salinas. Given that Cinnamon had the same sort of ownership over her tiny estate as Green had over his hill, they assumed this little section of land would be off-limits to the bad guys.

The crazy-elf-bitch-werewolf smell roiling through the grocery store was reminding Jacky of that truism about assumptions.

"Jacky…," Katy muttered under her breath. Jack nodded. They could spot or scent the ten or twelve different men who had entered the store right after they had, and none of them looked friendly. *They must have driven up*, Jacky thought, trying to be calm, *and they must have known where Cinnamon's line of safety would work and where it would not.*

"I see them," he said tightly. "They've blocked all the entrances, but I don't smell them back by the meat department. We can get out there. But first let's pretend we're stupid for another minute and let me call for backup."

The call to Teague was short, and he tried to keep panic out of his voice. "There's ten or twelve of them, and they've blocked the way to the car," he said as a greeting, "and we're going to make a run for it in a second. You remember when you were being chased by that thing at Sugarpine?" They were in the cereal aisle, and Jack looked unhappily at the big bag of fake Lucky Charms—it had been on his list of things to buy for Teague.

"Yeah?" Teague had his game voice on, but Jack could hear the thready blood of panic pumping through it.

"We could hear you bark for a good forty-five minutes before the birds saw you. Open the windows, open the doors, and listen, you hear me?"

"I will," Teague said tersely. "We've got backup on standby. Run fast, beloved. You and Katy keep safe, right?"

"I hear you, beloved. You stay put, and I'll trust in rescue, right?"

"Right."

And with that, Jack hung up, put his phone in Katy's strappy little purse, and knotted the strap to make it stay on her neck. Their eyes met as they passed the meat department, and both of them took an immediate and abrupt right through the double doors, ignoring the cries of the butchers in the back as they passed and shedding clothes as they went.

"What'd he say?" asked Katy as they rounded the corner to the dumpster bins behind the store and took a second to take off their pants and leave them in a puddle.

"I'm pretty sure he said he was going to do something stupid," Jack panted. Then both of them were naked, except for Katy's little tapestry purse, and there was another ruckus coming through the meat department.

Without another word the two of them changed form and ran for their lives.

In the past year, Jack had often despaired over his basic nature. He was not a fighter. He'd been told it often enough and had proved it more often than he cared to admit. He did not know when to fight and when to reason, when to be ruthless and when to back down. If he could he'd subvert conflict by moving around it, whether that was by sneaking up on Teague while he was sleeping in order to make him accept love, or by forming small conspiracies with Katy to keep their lover happy, or even by picking a fight with Cory to keep Teague out of danger because he knew Teague would never gainsay one of Cory's orders, ever…. God, all the ways he managed to slide under the confrontation radar. He could go around or under or over conflicts, but he was not very good at going through them.

Katy was decent at both, but she lacked his passive-aggressive instincts. Later she told him flat out that those were the things that saved their lives over the next two hours as they fought their way toward safety.

He would see an obstacle, such as a giant fence or a concrete cinderblock wall, and Katy would start the charge over it. Jacky would run down the side of it to go around, and sure enough, they would scent their enemy waiting in the most logical place for them to emerge. Jack, who had deplored his own nature, often cursing himself as a skulking coward, ran his beloved through the streets of a strange town, going around corners, under culverts, through crowds where larger groups of wolves could not run, and over piers to jump from rock to rock in the jagged stepping stones left by low tide. He would cover a suburban shopping center, the side of a terrifying freeway, the busy sidewalks of

Monterey's tourist district, and the ragged, frigid coastline that flowed to the south of it, the whole time making one big oblong semicircle from right next door to safety, far into the depths of enemy territory, and back to where, please Goddess, God, Cory, Green, who-the-fuck-ever, Teague could hear them push air from their heaving chests and howl for help.

They almost made it.

They'd been running, flat out and crafty as, well, wolves, when they rounded the corner of an alley in Monterey that should have gone through but stopped at a cinderblock wall instead.

They skidded to a halt and turned around to try to get out of the trap they'd laid for themselves, and found that what looked to be a pack of twenty wolves—all of them smelling like crazy elf-bitch blood—had come in through the bottleneck, snarling and pissed off at having to run that terrible distance.

Katy whined next to him, and he stood in front of her and started the series of short, sharp barks that could, he knew, travel up to five miles, if someone knew to listen. He could only hope Teague was listening.

Behind him, he sensed Katy skin-changing, and he heard his cell phone being quick-dialed even as the wolves moved in menacingly. He kept his wolf form. Katy was the smart one—if they were going to negotiate, better have them negotiate with her and fight with him.

"Cinnamon? It's looking bad…," Katy said shakily. "Could you tell Teague…."

There was a moment of silence that was one of the most truly terrifying heartbeats of Jack's life.

"He *what*?" Katy shrieked. From half a mile away at most, they heard it—the series of short barks that could only come from the throat of their winded, panicked, *dumber than shit on crackers* mate.

And then they heard the helicopter.

The helicopter gave everybody pause. All the wolves on the ground stopped and looked up, because it was flying really close for a vehicle that had no landing pad or even hope of one within a good four- or five-mile radius.

"Oh fuck," Katy muttered. Jack saw what she saw and gave a wolf bark that meant pretty damned much the same thing.

Teague came around the corner—his hind end scrawny, lacking in muscle, and flopping uselessly to the side even as he laid teeth into his first wolf, snapped its neck, and threw it over his shoulder to heal slowly behind him.

"Teague, if any of us survive this, I'm gonna fucking kill you."

Jack's yip told her he'd help with the massacre if they survived this one. Then, with the exception of Teague—who used the distraction to keep maiming werewolves with a terrible ferocity for someone who couldn't actually walk on all four paws—everybody looked up at the helicopter.

A person jumped out—a shocking thing to see—and everybody caught their breath in panic. He plummeted down, down, far enough down to be halfway between the helicopter and the ground. Then he was a bird, and Nicky started diving like a hawk, sighting a werewolf to harry even as he fell.

Everyone else ignored him, because there were two more people standing at the open bay of the copter.

"Oh, fuck oh hell oh no," Katy breathed. "Tell me they're not doing what I think they're doing."

But Jack couldn't. There, right about two hundred feet up, was Cory, standing on the internal platform of what looked to be an old Black Hawk helicopter with an open bay door. Bracken had his arms wrapped around her, and she was unhooking the harness that held them both in the machine.

Even from two hundred feet away, everyone looking up saw their eyes meet, saw Bracken's arms wrap firmly around her, and saw the way they trembled right before they leaped.

LEAPING

GREEN HEARD Cory screaming "Green, we need the fucking copter!" and then Bracken threw open the door to Green's room—broken magic lock and all!—and snapped, "You've got to fucking stop her, damn it! We can't let her go!"

Green swung his legs out of bed and looked regretfully at the pretty little werekitty who had just climaxed around his body. She stood up with absolutely no self-consciousness whatsoever, transformed into a cat, and bulleted out of the room. Before her tail had even cleared his door, Green slammed a sound shield around his room and got hold of his temper.

"Helicopter?" he asked first. Bracken nodded curtly.

"Werewolves are in trouble. I think Teague just changed form, and if he survives that, he's going to need backup. LaMark and Mario left an hour ago. They've got two more hours minimum, one if they abandon the car and fly. I figure the copter...."

Green looked blank for a moment and did a mind-to-mind with Arturo. He could do this with most of his people, although not as thoroughly as he often shared mind space with Cory.

"It's done," he said. "Now, about stopping her...."

Bracken's expression was pleading, and Green abruptly forgave him for his rudeness and panic and the fact that he had busted down Green's door while Green was in the middle of something delicate and personal.

"We've got to," Bracken muttered. "Green, we have to. She can't go. She's...." Neither of them had said the words, not since the night Green had lain next to Bracken and their beloved and forced Bracken to feel the beginnings of the life growing in her womb.

"I know exactly what she is," Green said now. "I helped make her that way, remember? But you know what she isn't?"

"Sane?"

"Bracken!"

"Sensible?"

"So help me, I will curse your speech for a week!" Green finally snapped. He could do it. Bracken was well aware that Green's power was greater—and more versatile—than his own.

"Okay, finish the sentence!" Bracken snapped back, and Green did.

"Helpless, okay, mate? She's not fucking helpless! Two weeks ago—hell, one week ago—you would have enjoyed the hell out of this."

"Well, that was before she was…." Bracken hesitated, and now Green filled in the blank.

"Pregnant?"

"In-fucking-sane!" Bracken roared. "Green, the whole reason she *got* pregnant was because her damned will eclipsed her goddamned common-fucking-sense, and then she had to prove to us that her will was all she needed!"

"Is that what you think happened?" Green asked, stunned. Oh, how could such a good man be so wrong?

"Yes!"

"Well, you're wrong, mate. What happened that night, what happened in our bed after that—we've been grooming her for that since she walked in the door and fell into Adrian's bed!"

"What in the fuck are you talking about?" Bracken wasn't yelling anymore. In fact, he ran his hand through his shorn, pine-tar-colored hair and sank slowly onto Green's used bed. Green sat next to him and wrapped a companionable arm around his shoulders. He and Bracken were partners of sorts in keeping their beloved alive, keeping her sane—and, in moments like these, keeping themselves sane when her courage and uniqueness seemed to overwhelm their good Goddess-damned sense.

"Independence, Bracken Brine. Self-belief. Our whole life with her, we've been trying to get her to believe in herself. Well, she does now. She believes in herself enough to contradict us and go her own way. But she loves us enough to respect our advice and stay right by our sides. Don't let the life growing inside her blind you to the person she's always been. She's fully capable of this, and she needs it, damn it! She needs to see that she didn't take that terrible risk for nothing."

Bracken nodded, because he was a smart boy—he was still *very* young for a sidhe—and then his entire face puckered with worry. "She's been so tired," he whispered, and Green tightened that arm.

"I know. I know. Redding wiped her out, and her body is getting used to the pregnancy… but she'll be up for it. You know she will. She's in no greater danger now than she has been for the last two years, and we've stood it. We need to stand it again until she's ready to hear the truth, to make her own decisions. If we tell her she can't go now, and tell her why...."

Bracken scrubbed his face with his hand. "Goddess... it'll fuck her up so bad...."

Green nodded and swallowed hard. Until this moment he hadn't known about his half-hidden hope that Bracken would come up with a really good argument to convince him to keep her there, keep her safe, with him.

But he knew better, and in spite of his basic optimism, he was also a realist. With a sigh he stood up and reached for a pair of jeans, which he slid on and buttoned hastily before offering Bracken a hand.

"Come on, brother. Teague's in danger. His family needs us. Nothing has changed."

Bracken's shoulders squared, and he stood and scowled, looking like the warrior he truly was. "Absolutely, leader," he said tightly. Green nodded. Green dropped the sound blocker and opened the door about a fraction of a second before Cory battered it down, her magic escaping her control because of her panic.

He embraced her before she could say anything—open her mouth to panic, to issue orders, to start thinking out loud all the things that needed to be done in the next ten minutes before she left him to do something perilous and painful and dangerous.

"Of course," he whispered, hauling her up until her toes dangled and giving a tight, worried smile into her puzzled eyes. "Of course. Our family needs us. Transportation is on its way. Just...." He took a quick breath and resolved to practice what he'd just preached. "Just be careful, beloved. Let Bracken and Nicky pick up the slack. Remember that you carry what's best of both me and Bracken with you, yes?"

She swallowed and looked at him soberly. "I'd never do anything to hurt you, Green."

He kissed her, drinking her down even as he heard the faraway sound of the helicopter that was coming to take her away.

SCREAMING

Teague was half a mile away and stumbling on all four paws before he realized he wasn't screaming anymore. Cinnamon had been right—the pain of changing to heal himself had damned near stopped his heart.

He reckoned it was worth it, even after his back end went out from under him for the umpteenth time as he ran toward Jacky's frantic yips that, just like Jacky had said, resounded from nearly two miles away.

The absolute fear thundering through his veins made every fracture in his still-healing bones throb with each pulse of blood.

Jacky and Katy, Jacky and Katy, Jacky and Katy....

He knew, had always known, that he was weaker than they were. He had always known that the most vulnerable place in his body was the place in his heart where the two of them dwelled, uneasy, hands wide over a balance beam of his own fear—fear that they would leave him, fear that he would let them down. He would rather have his heart explode. In fact, given the pain his body was in at the moment, he'd almost rather have his heart explode anyway.

But Teague was good with pain, and after all this time with people to care for, he was good at channeling it where it was needed. The first whiff of renegade werewolf mixed with crazy elf bitch turned that heartload of fear into ferocity. By the time he rounded the corner where his mates stood with their backs to the wall, Jacky ready to defend Katy with his dying breath and Katy using her clever mind for one last-ditch effort, he would have murdered anything that got in his way.

He ripped through the ranks of rabid-crazy elf bitch werewolves like a kid rips through a bag of potato chips, and he craved more. It wasn't until he drew up even with Jacky and saw Jack's horrified fascination with what was going on up above them that he realized the entire phalanx of werewolves was fatally preoccupied with what was going on above them as well. Finally his common sense kicked in, and with something *besides* blinding fear for his mates, he raised his muzzle to the sky.

He knew Nicky when he saw the first jumper, saw him change form in midair, and totally expected the fluttering of wings halfway down.

He identified Bracken and Cory about two seconds before they clutched each other like the lovers they were and fell out of the sky.

His entire identity spiraled with them. He realized with only a twinge of surprise that his life hinged on their survival as well. Here he was, standing in front of his lovers and certain death, while his devoted purpose for living, for being worthy of his lovers, plummeted from the sky in an attempt to keep them all safe.

He hadn't felt this dizzy when it was himself plummeting without bounds or hope to a place where his body shattered in defense of his realm. Oh Goddess. His lovers, his leaders, all of it whirled together, and he could not, even as he thought his heart would explode from pain once again, give priority to one or the other.

Then Cory and Bracken slowed in midair, stalled, hovered for a moment about twenty feet off the ground, and touched down lightly, right in front of Teague and his lovers. Nicky settled down next to them, and everybody, Nicky included, turned toward Cory. It was almost poetic, the way everyone was looking at Lady Corinne Carol-Anne Kirkpatrick op Crocken Green when she opened her mouth and spoke.

"Who in the fuck is responsible for this festering goat turd of a welcome party?"

By now there were over thirty werewolves in the bottleneck of the back alley, although nearly a third of them were recovering from wounds Teague had inflicted while plowing through that phalanx of bodies. One of the wolves in the lead growled low in his throat and changed, standing upright and scowling at Cory with malice and intent.

"Who wants to know?" He was ordinary—average height, average build, sandy brown hair, brownish eyes. In a way he could have been Teague, although Teague had more scars and a prettier face.

"I'm the consort to the leader of this part of California, asshole. You are threatening my people for doing nothing more than shopping by the beach. I want to know who put you up to it, and I want to know now!" Cory's brown-red hair was a mess. She was wearing cutoff shorts and a white T-shirt that was probably Bracken's, which meant that the neck sagged almost low enough to be indecent, but since she was also wearing a bright pink sports bra, it wasn't. She stood five feet two inches tall in her tennis shoes, and at the moment she would have looked like she hadn't slept in about two hundred years—except she only looked about sixteen years of age, period, total, grand sum.

And Teague wouldn't have wanted to meet her in a dark alley, for all of that. For one thing, the hum of power vibrating from her anger damned near turned the air red.

For another, Bracken was standing a little behind her with his hands out. Even as Cory spoke, he aimed that deadly power of blood at some of the werewolves Teague had injured, and they began to whimper and whine—and bleed through their wounds, which ordinarily would have been healing. Nicky was on her other side, and although he didn't look nearly as imposing, he did make them look like a solid team.

But the bad guy didn't see the threat—or maybe he didn't care.

"What're you gonna do if we just jump your shit, scary flying bitch? How are you going to find out what you want to know then?" The guy was looking sideways, his eyes shifty and frightened and, well, a little to the left of crazy. A little to the right of it too. Something about that off smell was not healthy—not for this guy, and not for the wolves that, now that Teague saw them whimpering, he shouldn't have been able to carve through so damned cleanly.

Cory took one look at that crazy and sighed. "Really?" she muttered to Bracken and Nicky, and probably to Teague, Jacky, and Katy too. "Does it always have to be buckets of nuts? Just once I want someone who's trying to take over the world to say, 'Hey, I've got a much better business plan… what do you think?' But no. We've got more nuts than gayporn dot com."

Bracken looked at her sideways. "That is the *last* time I let you stay up and play on the computer with Marcus and Phillip!"

Nicky chortled, but Teague glanced up and caught her sly, rather salacious grin in Bracken's direction and let out a little *whuff* to keep them focused on the business at hand. The bad guy realized he was being ignored and broke in.

"Hey, bitch, you didn't answer my question! What are you going to do about it if we just decide to take you out?" It was cold in Monterey, and maybe because Teague was a wolf and he was eye level, he noticed the guy's body didn't react well to the chilly fog that surrounded them.

Cory snorted and rolled her eyes. "I don't think you'll have to worry about it, chum bucket, since you'll be dead if that happens! Now, are you going to cough up a name and a location, or do I set Bracken loose on you? He was fucking cranky the entire trip here. He hates flying, and I gotta tell you, he really fucking wants to fucking kill something." The words were semifacetious, but Teague could smell the seething, terrified anger just oozing off the big sidhe. He glanced sharply at Brack and thought that someone who didn't know him would mistake the fear stink for fear of battle, but Teague had seen the guy in action and knew that wasn't what he was afraid of.

There was a movement at Teague's shoulder, and Teague looked sideways to see Jacky come abreast of him. Jacky whined and nuzzled Teague's ear, and Teague allowed himself to be licked. Yes, yes, why, he did need some comfort, why do you ask?

In that moment of peace, Teague scented something under Bracken's fear/hate musk, and his ears perked up. He whined and sneezed. Jacky looked at him, and then at Cory, and then at Bracken.

Passive-aggressive? Yes. Possessive and jealous? Absolutely. Shortsighted? Sometimes.

But nobody ever said Jacky was stupid.

Teague and Jacky both looked up at Cory, and Teague realized everything Kyle and Cinnamon had said the night before was absolutely the truth. That was their girl, their leader, their sorceress, and her body was gravid and quickening with the life of her lovers.

Teague and Jacky, as one wolf, growled low in their throats and stepped to either side of Cory, coming to stand between her and anything that threatened her.

Cory put her hand on Teague's head, and Jacky insinuated his head under her other hand. They both heard her surprised "Hmm," but that was all.

"Do you really think you can take all of us?" the lead werewolf was asking, and Cory snorted.

"Do you have any idea who we are? What we've done in the past?" she asked incredulously. "A week ago, we damned near took out Raphael's kiss in Redding for protecting a pedophile, and that was for someone we didn't know! Your people threatened my people. What do you think we're going to do to you?"

There was a moment of silence, and Teague saw something that looked like sanity cross the features of the crazy werewolf. "Whatever it is," he said quietly, "I wish you'd make it quick. She's killing us slow, and it hurts." Something happened then, a twisting, terrible thing, a line of crimson like an invisible wire cutting through the man's flesh. It writhed, it arced, it wrought a slow, wretched, painful line through his skin, and Cory swore.

"Oh fuck...."

Bracken also swore, and Nicky after him.

"Holy Goddess! Is that what I think it is?"

Then the man went wolf and launched himself at Cory with a howl that signaled an attack.

Jack and Teague launched themselves at him. Just as their jaws closed in on his throat, there was a terrible clanging like a bunch of pigeons hitting a cast-iron pan. Even as the head wolf's polluted blood flooded his mouth, Teague looked up for new enemies and saw the phalanx of enemy wolves hurling themselves against the shield Cory had erected between her people and their attackers with enough force to snap a wolf's neck.

Many wolves did just that and fell to the ground to pant and writhe in pain, awaiting an agonizing moment of healing.

"Jesus Christ," Nicky said after a few moments of horrible, horrible sounds and no indication of anybody stopping the madness. "Cory… Cory, I don't think they're going to stop."

"Me neither." Bracken looked at her, a very personal look. "They're being forced into this, beloved. They either kill us or die. I don't think whoever set them on us thought beyond that compulsion."

"Shit fuck sonuvabitch…." Cory shook her head and watched as what should have been a magnificent phalanx ocean of beautiful animals flung and broke themselves in wretched desperation. "I mean, Jesus. Don't they have to get tired of this? I just want to fucking talk to them!"

Her answer was more thudding, and she sighed. "The copter can't get us out, can it?"

Bracken shook his head. "Not unless you're up to levitating the lot of us up and over the buildings. I wouldn't try it. Especially with the chopper here."

"Emphasis on 'chop,'" Nicky murmured, in case she didn't get the danger of throwing a mass of people up toward the whirling blades.

"Yeah, yeah, I hear you. Shit—" That last sounded like she'd been interrupted, and Bracken's sigh had a distinctly relieved feel. Good. It was very possible that Green had stepped in with a plan.

Cory's people stood there and waited—waited for sanity to take over, waited for the wolves to stop killing themselves on Cory's shield and come to their senses. After what seemed an eternity of frenzied howls and horrible, cracking thuds, Teague looked up from the corpse of the head werewolf and spat out the heart he had savaged from the body.

Cory was still speaking to Green in her head, and the conversation wasn't going her way.

"I get it," she said out loud, her eyes looking decidedly elsewhere. "They're not going to stop. Green, someone's going to notice…"

She paused.

"But… they're being *compelled*. Damn it, it's not their fault!"

The shield around them flared and brightened, and when Teague looked up, he saw Bracken's hand on her shoulder.

"Don't fight him, beloved," Bracken said softly. "Please. For us." Their choices were obvious. She could take them out with her power—she was entirely capable of doing it. Or they could fight their way out physically, and that…. Teague felt his wobbling back end, looked to where his mates—not their best fighters—were listening tautly to the conversation.

Oh God. Teague's mates.

Cory swallowed hard. "It feels cowardly," she said through a husked throat, and Teague looked outside the shell that enclosed them and realized Green was right. He didn't even have to hear what Green was ordering to know he was right.

He was going to change so he could talk to her, convince her why it was a forgivable sin, but the thought of changing made him want to whimper. Suddenly Jack was human, wrapping his arms around Teague's neck and kneeling before his queen. He still had blood on his muzzle from the man—was it the leader? Was it Cujo?—they had taken down together, but he still looked beautiful and innocent for all that.

"Please, Lady Cory," Jack said humbly with clear eyes. "Please. You'd fight them by yourself, and you'd probably win, but we can't take that chance. Bracken would be by your side, and Teague and I would guard your flanks, but… but they're crazed. This whole thing isn't sane. They're tortured and in pain, and whoever is in charge, well, I don't think she's going to stop. This whole crazy-elf-bitch thing, it's big and it's bad and it's going to bite us in the ass, but not today. Today…." There was another horrible thunking clatter of broken necks and pitiful whimpers. Jack closed his eyes, and Teague licked his face.

Teague's body hurt, now that he was still. His body hurt, and his breath labored in his chest, and his nerve endings were bitching at him like wolf claws on a chalkboard a thousand miles long. The prolonged pain was starting to make him shiver.

But still he knew how to keep his pain to himself, so he didn't have to do what he did next. It should have hurt his pride like a mortal wound, because his whole life, of all the things he'd ever refused to ask for, refused to reach for, mercy was at the top of his list.

But Jack was in danger, and he wanted his mates, and his queen should be resting and nurturing what he and Jack could smell growing inside her, and damn it, what good was being a knight, serving his queen, loving his mates, if pride got in the goddamned way?

He whimpered.

He whimpered, and Cory fell to her knees before him and reached up gently to stroke his head. He leaned into her touch, and she sighed and looked up.

"Right," she murmured and stood up heavily, ignoring Bracken's offered hand. He grabbed her hand anyway and locked it between his, and she sighed and glared at the shield in front of them. It grew impossibly bright, a tiny solar flare in a back alley of a seaside town, and the next phalanx of furry bodies that hurtled against it caught fire and conflagrated before the tortured wolves even knew they were dead.

"Please take the—" Before she could finish the sentence, the next wave crashed against the shield, immolated to ash, and died. And the next. And the next. Every time a body hit or a werewolf howled, singed but still rushing the wall of death, Cory whimpered and tightened her grip on Bracken's hand until Teague heard him grunt. And the pretty wall of death flared brighter and cleaner until there were no more werewolves left at all.

They all sat there for a moment, staring into the vacant alleyway in horrified silence. Then the shield dropped abruptly, and Cory burst into tears.

Teague's back end flopped uselessly behind him, and he sank to the ground, resting his chin on his paws with a whine of concern. He watched as Bracken swung her up like a parent with a six-year-old and held her to his chest as she came completely apart.

Katy was suddenly a wolf again, licking Teague's nose and ears in comfort, in concern, but Jacky stayed human. By the time a giant black bird landed in the alleyway and turned into LaMark, Jack had hoisted himself to his feet.

"Jesus," LaMark breathed quietly to Jack. "What the hell happened? We got a call saying you were surrounded. Where'd everybody go?"

Jack grimaced. "Man, this is not my story."

Nicky leaned over and kissed the top of Cory's head, then sighed.

"It's not anybody's. Is Mario nearby with the car?"

There was a rumble at the end of the alleyway, and Mario hopped out of what looked to be Arturo's Cadillac. If nothing else, that broke the cycle of sobbing that had taken over Cory's body.

"Jesus, Mario! That man must love you like a son."

Mario grinned, the smile lovely in his Latin, lean-cheeked features. "Of course, *chica*! You ever doubt it?" The grin faded and Mario looked at the little group again, making eye contact with LaMark, who shrugged his shoulders.

Cory started to sob again, and *everybody's* eyes met, and Bracken suddenly took charge. "Mario, please tell me you have some pants in there. A shirt. Something. *Somebody* is gonna arrest Jacky and Katy for indecent exposure or something."

Jack bent down and, heedless of his junk just flapping in the breeze, put his arms underneath Teague to pick him up. Teague made a wolf grunt and picked up his own back end. What? He'd already asked for help once. He'd whimpered, for sweet chrissakes!

"Tough," Jack said roughly in his ear, sinking to an ugly-naked crouch and apparently not giving a shit. "Tough, you dumb Irish motherfucker. You're in pain, and I need to hold you, and you're going to let me pick you up because—" Jacky's voice about broke, and he had to breathe hard through his nose to finish. "—because if I have to watch you fall down one more time, it's going to break something in me, and I'm going to be like our lady, okay? We *are* a team, and you *are* my beloved, and she *is* my queen, and only one of us in our little group gets to lose it at a time, and right now, she's got dibs."

Teague sighed as only a wolf or an old dog can, and Jack hoisted him and stood. Teague wondered briefly if changing into a man might not solidify all the hairline fractures that were making him ache so viciously. It was not as bad… not *nearly* as bad as it had been the first day, and it was certainly not a *fraction* of the pain he'd endured to turn wolf, but it was irritating and distracting, and he felt useless and infantile with his forepaws dangling from Jacky's arms and Katy trotting along behind them. He must have shifted, made some sign, sighed, or tightened his body, because Jacky growled, "Don't even think about it, you stubborn asshole. I'm not kidding. I'll kick you out of my bed for a *month*."

Teague lifted his head and stared, surprised, because Jacky *loved* being in Teague's bed and they both knew it. But Jack's soft, wide mouth was firm and his pretty blue eyes were burning bright with anger and pain for Teague, and Teague suddenly knew how Cory had felt for the last week. He managed an ingratiating wolfy smile before Jack altered his stride to avoid some glass and the jouncing hurt worse than he was expecting.

He stopped a whine before it came out and flopped limply in Jack's arms. He felt like shit. He'd put himself in danger, and they were pissed. He wanted them to forgive him for that, because he needed them more than they could ever imagine, more than they could possibly ever need him, and Cory depended on him, so he needed his heart to be okay.

He raised his head to where Bracken was tucking himself into the back seat with Cory on his lap. Their little Goddess was down to deep breaths and little sniffles as she fought to control herself. Yeah. He knew exactly how she felt, he realized, and he forgave her a little too.

Nicky whispered something to Bracken, who nodded. With a leap and a flutter of feathers, he was a bird again, setting off toward Cinnamon's in the sea-scented air. LaMark followed, so there was enough room in the Cadillac without Jack or Katy having to turn wolf.

Together they huddled in the car as Mario drove them back to Cinnamon's tiny faerie hill on the cliffs of Pebble Beach.

Planning

GREEN'S VOICE over the phone was quiet as he planned and tried very hard not to panic or make assumptions.

"You're sure it was our mark?" he asked for the seventh time. As horrible as that moment had been, that image was not going away.

"I was there that night," I said softly. "So was Bracken. So, for that matter, were Nicky, Mario, and LaMark, if they'd gotten a chance to see it. I know what it looks like when our mark cuts through the skin of a traitor."

We were both quiet for a moment. Our mark—the tattoo of oak leaves, lime tree leaves, and twining, thornless roses I'd had etched voluntarily into my flesh, and my friends had gotten in order to show their allegiance to me. Anybody who joined Green's people had a mark like that blown through their skin. Bracken had one twining around his wrist. Katy's was on her ankle. Teague's was on the inside of his wrist and palm. Jack's was… well… *private*, for lack of a better word.

But we'd seen this mark the first night it had been issued, the night Green and I and everybody who loved us had blown touch, blood, and song through everyone in our part of the country and given them a choice. Follow us or die.

A few people had chosen to die horribly, that mark carving through their skin and flesh and bone until it finally reached their hearts.

That mark, which had been designed to guarantee the loyalty of the people who followed us, had been used to punish the disloyalty of people who followed our enemies. The ways this could happen… well, they were few, and they were terrifying.

"Do you know anything else?" Green asked at last, his voice heavy. I shifted on the couch next to Bracken and burrowed closer against his chest. We were huddling in the sitting room at Cinnamon's while Teague rested in the big hospital bed that overlooked the ocean. Jacky and Katy were stretched out next to him, naked and uncaring, because Teague had looked like shit when we finally got here to this little slice of fey in central California.

And we really didn't know much, sadly. We didn't know if that was all the wolves she had—but it had to be close!—and we didn't even know if the guy who'd spoken to us was Cujo. Somehow I didn't think so. I figured any guy flamboyant enough to take that name would probably have bragged about it a little, even if he wanted to die.

"One thing," I said softly, looking at the werewolves shivering in their sleep. "I know all the wolves said they smelled like crazy elf bitch."

Green made a sound particular to the moments when he was pinching the bridge of his nose with his finger and thumb. "Of course," he said. "There's really only one way to pass that particular magic along, luv. We knew that."

"She had to feed them her blood," I said out loud, for all of us. Touch, blood, and song. She might have slept with every werewolf there, that was true, but to keep up the power of the borrowed mark? It had to be done often, and it had to be done thoroughly, and it had to be done well. A combination, I thought now, sickly. It was probably a combination of sexual fluids, forced sharing among the pack, and a gift of sweet sidhe blood for those who pleased her.

There was a horrible, weighted silence in the fog-bright twilight of Cinnamon's sitting room.

"Do you think this was what drove the werewolves this last winter?" I asked, thinking out loud. I almost jumped out of my skin when Teague answered, shifting painfully on the bed and trying hard not to disturb his sleeping lovers.

"I'm thinking," he mumbled. "I'm thinking it had to be something. We never did get any explanations, you know? Why they were acting like that, why they'd come and take over. But the smell wasn't there— maybe she hadn't kicked up the magic yet to get them to do her thing."

"I'm sorry, weren't you supposed to be healing?" I asked him, letting my irritated bitch slip, and underneath my head I heard Bracken grunt with something like humor. Cinnamon had bitched Teague out but good for leaving the house AMA, and I was pretty pissed myself. All of this—what? He didn't trust us to have their backs?

"Now, beloved…," Green prompted gently on the phone— reminding me how much he could hear, actually!—and I sighed. Teague was looking at me with that angel's mouth all twisted, as though he knew *exactly* what I was thinking.

"I think you're right," I said by way of apology. He untwisted his mouth, and I rolled my eyes. "I think you're right—and you know what?" I brightened at this thought.

"Thrill me," said Teague.

At the same time, Green said, "By all means, tell us what?"

Bracken didn't say anything. He just sat there like a big giant breathing rock and soaked it all in. All the better to talk about later, I guess.

"I think there are not that many werewolves she can throw away at a time," I said. They both blinked as though they hadn't thought of that before. "That's why the first guy we killed last winter—the psycho. She was trying to recruit. We took out her first crew in November, and it's taken her this long to build another crew. I'll leave the vampires to look around, but I'm betting she's long gone, just like she blew out of LA when we took her guys out before. I mean, whatever this was—and I'm thinking it's just a matter of means and opportunity, you know? She smelled some of Green's people, and she thought she could take them out—she blew all her guys on it. She's not going to go after us until she's got another crew, and we've got at least a week or two to figure out what's going on." It didn't sound like much—not really—but given we'd been in Redding a week ago, it could have been worse.

"That *is* happy news," Teague mumbled. I smiled at him from the couch, and I might have moved to talk to him face-to-face, but Bracken's arm tightened around my chest, and I figured maybe not.

"It definitely means you can rest and heal up, wolfman," I told him softly. He barely nodded before his eyes closed again and he went back to where he should have been. Fast asleep.

"That goes for you too, beloved," Green said softly. Bracken grunted above me, and I remembered how tired I was. I'd fallen asleep on the helicopter ride over. In a thousand years, I would not have even *fathomed* that was possible. I'd never been in a helicopter in my *life*, and there I was, looking out the window and thinking, "Ooohh... pretty!" and suddenly we were over Monterey.

It had been Nicky who had spotted Jack and Katy, and... well... it hadn't looked good. I'd gone from drooling on Brack's shoulder to saying, "Hey! Let's jump out of a helicopter together!" in about two seconds. I guess the major guilt meltdown was something that came with the mood swing, right? I hoped so. I was known for long-standing, angsty, self-directed guilt/blame fests. The violent moments of remorse were sort of a new development.

But suddenly Green's voice in my ear, Bracken's arms around me, and that whole adrenaline-bleed/tantrum afterglow was working on me, and I was abruptly so tired I couldn't think. I felt Bracken gently take the phone from me as I mumbled, "'Bye, beloved," and then I was asleep in his arms. I didn't even feel him move me, but when I woke up the next morning—starving!—we were in a guest bedroom down the hall, with Bracken on one side of me and Nicky on the other.

We stayed for two days. One to rest up and kill the whole idea with discussion and see if the birdmen or vampires could sniff out any more crazy elf bitch, and the other to go sightseeing, because I'd been right. Crazy elf bitch was apparently nowhere to be seen, heard, or smelled.

Jacky and Katy took us around the town. Teague could hobble around by then, so we walked along Cannery Row and bought a zillion tons of fudge and ate clam chowder out of a sourdough bowl and sat on the beach for a long, long, peaceful time while I leaned into Bracken's arms, watched Nicky and the other birds fly above us, and reflected that Bracken hadn't been angry at me for nearly three days.

I cried on him a lot in those two days. Something about the awfulness of letting those bodies hurl themselves into death....

I wasn't sure I would ever get over it. That sort of violent mind-fuck leaves a terrible, sick wound.

But Teague and his lovers were at peace. That was the only way I could describe it.

From the moment Teague and Jacky had arrived on our doorstep this last fall, there had always been conflict, pain, and a terrible make-fit between what Teague's lovers wanted for him and what Teague was willing to reach for himself.

Jacky had hated me for it. Teague had wanted so badly to serve, and Jacky had resented the hell out of my place in Teague's life, and Teague had been so torn. Serve me, serve Jacky—the conflict had brought us some truly painful moments.

But not now.

I wasn't sure I'd ever know what impulse brought Jack to the front to guard me, shoulder to shoulder with his mate. I didn't know how I had rated that sort of loyalty from a man who had always seemed so sure I deserved nothing from him at all—especially since I'd been the one to let Teague down in the most real of ways.

But I did. And now that Jacky had declared his allegiance to us, I guessed Teague felt like his allegiances were perfectly clear. And Katy?

Well, Katy had always loved them both. Unconditionally. I liked to think her life was a little bit easier now.

The last day, as we were sitting at the beach, she came to sit next to me for a moment. Bracken took the moment to wander off in search of food—he'd been eating a lot lately and kept trying to drag me down into his evil vortex of calorie consumption as well. I wished he'd stop. Not only was I sort of queasy these days, but it was making me feel bloated.

"How you doing?" I asked, enjoying her pretty smile. Katy was always so quiet and self-possessed. I felt grubby next to her, and green and young, but she seemed to like me, and I was honored that she wanted to be my friend.

"I think we're going to live. How 'bout you?"

I shrugged. "You know us. Nothing's bleeding, Bracken and I aren't fighting, all must be right with the world."

Katy leaned in to me and spoke quietly. In the house, with all that wood to echo, she might as well have been shouting to the heavens—but here at the beach, with the waves and the wind, the gulls and the far-off sea lions… well, I'd never thought of it, but this must be what real privacy felt like.

"You know Teague bonded to us, right?"

I stared at her, surprised. Teague's lack of bonding had been a source of concern for him and contention with Jacky practically since their marriage ceremony back in February. He'd actually come to me and Bracken about it—an act of self-revelation that had been the equivalent of Teague going without his skin.

"That's wonderful!" I said, meaning it. I would never doubt his loyalty—I was just glad he was happy.

"You want to know why?" she asked, putting an earnest hand on my knee, and I blushed.

"If you're going to give me details about your sex lives, no."

Katy laughed, and it was low and charming. Then she shook her head. "No, not like that. He bonded because he and Jacky, they're on the same team now. They're on your team. You—I know you feel bad about what you had to do to keep us safe, to make that battle go. I know you do. But you protected your people, you protected yourself. It can be an ugly world, you know?"

I nodded, not wanting to think about it. Even here, looking out on the expanse of blue ocean, came with the knowledge of ugliness. Somewhere out there, man's dumb fucking ignorance and greed had made a place like this a sewer of filth, and men didn't have a corner on the ignorance and greed market—although they did seem to have mastered the self-destruction caveat that came with it.

"I know," I said softly. Oh Goddess. All the blood on my hands— how could I not?

"Well, you kept it beautiful for us," she murmured. I smiled back, feeling weepy. I really wished this whole aftermath thing or whatever that was just ripping my emotions all over the planet would go away. I hated crying.

"You guys make me believe in beauty," I told her, and we both looked to where Teague, in a rare moment of true relaxation, was leaning back into Jacky's arms like any other lover on the beach. He really was beautiful. They all were. Maybe like me and my lovers… or, well, at least my lovers.

"They almost don't need me," she said softly, and I shook my head, positive that wasn't true.

"They'd self-destruct without you," I told her, meaning it. "You're the chocolate in the middle of the cookie, sweetheart. They'd crumble without you."

Katy laughed, the kind of laugh where she threw her head back and shouted that laughter to the blue sky. "A good thing to hear, *mami*. I like to think that myself."

Then she stood and kissed my cheek. "I know you want to go home tonight, but you take care of yourself, okay? You don't go do no ninja-bitch shit without your men. Not until they're okay with it, right? We need you. We'd die for you. You gotta give us a reason to believe."

I shrugged, embarrassed, but before I could come up with a reply, Bracken was there with a couple of loaves of sourdough bread, some hummus, and some salami, and suddenly I was starving. We called the guys over and had an impromptu picnic there in the sand, and Mario and LaMark and Nicky came in from where they'd been circling over the waves and landed, and we fed their bird forms salami and bread with ginger fingers.

It was a good day, but I was still happy when it was over and we were purring through the night in the back of the Cadillac on our way home to see Green.

Jack and Teague and Katy would be along in a few days, I knew, and I hoped the privacy would do them good.

Teague—Being

It had been hard to see Cory and the others go, but she'd left the vampires there for protection on the ride home, and Joshua had doubled the hill's magic perimeter, and it was obvious that Cory needed the solace of the hill.

All Teague needed was the solace of his lovers.

When Cory and Bracken left, they were able to move the big hospital bed out of the living room, which made it a much more comfortable space, and Jack, Teague, and Katy all got to sleep down in the guest bedroom in the big king-sized bed.

Teague would remember forever the moment he awoke the morning after his queen had left and it was just him and his lovers, skin to skin, without any pain to come between them.

Cinnamon had kicked Jack and Katy out of the room the night before, laying hands on his shoulders, his neck, his hips, and his thighs for the first time since she'd relieved his pain so he could turn from wolf to man. Another less than stellar moment in his history—if she hadn't been there, he was pretty sure he would have thrown up or passed out. *Goddess*, he was tired of pain. Her touch was as impersonal as it had always been, but she stopped in the middle and looked up.

"You're bonded, werewolf."

Teague had blushed and nodded. He'd felt it earlier that evening when he'd offered Ellis a quick snack from his wrist. It was courtesy—all the werecreatures offered blood easily after their first months on the hill. Teague was no exception, and Ellis, a pretty kid with a hot temper, had reminded Teague a lot of Jacky, in spite of his smaller stature and slighter frame. But when Ellis had bitten and endorphins had flooded Teague's bloodstream— the pain cessation, especially after they had brought him home after the attack, had been exquisite—the endorphins had been all he'd felt.

There had been no arousal, no awareness, no… anything.

Katy had told him the night before that she'd felt it. He'd understood what she meant when Ellis licked his skin and he didn't even notice a strong hand held his wrist. Cinnamon's happy, clinical prodding confirmed it.

"I have," he said quietly.

"So what changed?" the elf wanted to know. She sounded concerned—and he couldn't blame her, since he'd set himself up to be the queen's bodyguard and all.

"Jacky did," Teague told her, his voice resonating chest-deep with pride.

Cinnamon looked at him with something approaching fondness. "So your beta wolf is truly your partner now. That is something. How'd you manage that?"

Teague blushed. "I didn't do anything," he muttered. "Jacky did it all by himself."

Cinnamon laughed. "Oh, aren't you lucky, Master Werewolf. As it turns out, some things don't need to be reached for—they just come to you if you earn them."

Teague thought about that whimper. The one time in his life he'd ever let weakness voluntarily escape him. "I reached a little," he confessed, embarrassed.

Two maternal fingers grasped his chin and forced him to meet a quizzical pair of red-brown eyes with more than enough wisdom for the both of them.

"Something you should never be embarrassed about, sir knight," Cinnamon said softly. "And you know in your bones that's something Green would tell you as well."

Teague's mouth twitched up at the ends. "Cory too."

"Cory too."

She'd pronounced him sound and whole, if still a little weak. The weakness would continue for another week or so—as well as the hairlessness where the plaster of the cast had ripped at his hair as he'd transitioned—but he was perfectly able to walk, run, and as she said, get in on some of the hot werewolf action that had been going on in his mates' bed.

Of course, when he'd gotten to bed the night before, Jacky and Katy were nearly asleep and just so glad to have him there between them that "hot werewolf action" consisted of lots of snuggling and skin stroking and that was about it.

This morning, Teague woke up between his mates and was very, very aware that his body was sound and whole and well and hungry.

He wrapped his arms around Katy and pulled her tight, pressing his erection into the soft flesh of her backside, and she groaned.

"Oh, I missed this…mmmm…."

"Missed this"—*snuggle*—"or missed *that*?" He thrust his hips forward. She giggled, and then Jacky did the same thing to Teague that Teague was doing to Katy.

Teague groaned, tightened his embrace around Katy, and shuddered. Oh Christ. He… he could barely *breathe* for the fire of want that pulsed in his belly and racked his limbs. Katy stopped giggling and with a quick move shucked her panties to her knees and then kicked them off. She took Teague's arm, which was wrapped around her shoulders, and shifted so his hand was on her breast, and her nipple butted hard and insistent and tender under his palm. Jack's hand came around his hips, and when Katy angled her thigh, Jack grasped Teague's cock and placed him at Katy's already slick entrance. Katy moaned and slid down him, and Teague's body flooded with desire and *must have must have must have must have*….

He was pounding into Katy hard enough to shake the bed, and Jacky was at his back, caressing his shoulders, his back, his hips, and Teague… oh Goddess, he wanted them both *so bad*… so damned bad….

Jacky's big hands framed his face from behind, and Teague leaned tensely into them. Two fingers slipped into his mouth, and Teague sucked on them hard while his hips continued to move. He wanted more pressure, he wanted more control than he could get at this angle, but he didn't want to lose Jacky at his back, so he kept doing what he was doing. Katy groaned and lifted her leg, throwing it backward around his knees, and he used that to move faster. Then Jack pulled the fingers from his mouth, and—

Oh Christ.

Jack had never done this before. He'd never even tried it before. He knew Teague had issues, he'd been respectful of Teague's boundaries, but his fingers… they traced their way to Teague's backside, to his entrance. He stopped for a moment, but Teague forced himself to keep moving, so Jack took advantage. Keeping pace with Teague's rhythm, he slid a finger inside Teague's asshole, and for a minute Teague's rhythm was actually the shuddering of his body as a new element of intimacy, a new pleasure, almost made him lose track of what he was doing.

Another finger joined it, and together they started to stretch. Teague made a noise, a throbbing, cracked cry into Katy's shoulder, and tried to keep his head while he thrust inside her with as much force as he could.

Jacky was going to… he was going to… he wanted to….

There was a snick—Jack must have kept the bottle by the bed—and then the fingers inside him grew oily and slick, and they were stretching, making him loose, easing inside him, making him ready.

Jack spoke into the hollow of his ear. "You have to want this. I know it feels good, but you have to want this. You'll have the rhythm. You'll have the control. And you'll have both of us. Do you want this?"

Teague could only grunt and nod. His pounding stopped for a moment, and he stayed still, quivering, while Katy whimpered and writhed around him, tightening her muscles and begging him for more.

Jack's fingers stretched him wide, and Teague whimpered just like Katy. Then Jack's cock took their place, and Teague couldn't help the sound, the roar that came out of him. He thrashed for a moment—backward until Jack was buried to the hilt, forward until he was buried in Katy, and then back again. Everything in his body sang fire. Every pulse of his blood screamed pleasure. It was them, his lovers inside him and outside him. He was cloaked in the flesh of those he loved best.

He lost finesse and reason and just kept moving, just kept fucking, being fucked, being loved, searing the feeling of Jacky's cock deeply inside his body and glorying in the wet heat of Katy as it sucked at him and gave him power.

Then Jack adjusted his angle and hit something inside Teague, and he came just a little. He thrust forward and then back and came just a little again, and again, and again, and again, until his eyes were blind and the screams coming out of his mouth and into Katy's hair were hoarse and ragged.

"*Papi!*" Katy screamed—in agony, she was so close—and Teague remembered his responsibilities and moved his hand down her mound, fumbling for a moment with the fleshy slickness of her until he found the swollen bundle of nerves that would send her over. Over she went, screaming into her shoulder, spasming around him, gripping him so tight it was almost painful. Then Jack thrust so hard into him that Teague was surprised *Jack* wasn't fucking Katy, and Teague's vision went black and stars exploded behind his eyes. His cock swelled and spurted, his orgasm burning through it, and even as he felt Jacky come in his body, he came into Katy's.

They couldn't speak for a few moments—none of them. They just trembled around each other, blind and panting and grateful.

Katy turned in his arms and kissed him. She tasted so sweet—God, he loved kissing her. She was everything a woman should taste like, sweet and tart, and wet and soft and willing. Then Jack's hand came around and cupped his chin, and they managed an awkward, needing kiss from behind, and Teague almost cried with the taste of Jack on his tongue. His Jacky—his and no one else's. Jacky, who stood beside him, who would stand beside him as they did their job and served their queen and made a life for their family that they could be proud of and protect. He didn't cry, because Teague didn't cry. But it was a near thing.

Eventually, though, their breathing stilled, and Teague's stomach grumbled, and Katy laughed and kissed him again and slid out of his arms. "I'll go fix you two breakfast, okay, *papi*? Let me shower first, and I'll be back." She stopped and looked at them firmly.

"And no fights while I'm gone. I don't want to get back and find Teague halfway to home because Jacky was an asshole, okay? You promise me, okay?"

Teague smiled his best fuck-me grin. "Sugar, I promise I have no plans today that involve moving far from this bed."

Behind him, he heard Jack gasp—because Teague was a workaholic and they all knew it—but Katy took him at his word. She came back to bed and kissed his forehead.

"I'll hold you to that. Us in bed, all day. Tonight we take a tour of the property as wolves. It'll be good. I love you—even you, Jacky, you asshole. Let me make you breakfast."

And then she disappeared, leaving Jacky—still inside Teague, still deliciously there even though he was growing soft in the come that had filled Teague just moments ago—chuckling in his ear.

"You liked that?" he asked, needing reassurance, and Teague nodded carefully.

"Not all the time," he asserted, because he did like to be in charge, and he *really* liked to fuck Jacky blind, but… but this morning, it had been perfect.

"Oh, of course," Jacky said, the smile evident in his voice. "I love you, you know. I'd do anything for you. I'd let you fuck me blind every day of the week"—and he often had—"but sometimes… sometimes I want to give to you too. Is that okay?"

Teague smiled a little and closed his eyes even as Jacky slid out of his body and warm spend began to trickle down Teague's thighs. "That's fine, beloved. You and me—as long as we're together and Katy's there with us, I think everything is fine."

It would have to be, he thought, clasping Jack's arm to his chest. Cory was pregnant. She'd be helpless. She'd need them, probably all three of them. But Jacky was with him. Jacky would help him serve. It was, he realized, all he'd ever wanted and feared to reach for.

He'd keep reaching for it now. He would, because his mates needed him, and he'd reach for anything to keep them happy.

Even happiness for himself. Even the contentment of just, for the moment, being.

Purple

Amy's Alternative Universe Romance

Amy Lane is a mother of two grown kids, two half-grown kids, two small dogs, and half-a-clowder of cats. A compulsive knitter who writes because she can't silence the voices in her head, she adores fur-babies, knitting socks, and hawt menz, and she dislikes moths, cat boxes, and knuckleheaded macspazzmatrons. She is rarely found cooking, cleaning, or doing domestic chores, but she has been known to knit up an emergency hat/blanket/pair of socks for any occasion whatsoever or sometimes for no reason at all. Her award-winning writing has three flavors: twisty-purple alternative universe, angsty-orange contemporary, and sunshine-yellow happy. By necessity, she has learned to type like the wind. She's been married for twenty-five-plus years to her beloved Mate and still believes in Twu Wuv, with a capital Twu and a capital Wuv, and she doesn't see any reason at all for that to change.

Website: www.greenshill.com

Blog: www.writerslane.blogspot.com
Email: amylane@greenshill.com
Facebook: www.facebook.com/amy.lane.167
Twitter: @amymaclane

Redemption comes in many forms.

GREEN'S HILL

Werewolves

Volume One

AMY LANE

In the world of the Little Goddess

Teague Sullivan and Jack Barnes work in the dangerous gray area between the natural and supernatural worlds, helping people who get separated from the safety of Green's Hill find their way home. Teague's in the game for redemption—but Jack's in the game for Teague.

Teague is damaged, haunted, and about the loneliest man Jack has ever met, but Jack sees beyond Teague's scars and gruffness to the kindness and bravery underneath. Teague is pretty sure Jack's a green idealist—a scarred old dog like Teague will never be good enough for a sweet young pup like his Jacky.

When Jack is injured, the two hunters are sucked into the paranormal world they've been defending. Teague must reevaluate everything he's believed about their relationship. While Teague is sorting out his life both with Jacky and as a member of Green's Hill, Katy steps into the mix. She's loved Teague since she was a child, and that love has only gotten stronger now that they've survived into adulthood. Teague Sullivan, who has lived "without" since he was born, is suddenly given all the things that make live worth living "with." Does Teague have the courage to reach for two lovers and a place on Green's Hill?

www.dsppublications.com

AMY LANE

The Green's Hill Novellas

A Green's Hill Collection
Companion to the Little Goddess Series

Welcome to Green's Hill, a small, secret collective of the fey, furry, and undead, existing unnoticed in the California foothills for over a hundred and fifty years. Whether your passion is exotic were-animals, angels, elves, or vampires, you can find them here—although things are changing on the hill.

Bound by love and honor, Cory, Green, and Adrian work to give their followers a home—but they have no idea that the effects of their true love will spread like ripples in a pond.

Be prepared for the unexpected, and ready for enchantment—you never know who will be awakened to the romantic possibilities of a vampire, a sorceress, or a pansexual elf who finds power in the force of love.

This anthology includes:

Litha's Constant Whim

It is on Litha that Whim meets Charlie, and their vows to return next Litha and finish what they started launch a thirteen-year tradition of celebration.

I Love You, Asshole!

It's a good thing vampires live forever, because it might take Marcus that long to convince Phillip that gender lines are for the living.

Guarding the Vampire's Ghost

An accident of divine politics has put Adrian, a twice-dead vampire, in heaven and under the care of angels Shepherd and Jefischa.

www.dsppublications.com

Vulnerable

The First Book of the Little Goddess series

AMY LANE

Little Goddess: Book One

Working graveyards in a gas station seems a small price for Cory to pay to get her degree and get the hell out of her tiny town. She's terrified of disappearing into the aimless masses of the lost and the young who haunt her neck of the woods. Until the night she actually stops looking at her books and looks up. What awaits her is a world she has only read about—one filled with fantastical creatures that she's sure she could never be.

And then Adrian walks in, bearing a wealth of pain, an agonizing secret, and a hundred and fifty years with a lover he's afraid she won't understand. In one breathless kiss, her entire understanding of her own worth and destiny is turned completely upside down. When her newfound world explodes into violence and Adrian's lover—and prince—walks into the picture, she's forced to explore feelings and abilities she's never dreamed of. The first thing she discovers is that love doesn't fit into nice neat little boxes. The second thing is that risking your life is nothing compared to facing who you really are—and who you'll kill to protect.

www.dsppublications.com

Wounded
Volume One
The Second Book of the Little Goddess series
AMY LANE

Wounded
Volume Two
The Second Book of the Little Goddess series
AMY LANE

Little Goddess: Book Two, Vol. 1

Cory fled the foothills to deal with the pain of losing Adrian, and Green watched her go. Separately, they could easily grieve themselves to death, but when an old enemy of Green's brings them back together, they can no longer hide from their grief—or their love for each other.

But Cory's grieving has cut her off from the emotional stability that's the source of her power, and Green's worry for her has left them both weak. Cory's strength comes from love, and she finds that when she's in the presence of Adrian's best friend, Bracken, she feels stronger still.

But defeating their enemy is by no means a sure thing. As the attacks against Cory and her lovers keep coming, it becomes clear that their love might not be enough if they can't heal each other—and themselves—from the wounds that almost killed them all.

Little Goddess: Book Two, Vol. 2

Green and Bracken's beloved survived their enemy's worst—with help from unexpected vampiric help.

But survival is a long way from recovery, and even further from safety. Green's people want badly to return to the Sierra Foothills, but they're not going with their tails between their legs. Before they go home, they have to make sure they're free from attack—and that they administer a healthy dose of revenge as well.

As Cory negotiates a fragile peace between her new and unexpected lovers, Green negotiates the unexpected power that comes from being a beloved leader of the paranormal population. Together, they might heal their own wounds and lead their people to an unprecedented place at the top of the supernatural food chain—a place that will allow them to return home a better, stronger whole.

www.dsppublications.com

Bound
Volume One
The Third Book of the Little Goddess series
AMY LANE

Bound
Volume Two
The Third Book of the Little Goddess series
AMY LANE

Little Goddess: Book Three
Vol. 1

Humans have the option of separation, divorce, and heartbreak. For Corinne Carol-Anne Kirkpatrick, sorceress and queen of the vampires, the choices are limited to love or death. Now that she is back at Green's Hill and assuming her duties as leader, her life is, at best, complicated. Bracken and Nicky are competing for her affections, Green is away taking care of his people, and a new supernatural enemy is threatening the sanctity of all she has come to love. Throw in a family reunion gone bad, a supernatural psychiatrist, and a killer physics class, and Cory's life isn't just complex, it's psychotic.

Cory needs to get her act and her identity together, and soon, because the enemy she and her lovers are facing is a nightmare that doesn't just kill people, it unmakes them. If she doesn't figure out who she is and what her place is on Green's Hill, it's not just her life on the line. She knows from hard experience that the only thing worse than facing death is facing the death of someone she loves.

Loving people is easy—living with them is what takes the real work, and it's even harder if you're bound.

Little Goddess: Book Three
Vol. 2

Cory's newly bound family is starting to find its footing, which is a good thing because danger after danger threatens, and Green can't be there nearly as often as he's needed. As Cory learns to face the challenges of ruling the hill alone, she's also juggling a *ménage* relationship with three lovers—with mixed results.

But with each new challenge, one lesson becomes crystal clear: she can't be queen without each of the men who look to her, and the people she loves aren't safe unless she takes on that queendom with all of the intelligence and courage in her formidable heart.

But sometimes even intelligence, courage, and steadily increasing magic aren't enough to do the job, and suddenly the role of Cory's lovers becomes more crucial than ever. Nobody is strong enough to succeed in every task, and Cory finds that the most painful lesson she and her lovers can learn is not just how to deal with failure. Cory needs to learn that one woman is only so powerful, and she needs to choose wisely who sits outside her circle of family, and who is bound eternally in her heart.

www.dsppublications.com

Rampant _{Volume} One

The Fourth Book of the Little Goddess series

AMY LANE

Little Goddess: Book Four
Vol. 1

Lady Cory has carved out a life for herself not just as a wife to three husbands but also as one of the rulers of the supernatural communities of Northern California—and a college student in search of that elusive degree. When a supernatural threat comes crashing into the hard-forged peace of Green's Hill, she and Green determine that they're the ones in charge of stopping the abomination that created it. To protect the people they love, Cory, Bracken, and Nicky travel to Redding to confront a tight-knit family of vampires guarding a terrible secret. It also leads them to a conflict of loyalties, as Nicky's parents threaten to tear Nicky away from the family he's come to love more than his own life.

Cory has to work hard to hold on to her temper and her life as she tries to prove that she and Green are not only leaders who will bind people to their hearts, but also protectors who will keep danger from running rampant.

www.dsppublications.com

Rampant
Volume Two

The Fourth Book of the Little Goddess series

AMY LANE

Little Goddess: Book Four
Vol. 2

Lady Cory has carved out a life for herself not just as a wife to three husbands but also as one of the rulers of the supernatural communities of Northern California—and a college student in search of that elusive degree. When a supernatural threat comes crashing into the hard-forged peace of Green's Hill, she and Green determine that they're the ones in charge of stopping the abomination that created it. To protect the people they love, Cory, Bracken, and Nicky travel to Redding to confront a tight-knit family of vampires guarding a terrible secret. It also leads them to a conflict of loyalties, as Nicky's parents threaten to tear Nicky away from the family he's come to love more than his own life.

Cory has to work hard to hold on to her temper and her life as she tries to prove that she and Green are not only leaders who will bind people to their hearts, but also protectors who will keep danger from running rampant.

www.dsppublications.com

Quickening
Volume One
The Fifth Book of the Little Goddess series
AMY LANE

Little Goddess: Book Five
Volume One

Cory thought she'd found balance on Green's Hill—sorceress, student, queen of the vampires, wife to three men—she had it down! But establishing her right to risk herself with Green and Bracken had more than one consequence, and now she's facing the world's scariest job title: mother.

But getting the news that she's knocked up takes a back seat when a half-elf hunts them down for help. Her arrival brings news that the werewolf threat, which has been haunting them for over a year, has finally arrived on their doorstep—and it's bigger and more frightening than they'd ever imagined.

Cory throws herself into this new battle with everything she's got—and her men let her do it. Because they all know that whether they defeat this enemy now or later, the thing she's most afraid of is arriving on a set schedule, and not even Cory can avoid it. The trick is getting her to acknowledge she's pregnant before she gives birth—or kills herself in denial.

www.dsppublications.com

Quickening

Volume **Two**

The Fifth Book of the Little Goddess series

AMY LANE

Little Goddess: Book Five
Volume Two

The elf queen who infected the werewolf population isn't going away—and neither are the two heartbeats that will soon be the children in Cory's arms.

Cory's used to throwing herself physically into the fray, but as their enemy gets closer and more dangerous, she's forced to choose between her safety and the people sworn to protect her. Her guardians are tired of worrying about Cory and her unborn children, and Cory is getting plain tired.

The preternatural world isn't her only worry—basic human birthing rituals are going to be a pain in the ass for a woman whose children will be sidhe. Cory's mother is still fuzzy on the concept of a polyamorous multispecies marriage and sets her up with an OBGYN obsessed with the inhuman silhouettes of her babies.

Cory doesn't want her children born in the middle of a turf war, but the people she and Green have nurtured and fought for aren't about to let her face this enemy alone. This battle is for queen and home, and the babies quickening in Cory's body are a symbol of hope. Cory's going to have to give up the idea of being a weapon and embrace the idea of being a mother, or she'll let down those depending on her most.

www.dsppublications.com